Will The Merchants Divide Him

with friendship —
— Jack

By

JACK HABEREK

Will The Merchants Divide Him
Copyright © 2019 by Jack Haberek

Library of Congress Control Number: 2019908660
ISBN-13:   Paperback: 978-1-64398-865-8
           PDF: 978-1-64398-866-5
           ePub: 978-1-64398-867-2
           Kindle: 978-1-64398-868-9
           Hardback: 978-1-64398-869-6

Printed in the United States of America

LitFire
PUBLISHING

LitFire LLC
1-800-511-9787
www.litfirepublishing.com
order@litfirepublishing.com

Contents

The Arc

Doctor Gloogla Pluplu opened the door and we entered the room. He had warned me before we did, he told me I was going to receive it as cruelty –and cruel it certainly was - but he also wanted me to know that it wasn't senseless: the man was held in the middle of the room by sort of a contraption immobilizing him in that particular point of space – physically; he couldn't move, if he wanted to, and the doctor told me that he did – Oh, yes, he did move; under heavy drugs, half way unconscious; he would move and that movement was extremely dangerous to the personnel as well as to himself; only then they used this sort of physical restrain.

The man stirred, slightly, in pain, like his liver was giving him hard time, I thought, to the right - a sudden grimace distorting his face. His head fell to the right, too, although his eyes remained open.

"The last story he told me, "the doctor said, "when he still spoke with me, was the bible, the old testament thing about the arc of the covenant, freshly built and now being painstakingly carried over the desert sands during the exodus time..."

"Doesn't he," I interrupted, "hear what you're saying?"

"I don't think he does."

"You don't think?"

"I ran some tests. I think, well, should I say 'I know for a fact', he doesn't."

"Yeah… What about the story he told you?"

"Yeah… They are carrying the arc on the desert. At some point the carriers stumble and the arc threatens to fall. One of them, none of the carriers, a bystander who is not meant to get involved into the process, if we may put it this way – obviously a guy to whom it is important, who really cherishes it as a value, his own personal value – jumps forward and tries to give it a support with his hands. He touches it, you understand, with his bare hands. Right? Well, he dies at the spot. See… When he was telling me this, he stopped at this point and kept on looking at something I couldn't see, something that certainly wasn't in the room (so suggestive that I turned around to look for what he was seeing - what was, or would have been, on the other side of the wall)," he points his hand towards one of the walls of the room we are in, "right about there, if you will. He looked, kept on looking, silent. I waited. That was, is… my job here, part of it at least. To wait and see. Then he sighed, as if coming back to life, you see, and then he said: 'Doc, do you realize that if he, that poor halfwit back there, took an A-frame ladder and opened it over that arc, and climbed it with no pants on, and from the top of that open and now solidly standing ladder took a dump on top of it, he might have survived… Right? We'll never know - at least that." He then looked through the wall again – for a long time. And I waited. And then he looked at me one more time, straight into my eyes 'But because he tried to prevent it from falling into the desert sand,' he said then slowly, in the same absence, that same sojourning somewhere else, not here, not behind those eyes I was trying to look into, 'and maybe fall apart, to pieces, to dust, he had to pay with his life…'"

Doctor Pluplu nods.

"I asked him then, if that was why he himself was here…"

"And?"

"He nodded."

"Affirmatively?"

"Well, sort of." The doctor shook his head. "Yes and no. Sort of. Strangely."

"Is he gonna come out of it?"

"What you want me to say. I'm a doctor. There's always hope...
Right? Gotta be!"

"Yeah..."

Kim

Eve came and we would have a drink – the bottle of the green stuff I
swiped from the Donovan's party; in fact I was just trying to explain
to Eve why would anyone swipe a bottle like that –you could buy
it, most probably, in any liquor store.

"Have you ever had the impression of..."I bit my lip, shit, of
what? "Of... well, that something from your past – like color, smell,
touch maybe, no, not touch – color or smell, yes! That it's there.
You got it, you're back, there's just that unbelievably little something
missing, ingredient, that makes you crap your panties, almost, but
you know for a fact you'll get it, yes sir, you will –you don't know
yet how, you don't know yet what the hell it is you'll get, but it's so
friggen close like it's never been so far and you know you'll get it..."
I was looking at her. That's what they call expectation, a painful
expectation. She shook her head, smiling.

"You mean – a sudden taste, of something, little thing,
meaningless, that moves you back in time to another place in a
different time –you're there, it's not just imagination – somehow it
is impression again. Straight and powerful. Right?"

She was laughing –although there was no smile on her face. I
was afraid she would. I knew it.

"That's Proust," I said then, "I know. Eve, but it's really like
that. Really!"

"This?" she wanted to know. "This stuff?"

"Yes! That's why I took the bottle. I felt like I got smacked over
my head with a sledge hammer."

"Where did it take you?"

"I don't know that either. I guess it didn't take me anywhere,
actually. No! I just got so bloody close to something important,

some kind of a start, you know, something that already was lost so long ago. Whatever it is. Was. Shit, will be…"

"Yeah."

We were sitting there in silence.

"What's with your exhibition at Donovan's," she asked then. "Do you have an idea what's it gonna be like?"

I looked at her. At the party I got drunk. I lost it. I would never talk about that kind of stuff to no one – not even Eve. Never. I am too superstitious for that.

"What did I tell you?"

"You were that bad? You didn't look it."

"That bad!"

"You told me he wanted you to make something. Nothing you already have. Something new. It would have to be about a man. A man, as opposite to woman – how he lives, how he dies. How he becomes a man, from childhood onwards. Through the woman's eyes. That's what he said it would have to be."

"Any ideas?"

"Yes." I was afraid now. Like hell; that she would scream with laughter, for instance. Some such. I was. "The dying Gaul…" I said, not looking at her. "Can you see it? I don't have a fuckin' thing here, I looked alread0y through all of that crap," I motioned towards the bookshelves and the table under the window, with a huge pile of books on it, too, "but I remember, I think, quite well, with details, how he dies – on his right arm, like resting, going to sleep, tired at any rate, his head already hanging down, but he is still here, on this side, with us, and somehow you have the impression that it won't be easy to kick him out of here, no matter how hard you'd like to get rid of him. See?"

"Anything else?"

"Yes," I said, I really had no idea what to expect; what would she do or say. "I thought… you mentioned at some point that Jack writes his memoirs… That!"

"Jack's memoirs?"

"Yes, sir! That!"

"You probably want me to steal them for you, too. Right?"

"That'd be great…"

"No! You'll have to talk to him. Besides talking to him, I think, will do you a lot of good. You just said it would have to be about *becoming* a man. You can talk to him about that too."

"Would you ask him, though?"

"Yeah. I will."

"Thanks!"

"Have a drink – of that green crap. Let's see what happens, huh?"

"OK."

McKenzie

I thought the TV was too noisy and I told that Jim, the bartender. He said in his book it was OK. He was always like that – a stubborn son of bitch. Loving to spite you. But other guys did not complain either. Yeah, I already knew well that at least for now he did not intend to turn it down.

Then Cluski came in and we started talking about the meeting we were going to have on Saturday, and what still needed to be done – I told him we are not prepared for police intervention should they be summoned; they would come, just like that, and chase us away, and we wouldn't be able to do Jack shit about it. I told him the only way is to confront them and hold one's ground – in other words fight back. Now, how do you fight back? They have nightsticks, the have guns, right? And them sonofabitches are ready to use both if it comes to that, they proved that in Detroit, in Cleveland, they proved that on the other side in Seattle as well. Possibly a thousand other places we knew nothing about.

"And, my dear fella, trying to tell them that they are Americans, too, just doesn't cut it; they have that up theirs –no, siree, we've gotta be able to fight back, and effectively at that: push them away and out of the way, wherever we might wanna go, right?"

Cluski wondered and pondered. He sighed a few times – I thought like a virgin before the fact. Goodness me!

We ordered drinks 'cause that always helps, donit? Then Irving came in and we told him, briefly, what we, I myself, that is, and Cluski, came up with. He basically agreed. We need training. Boxing. And some kind of a fight with sticks – like I saw in the movies. What movies now…? I saw it… Shit, man I saw it somewhere, I swear, guys fighting like there was no tomorrow, with long wooden sticks and nothing else – no swords, no guns. Finally it was Irving I think who decided to give me a break and agreed that most everybody saw a movie like that. Right? Yawp! Then we all agreed. The question now was where do we get something like that? Cluski got up, went over to the telephone on the wall and brought back from that shelf the yellow pages. We looked. Sure thing. Better than nothing, right? There was a boxing club in Southern Pittsburgh anyone could join according to their add in Yellow pages so we called and they confirmed – anyone who paid the fee. And what was the fee? Well, all three of us agreed it was reasonable, too. Irving said about then that his son was soon going to be twenty and he was a natural; he was six seven, you know, wide at the shoulder, narrow at the hip, he wouldn't give no lip, we all laughed, sure he wouldn't – but no, seriously, he could kick most anyone's ass without much ado, "I know," Irving said at that moment, half smiling and half serious, and I thought he was proud, "he could kick mine, if he put himself to it. I'm not sure he realizes that but that's a fact."

Yeah…

"They made an advertising I saw not long ago," Cluski said. "A young guy and an old guy, in shorts, in the ring. The old fellow throws a left hook and the younger one ducks it and then throws his right hook and hits the older in the yap. What happens? The old guy becomes a cloud of whitish dust that slowly floats off the ring."

"Yeah… Where did you see it?"

"On TV."

"Right."

Next Saturday we marched; with banners; and they chased us away, as usual, bruised and generally pissed off. I was trying to push away one of them and another hit me with all he's got across my buttocks with that blessed nightstick of his and the only effect of the whole thing is that now I'm unable to sit, yes, I'm standing at bar – my butt is blue-black with some yellow as I saw it in the mirror. Shit! Something's got to happen! Irving wanted to bring his son but we told'em not to because we thought it was plain no good – one guy didn't mean shit, he would've gotten arrested, most certainly, and in this democratic freedom we live in he might even get quite a few years for 'assaulting a police officer.'

We've found the club. The trainer told us for starters that it takes about four years of intense training to develop a real boxer. Four friggen years. I told him that – Cluski was there and Irving too – what we were after was basic self defense; we were not going after a championship of any kind. No! Basics. I guy approaches you, he is bigger and stronger than you are, he might also have something, like a stick, for instance in his hands, so what do you do? That – you see? Yeah, he saw it alright. We started. Basics, right? You wanted basics. He wanted us to run first, each time we'd come, for like half an hour. We obliged. And then, each and every time, just about when I am almost ready to go home and lie down, the training starts: punching the bag, jumping rope, push-ups, hitting hands, ducking and such. We followed the first time around and any subsequent time we went there –and that was three times a week; whatever he said. The first time I thought I was gonna puke my lungs out, but then I got a minute without anybody watchin' and that did me a lot of good, Cluski seemed to be a little better than me, Irving again about my level, give or take. Months were passing by like crazy, yeah, time-s-a-flyin', and then, at some point I've noticed it's become easier on me –well, all of us actually, still sweating, sure, still trying to catch some breath, and yet not dying anymore. One more thing: Cluski would throw a hook, left or right, and before we started this, all I could do was to block it off with my hands or take it on the body; now I can duck it, too. And I do. The guys do it as well. We organized a show where we live and that got us almost, believe it or not, twenty locals; they all want to practice. After a while, it's few months I mean by that 'while', yet ten more. After each of those training sessions we would go to a bar and there discuss our intensions: what's next? What needs to be done, such, that the democracy and freedom might stop sucking our blood in this leachy manner; how to stop it. Almost a year passed by and we marched again. Well, what can I tell you… I ain't exactly Joe Louis now either, but I managed to take the nightstick from the uniformed representative of democracy and with it to rearranged his face quite a bit, too; and then kick some more ass so that my heart grew to the size of Mount Washington. So did the others. Briefly – before they, them friggen cops, got reinforced they got chased away. The mayor came out and we talked. I said –straight to his face, my guys behind me – what is it we want and he stood there and listened. And then he said he shall look into it. I know, I'm not that naïve, that he'll look into it as soon as his wife spreads them on the bed, but at least he had to –you getting it? – *he had* to come out and talk to us, and at least pretend he was interested at all. I call that progress. We weren't a pack of mongrels that could simply be chased away by throwing pebbles at anymore. No, siree!

Irving's son had bloody knuckles on both hands – he really did it, with that little schooling we managed to organize for him he really contributed significantly to their acceleration rate while leaving the scene…

We came back here. And the next day we talked about the union – benefits. One of them guys died a couple of months ago because he had no insurance at all. We all have something in that territory that is more or less ridiculous, deductibles are so high one would have to die for that policy to really pay for something. And no dental. No ophthalmologist – and I for one really need one; my eyes begin to go; I got to this age were an eye doctor would be very, and I mean very much appreciated. And I got nothing. And where we work is quite a factory – the money is there, I know, it's just we have to pay for the yachts and excursions to the other side of the globe, and those pigs have no natural stop – there's never enough. Never. I saw at some point the son of the owner driving an English car I was told would go over here for three hundred thousand dollars – a snot, twenty maybe, I'm not sure… There goes my insurance, my ophthalmologist. Yes, sir, that one car sold would probably pay for all that. Maybe not for all of that. Maybe… But it would contribute considerably. It doesn't because a twenty-year-old-snot has to show off. All of one's life one does what one does because one expects, at some point, some kind of compensation for all the shit one has gone through, and then you see that nothing such will ever happen. The opposite: it'll only get worse. Now Ernie is growing and suddenly we have to buy stuff we did not have to buy before. Does he have a chance for something better? I doubt it. He ain't exactly brilliant, you know? To give an example: the other day we were talking about metals – what is the melting temperature of metals? He didn't know. My question was, though: would you be able to hold molten metal in your cupped up hands? And he said 'no' to it. Why not? Because it would spill... escape between my fingers. Can you imagine? In yet another case he asked me, because they had asked at school, what natural resources do we mine in NE Pennsylvania. I was tired. I just came back. God! I felt dirty and stinking and I wanted to take a shower, and there he was with his natural resources. I told him it was Styrofoam we mined there. Now here is something I for one had a hard time to believe: the genius repeated that word for word at school and they requested my presence to explain the mockery. What is he going to be? I've no idea. But I know one thing for certain: we, well, I have to fight – improve the system so that he too might find his place, his niche, whatever that might be. And I will. And I won't give up. Still seeing well or completely blind already, no, siree!

John (Fordham)

I wanted my son Jacob to study – as much as he possibly could and that was also why I pushed him as strongly and decisively as I could – to get his GED and then (the 'then' was not anything obvious: I had to help him go through with it any which way I could, including taking classes myself to be able to write 'his' stuff); then, finally, he 'made it', and after that I pushed him even harder to go to Fordham. The question was what could he actually study – grants were there, available, fortunately, hence money was not the real object here; what, though, what would be his interest, what would capture his 'personal disposition' as his major, then also as his minor. What? Good Lord help us! I remember him, of course, ever since he was born (he's Agatha's half-brother; Redhead was with a guy… hell, it's complicated and I believe it's plain boring, so to hell with it, except for what I already have said: Jacob is Agatha's half brother and I consider them both my own children), so I've known him since he was born and I – once we got to the point of choosing his major — was unable to tell what that could be: I just don't know about his interests, such that would qualify here. He, pretty much, had no interests that could from any possible point of view warrant an academic curriculum. He loved pot. Alcohol wasn't a big deal with him. He also likes to wander around in the woods, now and then shoot something, like a deer, for instance, well, whatever. University? I wondered. And pondered. Well… I went to his matriculation with the faculty: he was to study English literature there. And then I started to go there with him more and more frequently, to listen –in the beginning; but then also to talk, now and then, participate in the program, and all along I had to write 'his' things and I think that fact was known, became known over time, to the teachers there too, until one day I was asked, straight forward, to join as a regular student. And why not? was the point the main guy there, Josh was his name –I think a great guy - represented in that conversation with me – you show a thousand percent more interest in any of this than your son probably ever will. And then I repeated after him – to myself – why the hell not? And yet later, not much later at all, I simply became a real student. Redhead worked. I was part time taxi driver in Manhattan, mostly nighttime, and our incomes combined would allow us to vegetate along. We were renting a rat hole on Sedgwick Ave, a walking distance from the University, it was also easier to find parking space in the Bronx than probably anywhere else in New York, and that was the general manner in which we would very slowly get ahead – yes, I think, I would be inclined to call it that, all the counter-times notwithstanding. Yet later we found the employment with Jim in Connecticut, I was way into my studies, Jacob, my son, way after giving up any effort to remain in the program. Both of us now, Redhead and I, working together. Things started picking up rapidly from then on. Only some two years from that moment we bought a house (in real disrepair, that's true, but also with a great potential we were able to see right away) in Oneonta, New York, on ninety acres, which was pretty close to unbelievable considering our finances, and I was crazy, I was in true love with the property, with that entire area upstate – hell, with my life, probably for the first time ever since I was born. We had a lot of debts, that was also true, but Jim, our employer, insurance guy, big guy, really big, helped us to consolidate, and we were able to get along again. I would continue to study during the weekend, Saturday and Sunday, and I also started to write – my own stuff. I wrote a short story, over a period of time that was absurdly long, but nevertheless I finished writing it in the end, with considerable help of the Fordham people. I started writing a book then and it too met with good reception at the University (Josh himself and a friend of his as well – big deal for me!). I was slowly beginning to really believe in myself. Also among the students, other guys (gals) like myself I was slowly becoming sort of an authority there– they would come to me before classes to consult the quality of their home work with me, ask me my opinion about their opinions, and I tried, always, as far as I could, to accommodate them, however inconvenient their inquiry might have been at any given moment. Amongst them there was one who would come to me more often than the others, was my impression, to ask the same questions others did, but there also was something else about her approaching me in that long, dark hallway, I couldn't quite put my finger on. We would go now and then to a café to read and correct –well, change, modify, if you will, her texts written for the classes, discuss what she had to say about this or that part of the program in the class, but soon I realized that there was slightly more to it than just that. Her name was Kathy, she was of Hungarian descent, born in New York but still having traces of the ghetto accent, slim, tall, clear blond with beautiful blue eyes that I, sort of, more and more enjoyed looking into. She was in her twenties. My drinking – the fact, I mean, that I had my flask with me and that I would pour myself a measure of Jack Daniels into my coffee each time we sat there – did not bother her, just the opposite: she would say that all or most of the artists were drunks and that then there was nothing wrong with that – it would come to one from the oversensitivity, from the innate disposition to do great things other people were unable to do. We would go for long walks. And then the day came she took both of my hands in her one, smiling, looking me straight in the eye, as we were passing by an old building with a neon over the lintel - I did not realize it was an old Riverdale hotel - and we entered; she registered our names with the front desk clerk, paid, took the room key and then we went upstairs to the room she'd paid for, where the air was so stuffy that my first thought was we should open the window right away; but she took her cloths off so fast I didn't even have time to do that. I just took mine off, too, and we went into the shower, where, with the water already falling on us we made love, standing, I leaning against the tiled wall, and she with her legs around my waist. She never got pushy, she never asked me to change anything in the *status quo,* we continued to do things at the University the same way we did before, just now and then we would also go to that hotel. Redhead never said anything but I noticed certain changes in her: she got tired, sort of, older, I'd say. She smiled strangely –smiled to me, just as she would have before I did any of the above, we would take the same walks on our property in Oneonta, whenever we had a chance to be there, -there was a river down in the valley that still belonged to us and we really enjoyed walking all the way down there along that winding, sinuous path in the high grass and then along the slowly moving dark deep water, the path winding among huge old Oaks on both side of that water. After that we would come back to the house. I would have a drink or two – frankly: I would get drunk, actually, after which I would fall asleep on the sofa. Waking up in the middle of the night I would find myself all by myself, a glass of Seltzer on my nightstand, a bottle of Aspirin, too. Redhead would long be gone upstairs to bed. That was rare, though, the whole situation upstate. More and more rare, in fact - because we didn't have time: really less and less of it; we had to be in Connecticut, that was the job, our livelihood then, I had to be in New York at the university on weekends, so our times together in Oneonta shrunk suddenly down to almost complete nothingness. Jacob found a girl – fat and ugly, and it was actually me who pushed him towards marriage; I might just be old-fashioned, whatever, but I did, and then he did what I asked him to do: married her, officially, and both started living in Oneonta, on our property there and under her influence he started to sculpt – in clay (I would never have thought that clay can be that expensive; I was trying for a while to persuade them to just get a shovel and dig some up right there, behind the house, but no, that clay wasn't clay enough, no, siree, it had to be purchased for artistic purposes in some specialized store in town for the money they didn't have, and only then the process of kneading dough, as I would call what I was looking at, could begin. They would make pots and stuff, in some cases really hard to tell what the hell it was they were making, she also painted, landscapes, portraits, what have you, and so he started that to (she had an easel, an old one, yet from her past before she'd met my son but he had to buy one, the best one there was, of course, and I had to sit – long, hopelessly long sessions for both of them, and my portrait looked… well, I never thought I could look like an old sick cat with burnt off whiskers – twice!). She, Jacob's wife, got even fatter over time so that for a while I really thought that she might be pregnant and I'm about to become a grandpa but she wasn't as it turned out later, afterwards – they never had a kid, thanks God!

After classes I would go with Kathy to the hotel; I would call Redhead only to tell her that I had to stay longer and that there was no point in driving to Oneonta so late into the night and, hence, that I would stay at friends' in New York and we would see each other only the day after. The problem with that was that Redhead did not drive a car at all; she would have to stay in Connecticut, at Jim's, in our little room there and for Oneonta she could leave only when I got there; I already said that she started looking thinner, as if suddenly more tired than ever so far, peasants have a saying that someone 'is vanishing' and that, I think, would probably be the best description of what was happening to her; oh, but it was also happening to me: I too felt like I was, sooner rather than later, going to disappear; vanish; I would go to the church, whenever I was through out trysts with Kathy and at some point I would also start praying to God to help me –I certainly did not mean any harm to anyone and this was a point in my life where whatever I was doing, whichever choice I would make, I had a fair chance to do just that- harm, cause pain. Never before could I understand St. Augustine's prayer (I read the book in full actually long before we started going over it at school - Josh, the teacher, would go in the class by a three volume anthology, in which there was a fragment only out of 'Confessions,' but even in that short fragment we would discuss in class the passage I'm talking about was also included – it is the one in which Augustine prays to be saved some day; he prays because his mother, Monica, prays for the same thing, yes, he repeats her wishes and her prayers with a little clause, later on pretty famous, too – just not yet, Lord! I was just like that! Yes, siree, no difference! Oh, yes, I wanted God to solve my problem – I had no doubt it was a problem, I had no doubt I got myself into it (lack of power to decide, being too easy to manipulate, to push wherever others wanted me to be), I knew, yes, I had no illusions - but I also wasn't quite sure what was it I really wanted: I certainly did not want Redhead to get hurt; we had too many years, very good, even great years, behind us, together with her and I was certain all along and one hundred percent at that that she was there for me – me, as I am now and not me as I might become at some point, she accepted me as the little guy who, at least for now, would make his living pushing a vacuum cleaner and not a potential future Nobel and I don't think I was stupid enough not to appreciate that –I did. Yes, I think I did. Redhead was my friend, my dearest friend, hurting whom was killing me, and I also knew that she knew; not details, maybe; the TV little shit all the lowlife gets so excited about; I don't think, for instance, that she ever hired some sleazy PI to follow me like you see that nonsense in soap operas and such. No! And if one can be certain of anything in this life, she knew about my affair as a woman always knows about that (meaning nobody actually knows how or where from) and she had enough tact not to ever say one word about it.

Kathy would read my stuff. I liked her remarques –she was to the point, perfectly understanding everything I might ever have written, and she also treated my writing very seriously. She was the only one who took it like that: at face value, admitting that it was important part of my life and not just a hobby of some kind that I devoted my time and effort to because I was otherwise bored and/ or had – absurd view! – too much time on my hands… She thought I had real talent and if it could be developed… well, she thought it was sufficient for actually everything, given proper circumstances. Here she would tell me, try to convince me, that some people, she wouldn't say whom she might mean by that, no, but some people, you see, they just like it small; you get some little house, a piece of nothing really and they want the whole search, the big journey we're all about, to stop right there: by not pushing you, refusing to push, they actually slow you down – literally destroy your potential given to you yet at your birth so you may in the end really amount to something in this world. She would sit there, on the bed, naked, young, her body so firm and robust, associating itself with springtime, freshness, straightforward desire, - but turning the pages I would almost each time give her to read, she would also associate herself in yet another part of my mind with intelligence, culture: that future potential me I really would like to become at some point (there is that hope, I think, in any of us, unexpressed, not really sought after, but nevertheless also quite present, somehow, and pretty much, at least in certain circumstances, deciding one's actions or the not-taking-an-action type of behavior), and I would be sitting there and watching her, I myself having an unlimited and unreproached drink, the Jack Daniels bottle would be standing right there, on the night stand (as quoted above – all writers are drunks; drinking is not something one would want – let alone have to - control, drinking is a part of personality and has actually to be embraced as such – take Faulkner, Joyce, well, whomever, as the most known and renown examples). I would hear then a good, adequate and quite profound analysis of my text, showing me those shades of my own thought that were not quite clear to myself, and she would then talk about her reading during the week when I wasn't there: the last time it was LaBruyere she looked up in the library catalogue under the influence of her own Proust reading… She then talked about Musil and Broch, the latter my own enchantment of late; we were sharing the admiration for the 'Death of Virgil' I was still reading at that moment. Jack says I tend towards the complex, the bordering on non-comprehensible –which according to him is a sign of overaged youth. Mature! Whereas Kathy thinks Jack is just an old man (she doesn't mean physical age – we are, Jack and I, pretty much pairs), and also a bad influence on me - and I should decidedly liberate myself from that kind of personal relations because it gets you down – flattens you, if you will, puts a yoke on your dreams, crippling the propelling force those dreams represent in their essence. Jack doesn't like her either. But after I'd given him a few short poems of hers he read them and, in his usual, stingy manner, he even expressed something really positive about her literary efforts; he managed to surprise me, I must say. And I hear his voice –even, slightly monotonous, if he kept on going for a longer period of time it might even become boring: "only mysteries and portents, of which they stand in awe, can draw the attention of the faithless, for ignorance is the mother of amazement and when the sons of Adam forget you…"

I'm not that much of a believer. But I do think, like probably most of us, that there might - just might - be something out there, and in certain circumstances that some… thing may, again: just may, turn out helpful. In all those moments, situations, stuff that comes along and we don't know what to do with – with that precisely. Help! I tried to talk about it to Kathy but she just told me in answer I shouldn't get sentimental – man's job is to pick up the sword and cut his way through the jungle of the world: straight to the place he was meant to be at. Other than that he will remain a dishwasher for ever. To that Jack said, quoting again (he quotes because, as he puts it, it is already there – and if it is true, it's been someone else's pain that you're now allowed to apply to your own struggle without payment: 'the soul lives when it avoids the things which it is death to seek.'

I think I'll kneel down now and pray a little. It can't hurt anything, can it?

I see them both: Jack first and then Kathy. Then I see Redhead and I feel like… well… I'm kneeling, aren't I?

Kim recounting Ho's story

I am trying to sort out my notes from all the conversations with Pino referring to Ho's case. Those are mostly recordings – my own comments, as well as Pino talking, then also Jack, rarely, and then I also tried Ho himself – a couple of times in fact, just to have his voice documented somehow, yes, after a long, exhausting bureaucratic process I was finally allowed to ask him a couple of questions through Pino and get his 'answers'- even if it's all meaningless: it sounds like something from the animal world rather than a complex, as he later turned out to be, even in a way sophisticated human being. Communication with him was at any point very close to impossible, because he is def – almost one hundred percent. He was born def. He never really developed any skills as far as communication with other people – let alone people living over here, in the States; in China he was as isolated as he is here. The dialect he was able to say a few more or less articulate words in was not one of the great ones – like Mandarin, for instance. It was something hardly anybody over here could understand in the least. But is not only his linguistic skills what isolates him so terribly from others; it is also his personality: he has no patience, he is unforgiving to the extreme, and that is – probably more than the language – what builds that poured concrete iron reinforced bunker around him in which he seems condemned to live as alone as he is. Pino tried (I'll talk more about Pino later; I want to do it all one at a time, as it comes); hence, Pino tried; because he always does. Pino likes people and people usually like him back. Pino doesn't speak any Chinese, of course, and Ho never learned any Spanish, but they both know how to use gesture, sound – just that: sound, not words, nothing articulate, no, sound: a grunt, a laugh, hiss, (not as a sound – but as a grimace, mimic, a face that a grunt, a hiss, a laugh or what have you usually implicates…). And then you can also use things around you – as I have learnt - you can just point to them, whatever it might be at any given moment and that's, well, it becomes, part of the living and functioning language, too. Takes a while, believe me. If a thing isn't there you wait: that's patience, which Ho never had in abundance but with which Pino has been equipped quite richly. Pino is the one who really communicates; Ho receives the communication – for better or for worse. How do you explain that the young Ho would make his living fishing with Cormorants – how do you say in the language of gestures and grimaces 'Cormorant', well, you don't! But you do say, and quite easily at that, 'bird' instead, flapping your hands in the flying gesture and then you just dive, dive your hand, plooom:… into the water (a river drawn on the blackboard they had in the main room with a piece of chalk) after which you immerge from the water back out into the air, flattering fish in your mouth – the rest is encyclopedia research Pino did, internet (now and then they have access to the computer in the hospital's library and someone, at some point, taught Pino how to use the computer and how to surf the web), his English is sufficient to look up a word and then very slowly read the explanation, and there you are – all of a sudden in the know: Ho would stand on a low, almost flat wooden boat and he would let the cormorants – he had five of them – fish for him; then he would sell the fish on the town fish-market's bench thus making money necessary to cover his expenses – whatever those might have been. Ho had no family, no woman, no relatives. He lived in a hut made of clay and stones then thatched with wicker –a lot of that in his area. He loved the river slowly floating through the mountains, high, very steep mountains –no, you couldn't possibly climb those, no!

But they were beautiful. Oh, yes! That they were alright.

Pino slowly became an expert on China from those times – he would be able to talk about Cormorant fishing, little details he got from the internet as they were watching it together, Ho and himself, Ho laughing and at times also crying – quite a few times in fact, you know, he was so bloody touched he had watery eyes, and I be darned if you couldn't see real tears in his eyes. The revolution was long over and the fighting subsided, but it never really stopped: one could hear now and then about skirmishes, those who did not escape to Taiwan were trying to hide but if disclosed they would be dealt with in such a manner that suicide was definitely a preferred way of leaving this side of being; that for a long, long time after all the official dates, and that was also how Ho's career as a fisherman ended: at some point they fired a cannon at his boat, from the river, also from a boat – different than his was, a boat nevertheless: he was told that later, though, by the neighbors who saved him; all he could tell first hand was that at certain moment he stopped seeing anything – like the light switch had been turned off and a complete, one hundred percent darkness had ensued. But he didn't die. He woke up in the neighboring hut: they, those neighbors of his who had fished him out of the water and then took him there, to their hut were all there, just waiting for him to come around. And he did, too. His cormorants were gone and so was his boat. To make a very long story short the neighbors advised him to leave for America, for the land of great prosperity and great, unlimited freedom, well, everybody has heard something about America: wealth and prosperity, life, all the chances one would get, a true land of opportunity, he was told that in America money would grow on bushes right along the street and if you needed some you would just pick it up, right there, off the tree; he had a problem with that; he did believe, maybe just not all of it, but some of it, yes, but not all of it, no, never all of it, no, people, well, not really lie, no, but they surely like to tell stories, you know – but there was a group just about then going to San Francisco on an old freighter, everything already paid for, he had to contribute some, which he could do too at the time, his life savings turned out sufficient to cover that particular demand, and so he did use them and just covered the expense.

In the end he came to America. Well, again a very long story. Pino said Ho wasn't too loquacious about it, though, and he, Pino, couldn't force him to leak be it just a bit more of all those details that would probably make a fat book all by themselves; no; Ho kept silent and Pino had the impression that even water boarding wouldn't have made him more talkative, for some reason – whatever that reason might have been.

Yeah… We can only guess and it wouldn't take a very elaborate guessing, now would it?

From San Francisco they took him to New York aboard a train, with a group of other Chinese men like himself. Then he made a huge jump forward: in New York he got a job in the end and he was even allowed to retain some of the money he would earn working. Working with fish. Cutting, scaling, gutting, preparing, etc. He was still def. That didn't change, and he was still perfectly able, if he chose to do so, to communicate with the others in his strange manner, and still in most cases he would choose not to. It looked like he had no need to communicate in any way an average person usually does with people whom he worked for as well as those he met later and now and then would have a glass of Japanese sake with; he would sit there silent, polite, politely responding with a smile to indagations, pointing to his ears, though, and still, unchangeably remaining silent like the stone figures in the jungle he enjoyed telling Pino about (I saw his drawings on the board; the gods in the jungle, the gigantic stone gods whom the jungle was slowly swallowing up) – he liked sake; he never liked beer. He spent nothing. Fish he was able to eat at work, mostly row, would be nutrition enough for him. For years every penny he would be given for his work he would save up until he was able to rent an apartment. That was when he started thinking about a family. He always thought about that, Pino claimed to have gotten out of him – always as something distant, though, something that will happen some day, eventually, in the distant future nothing could be told about right now. But it was there. In the back of his mind, somewhere, yes, it was there. The family.

Jack and his father

I remember the park - of all things: our walks, I and my father, when I was a small boy, at first a long walk from town and then its continuance already in the shadows: trees, some of them really impressive, old gigantic oaks, a whole grove of those, from which the town would take its name, and bushes on the bottom– thick, stubborn, as if specializing in their silent survival, unsearchable and, hence, full of mystery; and yet farther up that way the river, moving, alive, the essence of the park and the natural end of it (*limes* was the Latin word, as my father – he never missed the opportunity – informed me at some point, once, briefly, but then to make sure I wouldn't simply forget the message, would keep asking about it each time at our arrival there, with the same unshakable consistency); and the flatlands beyond the river – wild meadows with yellow grass and dwarfy bush stretching all the way to the next town, the latter already beyond the horizon line except for a power plant stack that was one of the tallest in the whole country: it looked from the bridge perspective like they had built it somewhere in the middle of those fallows beyond the river only to make the two of us happy, a stop for our eyes weary of wandering through nothingness – no other purpose. We would have to take a bus in order to see that next town – all beat up, red, very old and terribly clunky bus, moving ridiculously slowly – and in such a manner at that that one knew about every stone and every hole in that road; made us smile, though… it was just a regular dirt road across the country, dividing those yellow endless meadows into two parts (we could ask the driver to stop anywhere in-between to get off the bus to smell the wind bringing to us almost all that grass with no end, heat up by the sun – the wind smelled blue, I used to tell father, not like the grass at all, no, a lot more like the sky), the road itself beginning right passed the tall wooden bridge (it was so tall in fact that seen from the level of the water, once you would get down there, it looked like something almost indefinable, scary shadow of an unnamable thing up there, standing on long wooden stilts) across the blue with slowly moving white cottons : and that indefinable something up there, the bridge, was disproportionately short as compared to its height, which made it look scary; a monster of some kind, stopped; waiting, only to pounce later; built of mighty wooden logs dried gray, hard as stone, spanning the two shores of the canyon, as already said above: the latter not too wide but really mysteriously deep. That is what I remember: it's there; all I have to do is close my eyes; and I also know that any view perceived out of a child's shoes is different, and at times completely different, from what an adult would see. Somehow I am almost certain now that today it wouldn't be so deep. The river wouldn't be such an impressive river as it was back then. Certainly. And…?

We would get to the bridge and we would stand on it then, both of us motionless, watching the dark water move slowly, majestically, towards the very distant steel mills – from here we could also see only the stacks: seven of them, built of dark red brick, very tall and slender, over the rolling-mill track, and then yet one more, a bit smaller, from the high furnace. The town was on the other side of the industrial complex separated from it only by a high fence. One could not see, of course, any of that from the bridge. There were two sets of tracks, though, once one would get there: tram – that was the town side, we would take that tram to go uptown or downtown, and then the other set: railroad, trains consisting of small noisy locomotives, capable of turning a Sunday white shirt of a walking person into a gray one in the matter of minutes only, and flat, funny looking cars behind them, carrying cinders in also funny looking containers all of it coming out of the steelworks gigantic atelier and, slowly and strangely, puffing very much a tired animal like, crossing the town to its other side, would dump those cinders in an area where we, children, would love to be, to play, we knew places there, things, Good Lord… yes, we did. Uptown there was a place where the shoemaker had his studio; the best shoemaker that ever lived on this earth. All my father's shoes were made by him. Custom made, as father would stress proudly, each time our conversation would go that way; of the best Chamois attainable, accommodating perfectly all the irregularities of his feet. And his feet were very irregular (not both of them, no, just one – the left one), unlike any human foot I have ever seen in my whole life, – but that is yet another subject, to which I hope to be able to get back at some point, more extensively.

My father, while shining them, would stop occasionally and, looking up at me, smiling, would knock with his bony finger on the front part of the shoe held in his other hand and, still smiling, would say to me: chamois, you know? Yeah…" His finger would then knock at it again. "Chamois…"

I haven't forgotten (and since I haven't forgotten yet, I think it is safe to say that I shall never be able to forget anymore for I am an old man as I sit here and do the remembering).

The day he taught me to swim – like birds teach their little ones: he just kicked me off that toll bridge: without any warning, any interruption of the silence, and I fell into the foamy wild water of the then spring swollen river only after a long (it really seemed endless as long as it lasted) flight through the ethers: that day, warm and beautiful, end of April or beginning of May, it - the river - was moving really fast, covered with yellowish irregular fringes of foam that would impose the impression of... rabies perhaps; yes, a rabid dog comes to mind, yes... I fought. I can't recall what I thought about the battle –was I to win or to lose... I just fought for my life without thinking anything at all, I guess. He stood up there all the time, on the bridge, watching. I swam ashore. In those few unforgettable minutes I got to know how to swim.

I still remember that as distinctly as if it had been yesterday.

I also remember (and won't be able to ever forget) *their* fights - for life; my parents against each other, that is – most of the time; my shakes, trembling; shouts - and a whole lot worse than just shouts, noise of whatever kind: they could really get physical; really bloody at times. From today's point of view, as families get 'counseling', my parents were perfectly dysfunctional; there was nothing but hatred; but I also think that there was a lot of love in that hatred, somehow. And –which is something from my today's point of view really appreciable – durability. They stayed together; separated by politics which threw, only a little later, few years, thousands of kilometers between them – by, hence, what would probably be by many people I got to know during my life grandiloquently called 'history' - they nevertheless never really separated from one another. She always knew how to find her way back... to everything we both, she as well as I, never got to know how to forget.

I didn't tell mother about the swimming 'lesson', once we, I and father, finally got back home. I just didn't want to wetness one more Peloponnesian war.

There was a pond in the park we used to go to, the swan-pond we called it. It was round and there was an island right in the middle of it with a house in the geometric centre of the island and some really big trees around that little green-white painted 'house' the swans would never really inhabit. We would slowly walk around the pond along the shady alley with a reddish surface made of crushed bricks. Now and then I would get closer to the water and standing right there on the shore, looking into the dark mystery the jungle of oozy weeds and all the other unnamables down there, yet closer to the slimy bottom, would surreptitiously offer to my eyes - a wonderland, slowly, almost imperceptibly moving in the almost non-existent undercurrents. I would watch. I would hold my breath and the expectations would grow quickly – almost turning the day into the night, filled up with dreams – dragons creeping out of the endless swamps, regurgitating rivers of fire, and heroic saints, all covered with soot, fighting them relentlessly, liberating the holy virgins offered to the beasts for their forgiveness and leniency. And then the swans would come.

Swans… There would be no point in describing a swan – most everybody has seen a whole family at some point in their lives. To me back then, though, that stately, dignified aloofness out there on the water was everything I wanted badly and didn't have; when Goethe says: 'entbehren sollst du, sollst entbehren…' and I still remember father's voice, slightly shaky, just for that particular moment while doing the reading seeming a bit out of whack, that 'entbehren' was right there, out there, on that dark shady water of the pond, majestically moving around, looking at us with quite a bit of contempt, - and my father wanted to know why. He would like to understand – out of so many things full of beauty all around us – why the swans. Why would I want so badly to touch the bird. What was so important about touching it. And I couldn't tell. All I knew was that I would have been able to give up a lot – a lot of things, as well as possible situations, dreams… For that one touch.

I watched father standing on the shore, concentrating, stretching his hand out towards the bird moving slowly, also focused, towards that hand, its fingers, to pick up his non-existent tidbit, and then father bent forward at the speed of a lightning and grabbed the bird's slender neck – God… in that one second it all changed from the stately, peaceful beauty of an old park into downright hell. I would never have thought that the bird might have that much power – he pulled father towards himself, into the water, yes, I saw father run like crazy into the pond, following, (both didn't want to give up) until it was all quiet again: the swan was simply swimming away with all his dignity regained in no time, as if never even touched, towards the center island of the pond with the green-white house on it, and father was standing there, up to his waist in the water, actually wet all over: even from his disheveled hair water was dripping now onto his chest and his shoulders. He spit. Wiped his face off with his hand. Then turned around and walked out, back onto the shore. Looked at me. Spit again. And then looked back, at the swimming swan and shook his head in a strange manner I can't recall from any other occasion. "Malicious rascal..." he said in a voice that gave me creeps, spitting one more time. His chamois shoes were now just two huge, dark, shapeless balls of mud and weeds – the latter all the way up to his knees. I remember. Having printed the page and putting it over the rest of them in the drawer I picked up an old clipping from a magazine where Federico Fellini, then perhaps not young anymore but still very much alive, explained the title 'Amarcord:' it's a word from very old dialect meaning 'I remember', - but to him, Italian, it was just a great word he fell in love with: it contained 'amare' as well 'cuore...'

Ernie

I had a little fall out with Mauna and that's why I am here – in the Totem Pole, at the bar. The TV is on, but I'm not watching. I was just talking to the guy next to me – I told him about the proposition I just had received concerning my job, my business, I should probably say. I own an automotive shop, specialized in transmission rebuilding – we do all kinds of transmission work: automatic, which is obvious, some eighty percent of cars out there have automatic transmissions, but we also do sticks, which is a lot less typical in this country of ours, and I do transfer cases as well, and it's been just fine so far – well, lately, because of the economy (it's unbelievable how everything affects everything else – even my size, little business cell), because then of the economy in the whole country that gets more and more screwed by the broken Washington DC crap, I feel like I've gotta be careful, more careful now than probably ever so far. I've had this business for the last, goodness me, almost twenty years… Going good! Strong! Yes, that was a sound business decision, those twenty long years ago. Very sound, indeed! Just lately… and that's how it came about, I mean, my conversation with a customer of long standing, a guy, who brought me quite a bit of work almost ever since I care to remember, certain John, employee of a filthy rich Jew in Connecticut. The latter needing –at least he thinks he needs – a mechanic, full time, on his premises. He owns – the Jew – a house, some fabulous architectural achievement, but he also likes cars. Owns a stable – Ferraris, Porsches, Maseratis, etc, and all of that stuff needs a regular maintenance, as well as – now and then at least – repair work done. The guy has a facility, supposedly, that beats most regular auto shops, he was able to equip his home garage with stuff a lot of independents could only envy, and that is where I would eventually come in. John is his property manager – I wouldn't even have to talk to him, the rich Jew, John would be the guy who would hire me, and with John it would be that I would discuss the conditions of my new employment. John predicts, based on what he knows (and what he knows goes way beyond what I do, or anyone I know - John knows and talks to people placed very high up), that the economy is not at the bottom yet, not by a long shot, no, sire, we haven't seen the worst yet and it's still gonna get a lot worse, in other words, we'll see hell, according to what he says, the global stuff is crumbling, they basically don't know what to do, how to save it. John's suggestion was that it might be a good idea to sell the business and look for shelter under the wings of a bigger – a lot bigger creature. I'm kinda hesitating. I don't know. I've had this business for, as said above, almost twenty years. I've been my own boss, shit! And now I'd have to go listen to someone else – although John says I wouldn't have a boss. I'd be the boss there as well. I'd do my own hiring, should I need someone else, should there be expenses, I would have only to present expense sheet to his, John's that is, approval. I am thinking. Yes, Sir! I am.

I ordered another Gin and Tonic.

"Where did you meet her?" the guy next to me just asked and I felt lost.

"Who?"

"Your wife. She's your wife, I presume. Right? The Mauna Gal you mentioned before?"

"Oh, yeah. Mauna. Yes, she's my wife. I met her in Honolulu. I was stationed there. I took her out dancing. She swims. She swam from Oahu to Maui, which was in the Honolulu paper. She also jumps, you know? The Waianae Falls, I saw her jump, that was how she caught my eye, because of the jumping, you know? After that I asked her out. I just went there, to where the swimmers, jumpers actually, were, and I asked her out. She laughed, she was a little bit embarrassed, maybe, but she said 'yes' and we went out dancing. We got married before I came back here."

"Nice story…"

"Yeah… I don't want to ruin it, you see?"

"I see, sure thing. I see that!"

"And that new business thing?" he asked then, only a short while later.

"That's exactly what I had in mind telling you that I don't want to ruin it. What I've got so far has been good. We are not rich but we live decently. Kids got whatever they need. She's got whatever she needs. So do I. But it's slowing down – lately in a way that started to give me creeps, to be quite frank with you. That's why I am even considering what the guy told me, see? Few years back I would have laughed out loud. Period."

"Now you don't feel like laughing, huh?"

"Not 'ny more!"

"Yeah…" He nodded. "You're not alone, pal!"

"I know!" I nodded too. I ordered another glass. I sighed and cleared my throat, coughing. I thought I was almost decided: we would sell the house and buy something that wouldn't depreciate – like maybe gold, or some such (I'd definitely have to consult someone on that) and then, without losing anything, just wait up; see what's gonna happen, maybe then make yet another decision, hopefully not as difficult as this one is – yet another shift. Yawp! One's gotta be flexible. These are times when one's really got to do things one would never had thought one would have to do or become… Times – I really don't know… Goodness…

Governor Cauldron

Eve turned on the TV – she wanted to check the weathercast but before she got there for quite a while yet there was on the screen an orchestra and then we saw the governor Cauldron – his face; and then the camera backs off – it's himself now, full picture, walking into the building, slowly, kind of stiff, he is not feeling well, although trying to smile, with his wife, he's never been so far too ostentatious with - I guess, I never really have seen them together up until now… A reporter stopped them in the hallway and Cauldron talks about music for a moment, about the therapeutic function of art in general, out of the corner of my eye I can also see the convulsive, quick movement of Eva's face muscles, a cramp quickly overshadowing her up until that very moment rather smiling expression. He says it was his idea, he always wanted to organize this here… As usual the funding, you know. That's never easy. Yes, he smiles, never, the young reporter smiles too, they talk about music for a moment, and then it is he, Cauldron, sitting and watching the orchestra, listening.

Eve turned to me.

"Did you noticed how he walked into the building?"

"Yeah," I said, trying to stay focused on the picture my memory kept perfectly alive for me, but also tying to figure out what was it she wanted from me now. "He wasn't feeling well, I'd say, or was he?"

"Gas colic. I am almost certain. That stiffness. He hardly could walk, right? Wouldn't you say, he looked like he had swallowed a broomstick?"

She made me laugh.

"Kind of, yeah."

"And now? Look! How wonderfully relaxed he is. Catharsis. Yes! Cathartic function of art in general. He was just talking about that. Huh? It did come out! You may ask how I know." She's serious. " Look at his wife!" she quickly points to the screen. "Her face! She's loosing consciousness! Her eyes are empty. Glass. She wouldn't know at this junction what the hell do they call her, I can bet on that! Look at the other gal, the one to his left. Whoever that might be. Same thing, ain't it? And he himself – his right eye seems to me to be on the seat in front of him, slightly to the right of his right hand, right? And his left eye's focus is somewhere up on the ceiling, isn't it? I think this could be a contribution to the second WW crime analysis – the immediate influence of the Cyclone B on the neural centers, wouldn't you say?"

"You don't like him a lot, do you?"

But she doesn't give in.

"What's got that to do with liking or disliking. What's happening there is precisely what's happening there, like it or dislike it. It's what they call a fact, my dear!"

"Tea?"

"Tea would be nice," she says and I go over to the stove.

After turning the crap off she threw the remote on the table in such a manner that I thought we might have to buy a new one again. I certainly am not in love with our TV and, considering the general level of TV programs as of late, I am really beginning to share the opinion of some of our friends – that, namely, TV in this country should be banned altogether. Yes. But weather, goodness… weathercast, although most of the time wrong, here in the mountains seems nevertheless to be facilitation to some extent of our very lives – allows you to anticipate at least a little bit what's coming to you. I didn't say anything, though. All focused on making our tea, I allowed that little tiny bit of me to still think about the cathartic function of art in general…

Rich

I met him on Union Square, at the Broadway entrance to the subway and he really surprised me, I must say: with his outfit: I knew he had found and then taken a cabinet maker's job, somewhere uptown, on the West Side, so the sudden sight of him in a blue suit with a very light blue shirt and a tie with a delicate rose touch, all of it fresh and clean, was a little bit of a surprise. He greeted me like he would in any circumstance, I thought, we both stopped and, smiling at each other, started talking (it's been a while, really since I saw him for the last time before this – I wondered: months, hell, more like years, quite probably...), so the usual: what's new? If anything – and nothing, really: although years, as said above had passed by since our last encounter, the same struggle, the same exhausting and boring, seeming at times just senseless, effort only to stay afloat, was there, very much on...

"Still living at the same place?

"Yes, no changes there. You?"

"Same, also nothing new at that point. Yeah... Any point."

"Work?"

"Same old. Yes.

"Agatha? How is she?"

"Thanks. She's fine."

"Eve?"

"No changes there. Thanks. A coffee?"

And I think right then, from the subway entrance a young woman came out, on high heels, white shirt, black skirt, also fresh, clean – bank employee type. Why would I look at her? Blond, lot of very carefully, meticulously dressed hair, blue eyes – she was smiling broadly towards us. That's why. I saw his sudden embarrassment, not to say panic in his eyes: like a cloud quickly passing over the ground on a windy day: no certainty if you really saw it or not. She came in almost no time to where we stood and he just had to introduce us. Then he told me he was applying for a bank loan, equity, on the house, you know, and they would be discussing the conditions over a dinner – that's a lot nicer than to sit there, inside, in a bank lobby... Whatever, right?

"Oh, yeah," I said. That is a lot nicer." I smiled to her too. "So good luck!" I added then, stretching my hand towards her.

"I'm sure we'll have it," she said and I thought it a littler bit strange that a bank officer in position to discuss an equity loan would have a heavy foreign accent like she did.

Then we shook hands with Rich and they were gone.

I stood there a while yet, pondering. The day was sunny, bright, the air felt wonderfully fresh, and I thought, since I had nothing really to do, that I would sit there, on the square, for a while, before I'd call on Eve upstairs.

A homeless black with a beat up, incredibly dirty and swollen face, was preaching Apocalypse in a very noisy manner and I thought he should be for his own good put to sleep ASAP– because that would really get him out of his present misery and a lot closer to the phenomena he was screeching about. Once he was gone, though, not that much later, I thought again about Rich and Agatha – something was out of their ordinary I knew relatively well from the past and I was forced now, sort of, to wonder what it might be.

Eve with Kim

I was walking all around the studio – Kim set up a fresh pod of coffee and the machine was now, a little bit on the noisy side, percolating the fresh load. Kim was still with it. I also saw – before I got really involved into what she had going on in the studio – a little silver tray with glasses on it.

Then I turned my head away from her.

Two big sketches on the wall straight across from the entrance to the studio- the dying Gaul, in natural size; she just copied the sculpture we all know from our school time: different angle – from the point down of his stretched left leg, clear left profile, the second one more *en face;* generally the same expression: fighting against death, refusing to accept his fate… On the one closer to the window he is much younger; two different positions, as if a little more suffering, more medieval, I'd say, Memling… No! Durer, maybe. Then I think for a moment about Mathias Gruenewald and his Christs. I wasn't sure how to put it in order. And then yet younger;

31

a teenager – open mouth, wide open, he could be shouting, it is not a shout, not clearly defined – it's modal, precisely that: he *could be* shouting… Then there's a child – eight, nine max, the boy suddenly reminds me of our last conversation about the green round bottle of Dutch alcohol we were having the last time I was here: the sensitive containing of the world around – fully translated into perception content, nothing left outside.

She came over, with the coffee and two cognacs.

"See," she says, "I got one shot at it; I gotta get him to like it or forget the whole thing. Right? Here it is," she put the tray on the floor. "This here, look!"

She moves the papers, bents them to see what's on them, puts them aside. "Here!"

She stretches one of them then in front of me and at first I don't understand: it is a couple of people having at first glance absolutely nothing in common with the dying Gaul: father and son, both naked, walking, the boy's tiny hand is in that of the father, much bigger, stronger (if that is his father – there is no indication to that effect on what I am looking at), and she now talks quickly, I know she is nervous, she cares about what I am going to say, I'm the first audience – and she tells me right about the stuff I was thinking about yet a short moment ago: "The child," she says, "is more about senses, it's the father, the adult, who is the intellect, the reasoning; but we also are both, - I think that's what Donovan meant talking to me, we may have lost something, sure, but we haven't lost everything, and the little ones have not yet gain what we've got, a long stretch of that road ahead of them to get there, but they also have got enough, right at birth which is what we say and that in turn means way before that, to make a sensible part of the expectation – our expectation; life… You see it? That taste… there is a world out there and it passes, sort of, indifferently by, and yet then there is that taste, that moment when you suddenly know that some of that absolutely overwhelming, quickly passing by and unstoppable infinity is locked up inside you even against your own expectations– that taste, smell, you feel pain trying to sculpt it into a remembrance of something more clear than what I'm now saying, it's a terrifically intense effort, pain to the point of dying and the refusal of death– life… Do you see…?"

She looks at me, all tense, waiting.

"Did you read Jack's stuff?" I asked.

"Time and again." she said smiling. "That's where it's all come from, to some extent. You bet!"

"You talked to him, right?"

"Didn't he tell you?"

"Very superficially. In a strangely… skimpy way. He obviously didn't want to talk about it, so I dropped it, quite quickly in fact."

"Thanks!"

"As to what you were saying before… This here really does make me see it," I said slowly, I didn't want it to sound light, like I was just appreciating a picture in a gallery – any picture in any gallery. No! "I think you got it, Kim, maybe just some of it and not all of it, on that one, the one where they are together, and I think Donovan is going to buy it before he even tells you he is…" I was looking at her. "You know what I was just thinking about, while I was looking at your boy, I still hadn't seen this" I pointed to the father-son drawing; my finger went all the way towards the picture on the wall – the picture with the dying, or whatever he was, Memling or Durer, nine-year-old. "I thought about the bottle of the green Dutch crap you swiped from the last party at Donovan's – we were talking back then, right here, about Proust and his concept of memory, senses, and how life can be enclosed in it and then dug up by something we would never expect might come our way at all, remember that? That's what I thought about. Now! While I was looking! Your boy did it, there's no doubt on my mind."

"God…"

"I think you did it, Kim! Your lonely boy on that one is also the boy with the father. And the father is what the boy will be some day. I do! Isn't that what Donovan wanted?"

"I love you!"

"Yeah, me too.

McKenzie

Cluski's head looks on the pillow like a broken off head of a monument of some kind, wrapped up in an incredible mass of bandages held together by band aids here and there; his mouth gives me the impression of not belonging where it is, seems too small, like a mouth of a boy almost, right now not reflecting any impression. He sleeps, or – should I say – is unconscious. I asked a nurse who was here before if he is in what's commonly called 'coma' but she gave me an answer such that I still don't know; sort of like when you listen to DC politician talking for two hours and then, once he is through, you try to recall for your own use and understanding what was it actually he had said, and you can't, so you ask the guy who was listening to it sitting next to you, and he, your neighbor, looks at you, he looks embarrassed, and finally you hear; 'you know... shit, man!' I think talking like that becomes a fad nowadays. Nobody knows anymore what the other guy said or what he wanted to say. Nobody.

I caught myself chewing my thumbnail.

We were marching in front of the mayor's office. They called cops. Usual. The cops came – they came in cars that looked like UPS trucks – they got out and started to chase us, well, they started trying to chase us and we responded, also in usual manner, only now, as said above somewhere, a lot more successful because of the preparation we've got in the meantime. In this particular case we were standing our ground, too, pretty good besides, and then I saw out of the corner of my eye Cluski fighting a cop, effectively, there was nothing to be worried about, the cop was backing off, and then another cop from behind hammered Cluski with his night stick, with whatever he's got, across the head. Just that one punch at full swing by a big strong man, trained to hit like that. Cluski went down like hit by a lightning. Then Irving's son got the cop who had hit Cluski – a wide right hook in the head, never mind that little plastic 'window' they have there to protect their faces. The cop flew backwards. The one whom Cluski was fighting with Irving's son got with his left elbow straight in the face sending him on paid vacation without any further delay, too. Boys saw what happened to Cluski and I guess that also got them going. It didn't really last long after that. Then we came here. Cluski was brought in by an ambulance but the rest of us followed as best we could and now here we are, watching, if you will, over him. The cop Irving's son hit was brought in, too. I know (I asked, that's how I know) that he is somewhere here in the building. Shit! Come to think about it he too was doing his job just as we try... What the hell is wrong? What is it?

The nurse came back – this time with a tray on which she brought coffee and cheesecake of her own making. She told us, as if trying to explain her former lack of clarity, that the hospital 'authorities' prohibit her to talk to patients, so she, well, they have developed that gibberish technique she just used on us; but she knew about us; she knew who we were and why then were we here, what had actually happened out there. She was on our side – in fact, her brother in law marched out there today with us, she gave us his name but we didn't know the guy and we told her we were sorry, she would have to understand there were few hundreds of guys like us on that plaza and there's no way in hell or heaven for any of us to know everybody else. She did. She made the coffee nevertheless and cake, well, even her mother in law admitted it was good. I was the first one to reach out for it. Irving got one then too. She looked at us while we were chewing like we were some kind of a genetic experiment she'd been planning on conducting for the last twenty years of her life. The cake was excellent and I told her just that. Irving did too. And then the others in the room, whoever had a piece. And we all did in the end.

"You've no idea how I'm glad to hear that," she said then. "All this time I wanted to do something, too. To help. To change that..." she hesitated.

"Crap!" Irving finished for her.

"Exactly! Just that there are no women out there."

"Not yet!" I said.

"I hope you're right!"

"I guess I could tell I am," I said, smiling at her. "When I was young nobody would do anything. Man or woman. That's changed a bit. See, why I am saying that is things have really changed a lot, actually. People are pissed off and have the guts to show it, not just here! Everywhere! There are books written about the beastly stuff that's done in this country, how it's been high-jacked to do dirty business of somebody else's, how we are pulled the wool over our eyes as to what is really going on, as far... damn it, just about anything. And women show in that process too. More and more so."

"Yes." She said. "I wish there was more of that! You bet!"

I told her in case she wanted to join the union where she would have to go and how things are done in general, and she told me she would think about it. I thought it was strange. Unexpected, to say the least. I asked her if she knew by any chance how the cop was doing they brought here together with Cluski, and she told me he wasn't doing well at all –they would have to open his skull, there was something wrong with his meninges, which is to say how his brain was attached to his skull. Something like that.

"He may actually die," she said, "you know?"

"Yeah... How old is he?"

"Twenty six."

"Defending democracy and freedom!"

"Right!" she said. "Democracy and freedom."

She told us then she had no more cheesecake but if we were hungry later on she could bring us some soup from the kitchenette they had right on this floor. No big deal: those are dry soups that hot water has to be poured into, but they are definitely edible and just plain good when one's really hungry. Irving's son asked if he could have one like right now and she told him, getting up, that there was no problem. Now or any time, dear. Just let her know. That's all.

We stayed there all the way until ten o'clock when Cluski died. We knew he did, without her, because the apparatus he was hooked up to suddenly beeped and then displayed the flat lines on those little green screens. We called her right away. They tried to zap him and what not – to no avail. Everybody left. Only I asked to be allowed to stay a bit longer and they granted me my wish. He was my friend; we grew up together, together we shirked for the first time, we've had our first campfire together, together we'd fish... First girls, yeah... That too. Together.

Nobody was here so I didn't have to be embarrassed by my tears. Didn't have to hide anything any more.

I kept looking at him.

His mouth looked now even more inadequate for his head made so huge by all that hospital dressing – more so now than before, I'd say. His lips were slightly parted, like he was just sleeping. I saw him like that, sleeping that is, so many friggen times. So friggen many!

Together! Fuck!

John (Coney Island)

We've taken a long stroll on the boardwalk, hours really, talking all the time about books we've read lately, politics in America (somehow it all fit together – perfectly, I'd say; I can't recall one single time we would have been bored, Kathy and I), and now the day was slowly declining; the music coming from the restaurants seemed to have gotten louder, more and more people coming for their dinner from the city – well, wherever from, and even the boardwalk would now look like it was more crowded than, let's just say, one hour ago. We were right at the Russian restaurant I knew well from my past escapades down here (I always liked Coney Island) when Kathy said she would like to eat something, too; so in we went, just like that, got a table at the window and ordered - fish. Food was always good down here and so it was also this time. I had a little vodka to it, not much really, a splash. And we talked about Smollet and Stern – literary inadequacy of personal memoirs, the Tistram thing itself as well as what it has entailed later on, how hackneycd and trite that form has become since, and that it should probably never be used again (your life is interesting only to you!), unless that someone's unknown, seemingly unwanted and failed life (isn't that what they all want to write about, for the most part – injustice, a genius – great man who never found any recognition?), unless then that single, personal life, hence, would really warrant the use of such a form – but then again it should be refined as much as possible, certainly never left in that formless chaff in which Smollet or Stern delivered their stuff to us. I had another vodka –they served it in almost frozen form, the glass covered with mist, and I appreciated its going down without leaving almost any taste in one's mouth: a really great drink. Great! The fish was very tasty too; just melting away in your mouth, without any chewing, leaving a taste of freshness, well, culinary satisfaction, if I may say so, without any objections, which with me is rare, kind of... Actually I did have an objection – how much was the bill going to be; I know Kathy is not stingy, she will pick up her half, or rather she would like to do just that, but then what should her half be? She had one glass of Cognac for just a few bucks, then her portion of fish, not expensive at all, and I ordered the bottle that's standing right there, now, in the middle of our table and looks shockingly empty: goodness, I really seem to know how to hold my liquor as of late, I don't really feel much, no!

After dinner we had some cocktails with umbrellas, the really good stuff from the bar, a New York cheesecake we both like so much to go with them, Kathy talks about an essay in which the guy comes up with the hypothesis that Smollet, Stern and Fielding prepare the ways of the Lord – they both announce Ulysses as the top, summit of all the literary efforts ever, and also the very end, the point at which according to late Thomas Mann the overgrown spirit of the European culture flips to one side, unable to retain steadiness on the base that became totally inadequate anymore... and art – any form of art and that includes also the writing, of course – becomes sheer picking up the pieces and putting them together again, not according to life as we know it, but according to the artist's imagination (I would swear she said arsetiste – but, of course, I can't be sure; or should I say - which is what becomes so much à la mode in this town: cunt be sure? Globalism has to do something with that, I guess...) And that's also the reason why artist's imagination is so terribly important, she said then, solemnly; and why it, in turn, should be so terribly important to himself - most of all.

We took a hotel room after that. Close to Coney Island, just a little bit up one of those side streets perpendicular to the boardwalk, also with Russians at the reception desk, where I was able to get a gallon bottle of Canadian Club without really much ado. At the regular store price, too, believe it or not. We went upstairs. In the room we took our cloths off and lay down on the bed that seemed wonderfully comfortable, and Kathy kept going about the twentieth century spirit that overgrew like a cancer growth, no proportions, no limitations, no mitigation at all, and then simply fell over and just apart, and I had a drink, lamentably in plastic toothbrush cup because there was nothing else, no real glasses, even though I managed to convince Kathy to do this very old man a huge favor, to put her night gown on and go downstairs to ask. Yep! She did. And: Nope! Had to be the plastic hotel bathroom cup. Shit!

Lying on my back with my right forearm folded under my head and a teethbrushingcup half way full of Canadian Club in my left hand resting on the unmade bed, I let my thoughts slowly slip away – if I may say so.

I felt good. Only now relaxing a bit.

I think there was smile on my face.

I thought (not me – my thoughts were thinking) I had late Thomas Mann, Smollet, Stern, Fielding and the Spirit, whoever the fuck the latter might have been, all of them right up my ass, and they could all dissolve in that wonderful warmth only now slowly building up in my belly, and I thought with real fear about the moment when Kathy decides to take my now dead dick in her mouth to suck at it as diligently as her usual manner was and then as soon as she gets it more or less hard , Jeeze, she'll get on top of me and will start riding me like an old jade whose only wish left there is to die as quickly as possible. Jeeze…!

I had another refill of the toothbrush cup.

I saw redhead, right there, in front of me. Wc, she was saying, - she was really pissed off all of a sudden and I started truly, since some time already, to listen to her words with full attention - bloody we, us, yes sir, you and I, and an army of the like, we keep this crap together. What does your Jim know how to do? What does his wife know how to do? Huh? Last months you kept alive all the machinery in this huge fucking house without calling in for anyone. No! You did! And more and more he uses you for his accounting purposes as well, doesn't he? I was there, I was dusting his fucking desk and then the bookshelf, when he called that prick from Manhattan, that big shot yid, the lawyer who makes in only one fucking hour a lot more than you make in a whole week. And? They discussed. And pondered. And debated. And fucked around, didn't they. And then Jim asked you about your thoughts, and they both, the fucking specialists, listened damn carefully to what you were saying. Damn carefully! I saw it! Yes, sir! Didn't they? And then they did exactly what you told them you would do. John, wasn't that so? Am I exaggerating here? You know I am not. We hold this thing, this whole big shit out there with all those billions and trillions, all the fucked up corporate business, we do... Because you and I know what we are doing, yes sir, only because of that simple fact they, that shit up elite out there, have time to invent all the 'high income occupations,' they have time to make all the 'high finance' money they make, so that there might also be the scraps from the children's table that we get down here and have to live on in the end. Isn't that the way it is? She stood there, in the middle of the kitchen, she looked Marseillaise, I thought, ready to start building the barricades, and my only regret was that my only son had so terribly nothing from the little Gavroche, not a thing...

I thought, suddenly Kathy's beautiful teeth felt a little too sharp around my flabby dick and her index wiggling in my ass was also kind of painful to me. For the first time in a really long time I felt thankful to my cock that it wouldn't want to get hard. All I felt like was to be left alone. Not even sleep. Just close my eyes, not having to pretend, to prove anything to anyone, just be there – without thought; relax.

"John, you do drink a little too much!" Kathy said lifting up her beautiful head from my belly and looking up at me. "Unless you're fed up. Are you?"

She wasn't really looking at me. I coughed. Shook my head.

"Let me take a shower!" I said standing up.

"Yeah... Take a shower. Sure thing!"

"Shall I brew some coffee?" she asked then and I said a loud 'yes' to that.

Part of the room equipment was also the coffee machine.

While I was still in the shower she came in too. She washed my back and asked me to wash hers, and while I was doing that, looking at her butt, I felt like also grabbing her breasts from behind and, while I was squeezing them and pulling at the nipples, I started kissing her neck. Her hair cropped as short as it was had here under the shower a rainy smell to it, which in turn made me think about dogs making love (if that makes any sense) in the street during the rain, and I told her, pulling back the plastic shower curtain, to bent over and after she did we did it doggy style and it felt great again. It did. I couldn't finish inside her because she told me she wasn't protected in any way and it wasn't the right time, so I had to interrupt for just a moment, to –as she calls it –go up one flight, and then I finished. Gloriously! In those moments I understand – not in the moment itself – but shortly afterwards, after one regains the capability of thinking more or less clearly, that, yes, I understood circumcision. Without a concrete sex example I never did. Why would the almighty God be interested in Abraham's foreskin? Does that make any sense? Any sense whatsoever? Not to me. I suddenly heard Jack's voice, quite clearly – a little monotonous, in perfect agreement with me, for once… But then in those moments, like the one we just went through, you see, he says, that he's saying, God, that is, to his chosen one to just be careful – to understand that precisely his sex is the power he cannot possibly be any match to; cut off everything that's not absolutely necessary (and necessary it is because I want you to multiply–without it you would cease to exist rather quickly, isn't that right?); he talks then about the 'nations' and not the 'nation' which a lot of people don't really understand and that is of extreme, really utmost importance: absolutely necessary, hence, he says then one more time, you got it? Make sure you got it! I see him smile then (Jack), his face a little tired and I think he should get a shave: Because this is the devil's property, too, and he –whenever you call on him, will also come; and he isn't exactly someone you can show the door whenever you get bored or pissed off. You got that?

We went out of the bathroom and back into the room, with the now wide opened widows letting the sea breeze in.

We went then back to bed and she fell asleep almost right away. I couldn't, as usual. I just lay there with my eyes open, we had the little night lamp on the stand at my side of the bed still going and I thought. My thoughts teeming, moving chaotically towards something I had no idea of what it was or ever would be; I just let them. Yeah... Lately I almost didn't give redhead any help. I was the big mister student – and I had to do homework and the reading, and the rest of the bullshit, if you want to bullshit someone, and I think I wanted to. Just that! So she would cook, wash in the kitchen, clean – doing also the regular housekeeping work that was supposed to be mine; yes, she worked for both of us, so I may study, mind you. Study. And ain't that what I'm doin'? Huh?

Kathy sighed and stirred slightly at my side. I passed my hand through that incredible hair of hers and she nestled her head against my breast, strongly, as if afraid that I might not be there at some point. I kept caressing her head. And not that much later I just turned her around, onto her belly, her beautiful butt right up, and climbed on top of her. At first it was me who was doing it, but then she also joined in, if I may say so, and so we did it again. I had a cigarette and a drink, and I was just lying there, thinking again about Connecticut, about the house, the great work I was getting paid to do –and in the end, of course, about Redhead: she stood there, right in the middle of that kitchen that was bigger than some country churches inside, and her face suddenly seemed strangely pale to me. I asked her what was wrong and she said it wasn't anything really, it was gonna be over in no time, here, in her belly, probably just a gas, you know, nothing. Then she sat down at the kitchen table and I made her tea with lemon. She drank it. I never thought she was so small physically –so fragile, her back, now bent forward, seemed that of a little girl, showing the well pronounced vertebrae through the thin dress she had on. No, I never saw it so far like that. Never. She looked at me and thanked me for the tea – it did her a lot of good, yes, the thing, whatever the hell it might have been is over now, yes, she'll just have to go to the bathroom, you see, that was all it was. Yeah!

Kathy stirred and opening my eyes I saw that she was looking at me, propped on her elbows. I saw curiosity in her face but also as if a grain of fear... I'm not really sure.

"Why you crying?" she asked.

"I'm not crying."

"Your face is all wet. How can you say you're not crying? You tellin' me you pissed on your face?"

I pulled her towards me and kissed her and she returned the kiss. Then, although she did not stop looking at me, still propped in the same manner as before on her elbows, studying my face, sort of, she seemed to relax a bit, give in...

"Not sleepy?" I asked.

"I don't want you to be tortured," she said. "I don't want anyone to be tortured. You know?"

"I know," I said.

"It's your decision, John! And yours only! At this point I can't really help you in any way, you know?"

"Yes," I said. "I do."

"Stop crying!"

"I'm not crying!"

"Stop the bullshit!"

"Not sleepy?"

"I don't want you to be tortured, that's all!"

"I know. Go to sleep now!"

She kissed me good night and I kissed her back.

And then I finally fell asleep and I had dreams I wouldn't be able to reproduce in any possible way: the Death of Virgil, the boat moving through the jungle of life itself, getting thicker and thicker, and I saw all that in great and greater awe that kept on growing, until the very morning. When I opened my eyes, thirsty to death, the small square of the window was already fully filled with the daylight that seemed to be dirty. Kathy was still asleep. I had a drink, which made me cough – I almost threw up, but then it was a little better, I thought. Just a little.

Kathy got up and took a shower, after which we went downstairs to have some breakfast. She asked me if I could drive her to a hospital not far from where we were, because she had an appointment there, made yet a few days ago for this very morning. She almost forgot all about it. Hospital? What the hell for? Mostly, she told me, general stuff, ladies' undercarriage has to be inspected now and then, but also, and she wanted me to know about that too, she had a lump... well, something in her right breast, close to the armpit; so close in fact that it was very hard to detect; "you didn't, right?"...something she simply didn't like. She looked at me and smiled, spreading butter on her toast with a wide, awkward knife they gave us yet back at the counter. It may, of course turn out nothing, just as most of those things do, but it may as well be something and then one is a lot better off if it's diagnosed early on. Certainly, there was no problem on my part, I would take her there and then, after she is delivered to the door, I'll leave her at the very same and then drive to Connecticut to take Redhead from there to Oneonta.

"Let's go then!" she said, taking a large sip of her coffee and then putting the cup down on the table.

"Let's," said I, smiling, I too having a sip of my coffee that felt really wonderful.

As soon as we were through eating, we paid and got out. The car was a short distance back, towards the Coney Island and walking in the direction where the particular lot was I thought for the first time this morning that the air was fresh although it also smelled the sea and fish.

She stopped me then, holding suddenly both of my hands in hers and looking me straight in the eyes, she said:

"I want you to know, John, that I love you."

I kissed her eyes, both.

"I love you too."

"One more time: I didn't mean any harm..."

"I know you didn't."

She let go off my hands and we started to walk again. The sun was already high and the air was quickly getting hot. It was going to be a hot day, I thought. Hot like hell.

Jack. Father's travel from the North

Mother's face: all focused, deep crease between her eyebrows, her hands on the table, immobile; she tries to remember as best she can and it's a story she, too, knows only from telling, it's his – father's - story: he came to Ismaning, where she was settled with the rest of the family, one sunny day, limping, yes, he had a heavy limp, his foot was healing over from the injury he had sustained back in the North (where exactly in the North she wouldn't know –all he knew, I think, (I am not really sure) he told her without holding anything back: it happened somewhere close to Hamburg, but he himself seemed to me, at each and every single one of those times of recollection, to never have gotten to know the details: what town, for instance; she wanted to know, she insisted - later on, years later, her curiosity suddenly awakened after she then found out for the first time - good twenty years later - about the Volkswagen Fabrik on Lüneburger Heide, if that could have been it, yes, she asked and asked again, but he couldn't tell then, with those new details, either – I see him even now, trying (I think he learned that from her – when people are together for a long time they unknowingly pick up each other's mimic and this, I would swear was hers: the teeth of his lower jaw biting lightly on the upper lip) his forehead all wrinkled, each time taking a deep, deep breath: it looked - after each time having gone through all the still available, by now almost meaningless details - like really nobody still on this side of being could answer her questions anymore); from somewhere in the North then, somewhere near Hamburg, he walked, yes, walked on foot, helping himself only with a wooden stick he made of a dried up tree branch, he walked all that distance, limping, his foot never actually properly healed after the accident, with no regular supply of food –walking he would ask people now and then if they could help him and some did too - he slept in the fields in good weather and in the woods, trees of some kind - in the time of the rain. I see her face again with the same sharpness: she talks about the rain, her words suddenly having a strange, strangely bitter taste in my mouth - I think they are greenish-gray of a still wet, dense paint slowly drying on an old wood, hardened by endless years into almost a stone: big first drops just hit the dust of the road, raising the unavoidable strong smell of the summer rain between us, here and now, in the kitchen. I have to shake my head quite strong, and then even stronger, to get over that. More rarely it was a barn – someone would actually give him permission to use their barn. Yes, that too. She sat there, nodding. Wondering. Much later I sat there, too, I, too, wondering. Nodding. Shaking my head. Or the two of us together. Why did he go south, towards Bavaria and not south - east, towards Silesia, where he had been schlepped away from? According to him: somebody told him up there, still in that factory where his accident also had happened that there was in Munchen's suburbs a community of people, migrants like himself, originally from that very region he had been taken from and where he also came into this world at that one moment appointed for him, and he wanted to see them, wanted to talk to them, tell them about himself and what had actually happened to him, as he reported that to my mother shortly after they had met – here then, yes, right here, talking, facing that old house belonging then to grandma, before he would eventually go back to 'his own country'. And that 'his own country' was also a thing quite out of the ordinary (Poles were pigs, and Germans were swine, which would unchangeably provoke the question about his own allegiances – her simplistic: who then would he be? provoking each and every time the also unchangeable growl: Silesian).

People who met him back then, my mother's grandma, my mother herself, and yet few others, seemed to agree on one thing: he looked like an apparition. Like he was about to die from exhaustion and starvation - a ghost out of a bad movie, as my mother's mother put it later on. My mother would work on that: maybe more like a ghost from a lousy religious movie, who at the end of his penance in Limbo or Purgatory had decided at the last minute to put on the human shape again – for whatever reason. There was a crust of dirt on his face. God, he must have been like that all over, she says, sighing, and she wipes her face off with her hand. All over. He soaked for hours in the cellar zinc bathtub –hours and hours on end. He also slept in that very cellar until they left Ismaning together (to, then, both of them travel to Silesia he wanted at any rate to get back to – that was something he just would never give up). He would get meals upstairs, in the living room, though, together with them.

She nods again; and she sighs.

His job in that factory consisted in hitting a heavy artillery shell coming down on a conveyor belt, straight from the casting graphite form, yet before it would get to be treated and improved any further, made suitable in the end for that one particular moment of leaving the canon barrel carrying the best wishes to wherever it might be sent entering the human world for good - at the moment, hence, he was talking to her about that blessed thing would still be standing upright, yes, he would have to hit it with a huge sledge hammer - most everybody around him was out of position to even lift that hammer off the floor - hit it time and time again, until the form's graphite left-overs inside the shell would come off and out, all of it nicely loosened up and ready to be simply swept off that belt. At some point he hit it with that hammer too strongly or, perhaps, the shell was sitting there unevenly, there's never been any investigation, nothing such, suffice it to say, it just flipped over to one side and before he knew that shell weighing good quarter tone was on his left foot – what was left of it. They took him to what they called 'Lazaret' (field hospital of sorts) and just left him there. He would get not only no medicines, but also no food. They took him there to die. To them he was just a Polish swine, cheap work force worth feeding only as long as he was able to do what they were expecting him to do – hence, why would they waste food (or anything, for that matter) on something that just wasn't worth it anymore? They (he himself and yet another lucky skunk just like him - in pretty much the same predicament) would catch roaches – there was no dearth of that there; once or twice they got even more lucky: 'Schinken'- ham: a big fat rat -- one had to lie still, wait up for the right moment, and then reach out – as fast as possible, reach out, closing one's hand really quickly, catching. Rats were relatively easy to find (they would actually find you) in that 'hospital' and thanks to those, probably most of all among the other 'help' he had, he also survived. He was too weak, after a couple of months of that kind of 'cure', too exhausted to go back to his former work, so they, stunt by his being alive at all, just let him go as soon as he was only able to stand upright. Go! You're free now! Just go! The sun was up high on the sky and he started walking, too – as best he could. Down south. To be able to talk to his people again as soon as possible. To live.

My mother nods and I do too.

Many a time I have requested to scc his 'hoof' – as my mother would call it; in the evening when he was changing to go to bed, his shoes off first, then socks, I would ask him to tell me about it (again and again – his story would never actually bore me; not once). And I will always remember his hand on my head and his smile when he did that the first time - and only a little later I was able to faultlessly point out the spots out of which pus would come out back then, whenever he would sit down on the side of the road and unwrap the 'hoof', taking off the rag that was getting, according to his own words, stiffer and stiffer, and more and more smelly, but of course he didn't have another one to replace it and he couldn't expect miracles, right? – well, yes, once there was a river, like a miracle, sort of, yes, and he carefully descended to it from the road he was on, and he soaked the rag for a longer while, quite a while in fact, in that slow moving water until it got cleaner – there was no soap. No! Yes, there… And there, too. Yes! He could now touch it delicately, timidly, sort of, still apprehensive, as if still expecting pain, and back then the yellow stinking dense liquid would slowly come up to the 'surface' and out, over that rosy, young, strangely delicate, as if not yet quite formed flesh, only a moment later joined by an admixture of dark, also hellishly stinking blood. At least he thought it was blood… Was he afraid? And at that moment he would slowly, with that same smile around his mouth, explain to me that every living thing is afraid of dying, yes, he too was no exception to that rule, and it was pretty clear to him that if he had gotten gangrene or some such, the only thing he could expect was a slow and probably painful death on one of those dusty roads. The only thing people would make sure of back then and there would have been that he wouldn't die on their property. They would probably carry him off to a local cemetery or some such, would be his thought. Maybe someone with a touch of pity would mercifully use their shotgun to put him out of his misery. That too seemed possible to him. Maybe… No, he didn't feel too well about any of that. Nope! Yes! Right there! Right there! He would quickly confirm the deep scar I just put my finger on. Right there! That one could have been the worst. But it too healed before he actually got to Ismaning. The pus stopped and a scab appeared on it. Tough as nails. Black. That was when he knew that he was gonna live. That he had made it. He never met Hans afterwards – the guy he was with in that stinking hole they called 'Lazaret'. And I see his eyes now again – gray, deep, like the sky reflected in the sea; the wind not too strong, just sufficient to slightly wrinkle the surface. "I would love to know if he had survived…" there is a strange sadness in his face when he says that. I wish… He didn't even know the guy's last name. He never asked. He lowers his head, looks at the floor - seems like it - and then, when I already ceased to expect anything, he would suddenly say: 'God uses evil to bring us closer to him, you know?'

Ernie

The house we would live in wasn't much bigger, if at all, than what we had so far. From my room, though, there was a view – the house we were supposed to be in had been built on the coast, on top of the Connecticut high cliff, and the view of the sea from my window was really breathtaking. Mauna would have her room all to herself, if we had little kids, they would have a separate room each of them, too. I thought we all liked what we saw. But I don't think the house was what made me make my final decision. It was the shop – if one could call it that; some – I still don't really know the exact amount – hundred cars, thereabouts, yeah… most of them in perfectly drivable conditions, cars, whose price I wouldn't be in any position to asses without consulting professional sources; there was one Duisenberg, for instance, - Jeez… there was a 917 Porsche, and then a 962, both with respective LeMans and Daytona credentials.

Lifts. And tooling – quality I'd never seen so far anywhere in my whole life. The first job I got – even before I said 'yes' to any of it – was the owner's Carrera 4 he would drive in everyday life, hence an incredibly high mileage, in which the engine seemed to be slowly going. I jacked the rear end up right then and there, and looked. I told John who was there with me that it was an alusil engine, which I expected anyway, and that there were a couple of ways to choose from – buy new from Porsche, second: buy two blocks from the above, third: sent to England to have it cast iron re-sleeved, the latter being my personal recommendation. I would then put it back together right here. There was a small guy there, kind of grayish, a common little birdie you wouldn't even look at, whom I seemed to see wherever we went, John and I, always – as it, again, seemed to me – pretending to do something more than actually doing it. When I expressed my opinion as to what should be done about the Carrera's engine, he just said – he was very close, I'd say, he was next to us, strangely, at that very moment – "So you accept...?" He stretched his hand towards me and introduced himself as the owner –John's boss. I looked around. I smiled to myself. Then I just said: "Yes, I do!" like people say it in the church to one another.

John organized the moving. He also organized the sell of whatever we had back there that could be sold, except the house – I insisted on that one. John would be the guy to issue my paychecks from then on.

We moved. And shortly after that John told me to call Autofarm in England and have the job arrangements made – whatever was necessary. I did, too. Then I took the engine out and apart and together we took the stuff to the airport, John was actually driving the van, where I found out that the engine was going to be taken to England aboard the private jet that belonged to my new boss – by a crew that also was on his payroll. John told me that the plane would fly once, and sometimes twice a week, to Paris or London, with our boss' wife as its sole passenger. Because she liked it there. Son of a gun!

Because she liked it there.

Since we'd moved I got a new habit of getting up earlier than ever before – and that's because the sunrises out of the sea. I get up and just sit there, on a chair, in front of that huge glass window that is actually one of the walls of the room, giving onto the waters down there and the sun –well, light, slowly at first, but then a lot faster, and then yet faster, immerging from behind the horizon; from where I am then and there the night ceases to be in a matter of minutes – darkness turns into a full blown day, and I am sitting there, rubbing my eyes that are each of those times a little blinded. It makes you think: what is all that? And who are you? What's the scoop here? Is this it? Or is there something else we should probably consider – like what they used to be talking about in the church when I was little. Well, is there? There are no answers – just that feeling of satisfaction, like when I was a child and would come back from the yard after having played for a longer time, hungry, I remember being hungry probably better than anything else, and cutting myself a piece of apple pie – right there, without having to ask – yeah, that feeling now all back –whenever I see the sun getting from behind the horizon like that...

This morning Mauna came in from her room (since we moved she took to spending her nights in her room, dammit!), she grabbed herself a chair too, and we were sitting together and watching it. I put my arm around her shoulder and suddenly I thought I did that for the last time yet back in Hawaii. Did she have the same questions I have? Maybe not. How would I know... But then she said:

"Have you ever thought what were we before we were born?"

"A time or two."

"And?"

"Look!" I said. "Just look!"

"Yeah..."

A half of the gigantic disc was now out of the water, blinding; there was a wide road over the ocean leading broadly to that disc, itself also blinding; I thought about it, too.

"I think we are lucky," Mauna said.

"I guess you got that right!"

"I'm sure!"

"Yeah, me too."
"Luck…"
She sighed.
"Luck…"

Eve & Kim

I saw right away, almost the moment I entered, that she did something with the wall: the wall across the studio, with two windows giving onto the street, that had never had any plaster on it, she did something… painted it with clear lacquer of some kind that brought out the dark depth of the bricks, that old, almost, somehow, historic red, yes, she also put a filter onto the shade of the big, steel movable lamp with the long arm– the red was now deeper… well, still more than that.

Right in the middle of the room there was a blanket spread on the floor with a pillow, beside which there was Jack's writing.

"Do you read it a lot?"

"Yes," she answered me. "A lot. I can't stop. It gave me the idea that there might be color to the drawing… I started experimenting with the light – I think I am slowly getting it. I do. By the way," she looked quickly at me, changing the subject like that, which I didn't expect, "did he ever try to publish that stuff?"

I shook my head, undecidedly.

"Do you know anything about the publishing business?"

"No!" she said. "Not really."

"Suffice it to say that he sent it to a 'publisher', here in New York. They in turn sent it to a critic and the latter typed a true panegyric; the word 'great' seemed to be plain abused… But that's not what I wanted to tell you… See, before they sent it to that gal, he, Jack, talked to the senior editor of that publisher. The guy wanted to know where Jack's writing comes from, you understand, who from did he learn to write. Jack told him it was Proust, Joyce, Faulkner, DosPassos and… yet somebody else, I'm not sure right now. Then he, Jack, made a joke –he thought he was making a joke- asking if the editor ever heard any of those names. He was really stunned hearing the simple: 'doesn't ring a bell…"

"You kidding, right?"

I laughed now.

"No, I am not kidding and that was also Jack's question: 'you kidding, right?' exactly as you did just now, and the answer to it was 'no, I'm not, why?'"

"What the fuck was he doing in that business? Why not sell cars… Or something…? Huh? Soft rubber dildos?"

"Very much Jack's question too. See, that's why I asked you if you knew anything about the writing business – there are things one has a hell of a hart time to even believe. It's all automatized; computerized. A guy who actually reads books in the book publishing business that is by today's standards an anachronism. Dinosaur. A Malcolm Cowley today wouldn't probably be able to find a job at all. Faulkner – forget it! Forget it doubly!

Talking to her then I didn't know yet what was going to happen to Jack - not that much later. And even then, after it already had happened and Jack was all of a sudden taken away from us in a way we simply couldn't comprehend, she turned out to be a true friend – she really helped a lot, she was the one who kept me alive during the first period of time afterwards, she was just there – for me, as well as for him, she never said 'no' to any of our requests, although she had in the end received the contract from Donovan and started working on the project which would take all of her time, well, most if it anyway; I always wanted to just thank her; thank her – somehow; hug her maybe. I never knew how to thank her. And I never did, too.

"And?" she asked then.

"Nothing. Jack got pissed off. You know him. Told them all to go ahead and fuck themselves – to each and every single one of them. Because they kept calling, I have to tell you. Oh, yeah, they did. Like those telephones about mortgages or credit cards. Like that. You know?"

"That shit can really get one going!"

53

"Got him going too. Enough to call the FBI and ask to put a stop to the crap."

"Wow!"

"Yeah… What's with the light? I asked her then. "Could you elaborate a little on that? Why that wall?"

"I'm not exactly sure, "she said. "See, when you feel something it shows in your attitude. In the way you move, talk. Your gestures, right? All that."

"Clear."

"Yeah. Here I am showing what I think I should be showing in drawing. Line. Thicker. Thinner. Less or more deep – into the paper. And drawing seems OK. You like it too, right? But then I saw this wall – its color. It was like that green stuff: here it's not the taste, though, it's color… As children we are more sensuous, right? There is more of what I'm talking about now in us, both, boys and girls. Only then… the A then B, then C type of thing starts and once really having started, it takes over, it simply eliminates color and smell and taste… You see? I'll leave the drawing the way it is. But there also has to be that wall – somewhere. I don't know yet how or where but I know it'll be there, just as you see it now, and they'll be walking, they'll just keep on walking, like they do now, too – not for the wall, see, for the color; and the color is not there without the wall, so the wall will have to be there, too, somehow. Shit, I'm working on it. You know? I don't quite understand what the fuck I'm talking about right now, but I know one thing: I am on my way up there. When I am here, on that blanket, looking at it, everything I am, my life, all of it is right there; not in the wall; but also not in me; I and that wall –got it?- me and it, we, then, are my life… also the pain of realization and translation. Are you getting any of this?" She looked at me with great, it seemed to me, concern. "I'm asking not to question your ability to understand, but I simply know that I am babbling, it's all chaotic, not really thought through. That's why."

"I think I am getting it, Kim," I said. "And I also think it's pretty much impossible to express what you're trying to express in any more ordered way… It's the nature of that stuff. I know your mother was half Polish and Half German."

She looked at me, surprised.

"Why?'

"Do you actually speak any of the two –Polish or German?"

"Some German, why?"

"I could give you Ingarden to read. Precisely about that. But I have it only in German. He's one of Jack's favorite also. Reading him might help you put it a little bit more together."

"I read Hildebrandt," she said, surprising me in turn. "I know some of his thought through my mother." She shook her head. "Not now, Eve! No! Not now! I've got too much work right now, I've gotta do a lot of thinking, a lot, nothing is really ready yet. I think," she smiled at me, kinda sad, "whenever I'm through this project, I'll ask you to lend me the books…I would also be curious how I would get along with German reading a phenomenology manual… Jeez!"

Zebek (Jack's mother tells the poor boy's story)

He was born in a house, well, house… a mud hut, where other people's houses would end and empty meadows begin. His mother would go from house to house to do the laundry or whatever they might have had to do at any given moment, yes, she would make her living on a boondoggle like that… No one knew who his father was. Just at some point people noticed that she was expecting a child and then he, Zebek, was born. Yes, just like that. Nothing changed in her life all that time, before or after, or, for that matter, during her pregnancy; she kept on doing what she had been doing ever since anyone could remember.

Mother sighs now, her eyes focused fully on the past.

"My friend, Maria Otto had been here longer then we have so I asked her, since we were always on friendly bases, ever since we settled down here, really, as the saying goes 'from the day one'" – Mother's face is now all wrinkled and she is faintly smiling, remembering, making me wonder again about the miracles of our memory – "but she knew nothing more than that either."

Nothing! Ever since he was little, but also grown enough to be called something, anything, everybody would call him 'Zebek'. Just that. Does it mean anything? In vernacular, dialect... No! Not that I'd know, anyway. They just called him that, period. Whatever it is. However it came about. Ever went to school? Nope! His mother most probably didn't even know there was such a thing as school, - I don't think she did.

They kept on like that until the angel story happened. I look at her and she smiles. Is she sad? At least now I don't think she really was. No! She was more of a reporter at that moment, a story teller, perhaps, no, she did not display emotions, if she had any about the facts she was reporting to me. A very simple story. There were angels in the church, very realistic sculptures, finished with oil paint in such a manner that they looked... well, one would expect them to really be able to speak to one and when they did not one was kinda disappointed. One was. Three on each side of the altar. Zebek asked the priest Goettowski about them. He wanted to know something, whatever it was... Goettowski remembered that later. Later, yes! One was missing – broken off its (his? her?) pedestal, obviously, and just taken away. Goettowski called the police. They arrived 'at the scene' and he told them, in a general conversation, not really as some separate, stressed detail he would attach some special attention to, no, about Zebek's having asked – trying to collect information of some kind at some point about the now missing sculpture. They went, of course, straight to the mud house where Zebek lived, first thing, and, sure as the sun up on the sky, they found the sculpture right there, no further ado necessary! She looks at me, smiles, and I know she is thinking very intensely about something she doesn't want to share with me now – her forehead is all wrinkled, her crochet stopped in midair, and so has the story. Yeah... She nods. They took him. She nods again. And sighs. He came back as an adult. His mother was still alive, although not quite well – there was something wrong with her head, she could talk, yes, that was there, but she didn't make much sense. People stopped giving her those little chores to do because they didn't think she was capable of handling them anymore, not even that, so it would really be hard to tell what was it she would live on. Must have been ravens bringing her food – as the bible says: flesh and hearth cakes – whatever that might be. But she stayed alive, oh, she did! Yes, all those years she managed to stay very much alive. Mother smiles, sadly. Perfectly. Little, sick, obviously cuckoo, but perfectly alive. Shrinking, though. Whenever I saw her on the street she seemed smaller each time. Shrinking. Loosing substance, if you will.

Looking at her now, in my memory, I think about goodness. Infinity. Eternity. I just can't stop.

She works for a while like a machine, faster, I think, than usual.

His first victim after they'd released him was Maria Otto, my mother's dear friend. He took her purse, that was what he was after, but in order to get it - she wouldn't just yield to him – he'd beat her up badly. Hit her face with his fists several times. And he was a big guy – yes, he came back as a big strong… God, please forgive me! She nods her head again. I couldn't recognize her for quite a while after that, you know? She spent some time, quite some time… in the hospital in the city. I paid her a couple of visits there, made her cheese cake she liked almost as much as you do, apples, and poppy seeds cake also – she like that one very much… Your father was getting better at the time, they moved him from the passport division up to… I'm not sure what exactly, but he's got his promotion right about then, if I remember correctly, and I think I do. Yes. They just did things, I mean, he and his blessed friends in that division. That was also when he came up with the communist sympathies and when they started to warn him… I thought we had too much money, believe it or not, and that too much money is never any good – never, any good, to no one. Remember that!

I tried to redirect her back towards her beat up friend.

Oh, yes, Maria got out then, they released her and I was there to help her, and the same week, I think, she applied, precisely in father's division, for a gun permit. She wanted to be able to defend herself. Your father helped her, they went together to get, you know, physically get, after all the formalities, that endless paperwork had already been done, they went together to get the gun from a store they had downstairs in the same building, and then he also taught her how to use it in the bathroom in that building, in the same bathroom he told you about himself, I remember well, I was there, where the rich Jewish merchants from town would get their armament and then the 'training' he'd offer. Right? We talked, Maria and I, she too did not have anybody else to talk to, we talked and we enjoyed being able to share things, and I told her at some point that I was happy, that I enjoyed my life or, rather, that I would enjoy it, if it weren't for all those things I did not enjoy – then or ever. The balls. The coming back at night, bubbly, not making much sense, if any at all, sleeping then and snoring like an animal or some kind of a senseless machine at work nobody wanted, waking then up, totally disoriented, in the middle of the night to get a drink of water, and then snoring again. She nodded. We're getting there...

She put her crocheting aside and, having stood up, went over to the kitchen stove. She lifted up the porcelain cover on the miniature porcelain kettle for brewing tea essence purposes and, disappointed, said loud, looking back at me: "We don't have anymore tea! Did you know that?" I don't remember if I did or did not know about the tea, but I do remember her making it and I do know I shall never be able to forget the process itself, the ceremony, whoever ever of the two, father or her, would be doing it at any given moment– that pouring the dried up, making the for me quite audible impression of a field of rye rustling in the summer wind, black stuff from a cubic metal box into that toy-like porcelain kettle miniature, then pouring water onto the layer of that essence of dryness on the bottom, later – the water in the big kettle had to be boiling first (she had to add few pieces of anthracite into the stove and set that big black metal water kettle (the real thing) onto the fire, the small porcelain toy sitting right on top of it). The water would boil in only a few minutes and she would pour it onto the black tea leaves, letting then the whole arrangement sit there, on the fire for yet some time to come. And then she would ask me if I wanted tea also, and that I would answered her question unchangeably in the affirmative, she would pour the by then also almost black tea essence out of that tiny porcelain kettle into the two pieces of old gold rimmed china we still had at that time, thinning it down with the boiling water from the big kettle, after which she would let those too sit there for yet a few minutes, before declaring them ready for the final consummation...

"J'avais vraiment soif," she then said in French, although that was not the time for my lesson. But she would teach me French whenever she could. She would read to me books she liked. Her literary choices... Her favorite – and my eyes just wander unwittingly to the shelf with her books and the good two feet, right in the beginning, of the 'Comédie humaine.'

"Where were we?"

"You were telling me about father becoming a drunk. The balls. The drunken nights. That."

"Not a drunk! No! He would never get a bottle to get drunk by himself. No. The blessed balls, precisely. Lots of money. Bribes. I'm sure of that. All that societé de... Bon Dieu! Yeah..."

"And what about that guy we started with. The "Zebek" fellow?"

And she re-starts, after having nodded a couple of times, having sighed deeply and finally picking up her crochet work, telling me that the guy became a regular bandit, that he would molest people in the street for money and not only, actually, for money – but for the fun of it: you see, there is a point you can't go beyond, because if you do that is exactly what's gonna happen: you lose your feeling, your humanity, you lose everything... He would beat up people simply because he enjoyed beating up people, seeing them in blood, down on the sidewalk, moaning. Police? Well, if they could catch him *in flagranti,* they might, just might finally be able to do something at some point. The thing was that they never did. He knew how to do his mischief without witnesses, and so it was pretty close to impossible for them to really do that something most everybody was expecting from them in vain. Usual, isn't it? The system, as we call it today, just doesn't work in cases like that. I interrupted her by saying that they were able to put him behind bars and that for long years –for a stolen wooden angel... That worked. And she nodded and smiled again. Yes, that worked. It's us! The so called modern society, OK? Or better yet: highly developed society, huh? Next was the guy down the street, the what's his name... She thinks, then she does recall, gives me the name, and says that the one after that was really bad, had to be hospitalized and after that one they really tried to get to him but he just vanished into thin air for months on end. His mother by then couldn't be talked to anymore at all, complete dementia, so they just dropped it for the time being, one more time. One more time hopeless and helpless.

She had a sip of tea. I remember her looking then at the window, her head slightly turned to the right, for a longer period of time. I knew she wasn't really looking at that window the frost had covered during the night before with all the Hans Christian Andersen's fairy tails I loved so much, or rather she was looking that way - through that window - at something she was trying to tell me about.

How hard it is to tell something –to do your subject justice; how really hopeless we feel at times, trying to measure up to that immensity of the memory, that almost immeasurable, gigantic edifice our memory turns suddenly out to be, almost as soon as we decide to cloth it in words; to deliver it out of the isolation of our own soul to our listener out there.

I see her quite clear now – although she died so long ago.

She starts, awkwardly, obviously intimidated by her subject, uncertain… She paints slowly the late afternoon light, the dust on that road, heat, visible through that window she now had moved herself to, and I also see him, father, coming back, drunk - he was swaying, not all that much, no, he would know well how to hold his liquor, coming back home, in that late summer afternoon heat. And there was also, coming from the opposite direction, 'Zebek'… She saw both of them, Zebek approaching father, obviously asking for money, that was always his start, and father just nodding, reaching into his inner pocket, getting his wallet out, and then she saw instead of the wallet his revolver and the first shot really sounded like a thunder. Father emptied the cylinder into the body. And then:

"Mon Dieu… I'm not really sure that I should tell you that…"

She bit her lower lip, looking at her work, thinking, deliberating with herself – should the story be told, or maybe not…

And then she looked straight at me. Quickly. Furtively.

"His back was to me then but I saw it nevertheless… He opened his fly, your father, God… and desecrated the body from head to toe.

Then he came in. Humming. I cried for days after that, you know?
I'd lived with a Landru... Mon Dieu Sénieur..."
"Why don't you have some tea?" I said.
"Yeah..."
She nods.
"People around here loved him for that..."
"I would imagine they did."
"People..."
Her head moves slowly in the same sadly nodding gesture.
She looks at me. Or through me at something.
"Yeah..."

Wyatt Erp

Eva was better now – this time the printer spat out the picture she
has been after for quite a while by now, but all this time up to that
point something would unchangeably go askew, no mater how
carefully she would set it up: she wanted to print out from the internet
'the view of Delft' by Vermeer, to look at it while she would read
(look, put down the picture and read, then put down the book, raise
the picture and look at it, remember, feel, recall, think, then read
again), the fragment she thought was the greatest literary analysis
of musical effort the geniuses throughout the history of mankind
ever managed to bring about: the end of the first volume, when
Swan is at the Verdurins.' She thought the view of Delft she's been
trying to print out now and couldn't succeed was a perfect *pendent*
to that fragment. Proust himself says something to that effect, too,
somewhere, she couldn't recall now... Clarity in the fog: something
we know well, we just can't recognize: that stage of memory we
are sure we know we are close to the subject (K.G.Jung, according
to her, would say that the content's energy level is almost sufficient
to surface – there is only the simple compatibility problem with the
rest of the field) - but it's coming, yes, it's almost there, I know, I
just can't be sure yet, one more effort, it's on the tip of my tongue
really, just bear with me, a little patience...

"Yes, this is it," she said lifting up the page from the printer. "Finally."

Then she looked at me, smiling, the dark cloud from the middle, dissipating, disappearing in the sky, quickly becoming closer to the blue that must bloody be somewhere, better be somewhere in that background.

"Why are you not writing?" she said then. "You haven't been at the computer for days on end." She cleared her throat. "Do you feel lazy?"

I smiled at her, but she shook her head.

"Do you?"

"I can really relate…" I said, "even appreciate the fact that you want me to keep writing. I mean that you're interested in my work at all. I do. But I always have to know first, Eve… It takes time, always. You see? Why do I actually decide to write something… Why do I think it is, or just might be, worth telling others about it. What is, for instance, so important in the scene you appreciate so much, in which my father, still in those times I wasn't even around, shot a hoodlum everybody was sick and tired of. Do you see that? That's not something characteristic of a national hero, is it? Not back then and, particularly, not now. Why then? You see…?

She just kept on looking at me.

"A national hero in this here country was Wyatt Erp – a guy who would take the shackled hoodlum and, all submerged in the armed to the teeth crowd of other hoodlums at large, hardly able to watch his own back, would escort that subject from such metropolis as Holy Piss Valley all the way to Tucson to be hanged there in all the majesty of the law. There is something almost Greek in that. A true drama. Greatness, if you will – not even the greatness of the great Wyatt himself, but of the human being in general: sacrifice to the transcendental; being at one with God, living by every word of the creator, right?

She laughs. She shakes her head. Then, not looking at me anymore, she starts talking, a smile still erring around her mouth:

"The train robbers figured out, though, you see, and that seems to be the point here - that might be your 'why' - and not that much later at that, that all those people, shaking, emanating all that almost tangible hatred towards the guy with the gun, with a trembling hand handing over the watch nevertheless to save their meaningless, unwanted and totally failed lives, those earrings, the wallet, the whatthehellever… that they can be made to do the same without all that hatred, hence, without all that risk. Right? That there doesn't have to be anyone behind the robber's back to watch it (the one who also unavoidably misses something time and again – in which case they would both – the watcher as well as the watchee – just plain be dead at the spot or later on, as alternative to that, being taken by our heroic Wyatt from Holy Piss Valley to Tucson to be hanged), oh, yes, sir, they – your Zebeks – very soon figured out that they can get all that without the slightest risk on their part… By becoming a Legislative Body themselves and then by creating proper legislation, respective to that." She dallies with the word –stretches it, goes syllable by syllable one more time: "Le-gi-sla-tion…" And then: "Ju-ris-pru-dence. You see? They now can even hire the great Wyatt to take to Tucson to be hanged those who refuse to give up their wallets, watches, or whatthefuckevers, now can't they?"

"That's a business," I said, I, too, laughing now. "Isn't it?"

"Yes, sir! Big business! Those very same poor chops from the train, this time without a slightest trace of hatred, would now come to the legislators of their own will and just hand over those earrings (their hands still trembling a little from the pain of having to part with the goods), watches, wallets and whatevers… right? And they (whoever that might mean now) wouldn't be stupid either (they also got some schooling in the meantime), of course, no, they wouldn't use that old threadbare terminology nobody likes - to call their actions at present 'train or highway robbery' anymore, 'train stopping' or some such. No! Now it would be 'fiscal politics'. 'Fiscal responsibility' – even better. The ones who take stuff are now 'Federal Reserve'. How do you like that?" And then, I just can't help thinking that she really enjoys herself at this point – it's like a cabaret: Good morning, bienvenus, welcome… She looks at me all the time: "Look at DC, at the, what we call, for some reason all along unfathomable to me, 'Government' – those 'faces' - isn't that sheer Zebek? And wouldn't you like for your father with his gun to be there this time as well, to do it all over again?"

"Defining the new hero, huh?"

"It's an easy definition. Simple."

Her telephone rang and she was talking to someone for a while, before I realized it was my agent she was talking to and their conversation was about me and my work. Good. I didn't want to talk to him now – didn't feel like talking not just to him, jeez, him or anybody else, for that matter. Then she turned it off. She picked up the fresh print of the Vermeer and looked at it. For quite a while. And after that, putting it down, she looked at me again.

"I just thought about that guy in the train with the gun in his hand, you know?" she said. She nodded a couple of times with conviction. "I think it was simple. It was straightforward – frank, if you will. There was nothing in that what is in it now – all the sickly mockery... Bullshit. People around you loose in a hurry everything they ever worked for and then got to have, and an imbecile with a face that one automatically wants to suggest taking lessons in how to sit on it shows up on the screen telling you that 'the economy is solid.'" She nods again, with the same conviction. "That frankness (that guy is the good one, and this one here is the scoundrel) is gone. That is gone for good. Yes!"

I think I would have nothing to add to that. I feel just about the same way about any of it.

We talk then about Vermeer: the half shadows, the almost transparency of colors, perfect definition of objects on one hand and yet how strangely they express the ineffable they are there to express – those... touches, those tremblings of that dark immeasurable cloud in the middle, that immense endless night of the soul suddenly (it is always sudden) confronted with being, whose first and foremost characteristic is that ineffability the picture, somehow, is about – we know them, yes, they are familiar, perfectly so, recognizable each and every single time, we just don't have any idea whatsoever, not the faintest one, what they are. And here we get to see them. Captured."

Eve looks at me. She slowly bites her upper lip with the front teeth of her lower jaw, which gives her a little strange, tenderly-pensive look

(I have a quick reflection that I know the mien – it too belongs to the past), that gets to my heart the fastest and leaves there the probably deepest traces of, who knows, maybe even all our times together. Those little things so incredibly important, that we are unable to forget, ever; they just stay with us through whatever happens.

"Is art really the only thing we have down here?"

I don't know.

"Sometimes," I said, half way to myself, I too suddenly made pensive, "I think it is. Yes…"

"Yeah…"

"I think," I said then, "you should copy it." She looks at me, waiting, trying to figure out what am I talking about. "You just reproached me my not doing anything as of late. And yourself? Shouldn't that be your 'something to do' now?" I look at her and she smiles. "Copy it! The way you understand it. Doesn't have to be Vermeer at all."

She keeps on smiling.

McKenzie

I've been watching Irving for the last few minutes – we sit across the huge mahogany desk that by itself could be a good intimidating tool, there is a bottle of water in front of everyone of us and a piece of paper with pen; Irving is great in my opinion: he talks at a low voice, very calmly, very much to the point, his legal preparation is amazing to me (considering he never went to high school – it is just his private reading, he wanted to know, you see, he always wanted to understand what is it that makes this planet of ours a paradise to some and hell to most of us. Now he talks about it: he talks about the added value and its division (it's his reading but also my lectures on 'Capital'- I remember all the questions he asked me when we were talking about that and him writing it all down for later), the distribution that is so unjust that it really, considering the means of production today, stinks to high heaven –which in turn shall in a foreseeable future also lower the production, lower all the capacities, and then it also shall be that they, the owners shall discover how little equipment means, if people say they've had it. He is not naïve. Oh, no! He is not, and he would ask anyone in the room whoever might have made such an assumption, to give it up, please, better now than later, it would save a lot of time. He came here to negotiate and he knows perfectly well what is negotiable and what is not. Last month we've had two victims; two dead guys, one worker, and one cop. That is what's got to stop. Can the factory afford benefits? Of course it can! Can it afford paid vacation of reasonable extent? Of course it can. Do we have to follow the state minimum as far the wages? Of course not! It's up to us. These things shall finally be granted to those people who are killing themselves in the production ateliers in order to meat the norms. Or – as yet another possibility – a strike shall begin tomorrow. It's gone too far. People are not going to back off now. No, Siree! These papers shall be signed, and the changes shall be made. The world has to go forward and not backwards, gentlemen!

The general manager responded that they would need more time, a few days, the board will have to be consulted, those are decisions that cannot be made without the board's approval, he, Irving, can surly understand that, there'll have to be another meeting and more people should be heard. That'll have to also be arranged. Right?

Irving said to that he wasn't so sure if that was right or not, but he could relate to board consultations, and then there was a lot of push-pull type of thing as to when should that 'another' meeting take place. They made a date and that was that for the day. We left, went to our bar, had a couple of beers, and then went home.

Next day, I'm not sure, the day after… I found out – his son called me - Irving was dead. He died overnight, heart attack. I went to his house, of course, and his wife, not herself at all, squealing like a poor pig jumped on me – it was all my fault, they killed him, those pigs, they killed him because I pushed him into that crap and that's why they killed him, those fuckin' pigs… She started at some point drumming with her fists on my chest and the only thing I could actually feel was pity – such that I had tears in my eyes. I just stood there, Irving's son was trying to pull her away from me, delicately,

sort of, but I mentioned him not to. Just let her be. What the hell.
I hardly could feel her fists on my chest but inside I could feel my
heart – that was a real pain I could hardly bare. I put my arms
around her and pulled her to me. With her head on my chest she
got quieter, she just sobbed. Then I lead her to the table and made
her sit down. I wanted to know how he died. What happened? Did
anything happen at all? Anything they could tell me about? And
the answer was 'no.'

I too had a hell of a hart time to believe that he died of natural
causes, just like that. In these circumstances. Huh? We are on the
eve of signing something that changes the position of a worker,
obviously decreases the net profit of the owners, board, and the
rest of the crap, and here he is: he – conveniently – dies. Just like
that! Huh? On the other hand, though, they were all here, in the
house, all of them, his son, his daughter, his wife, and nobody heard
anything. No breaking in. No, not a trace of that. Now, how would
one explain something like that. I know I can't.

But then the meeting came. We were sitting at the same table,
with the same water and paper and pen, and what else BS have you,
and they were trying to tell me that our conditions are not acceptable
and they will have to be 'adjusted down a little', and I told them that
nothing, not one thing in that petition shall be changed. He, Irving,
paid for it with his life and it shall remain just as he had prepared
the whole thing. Even if - I said that clear and loud - if I were to
die too. I represent the union of the workers of this factory. I have
consulted my opinion that I just voiced with them. If there's a trial
to change anything in that petition first thing on Monday morning
people are going on strike. Period. Indefinitely. We know that some
of us can be replaced with the Mexicans. Yes. Not too many of us,
though. The process is to complex, it takes a lot of schooling to be
able to do what that crew out there does in its daily endeavor, and
I think, well, we all do, that sooner rather than later we'll get what
we want, so let's not waist each other's time. Shall we?

The general manager wanted to know what have I meant by
'were I to die too'. I looked him in the eye. Hard. Long. He lowered
his eyes in a certain manner and I knew - I knew, no supposition,

no guesswork, no, I knew at that moment - that Irving did not just have a heart attack. I knew there was no point in trying to nail the suckers, they'd hired somebody from New York, some top pro hit man from the Wobs or some such. But I knew. And everybody will know. Irving died for the cause. If anyone gets a penny more they should thank him for that. He put down his own life for them. It doesn't matter, in my humble opinion, if he knew that they would go thus far, or if he didn't. He's lost his life doing what he believed in and that's what counts. Right?

So many people got injured or even- like Cluski or Irving here – died, but we also have achieved something, haven't we? The American worker –the blue color little guy – cannot be prodded by means of a nightstick, water canon or tear gas wherever the organized greed wants him to be. Not anymore. And what are they gonna do now? They can fuck themselves for starters. All they'll ever be able to do shall be… to make it global, would be my guess. To take American industry, our ingenuity, inventiveness, intelligence, the good two centuries of preparation and schlep it to somewhere else. Sign some kind of global treaty that would allow them to take the production to, let's say, China or some stinkin' Mexico, or some such where the local poorer than poor cockroach will work a day for a dollar - without having to pay border tolls; use the poor on the other side of the globe, those who have not yet learned how to defend themselves while to the ones right here an explanation shall be given that I, for one, was just a 'boomer,' we, Cluski, Irving and them other guys (without any degree of generational accuracy – there finally are people six, eight, ten etc. years older than I am, just as there are those who are younger in the same way– all of which doesn't matter) we shall all be boomers, mind you (just lucky schmuck- it happened to have worked out for us the way it did, some strange, unexplainable thing occurred in the country's economy); the fact that I could buy a house and sent my kids to college (well, Ernie wasn't exactly a college boy type but his sister was and college also was where she went to and graduated from) being a factory worker - that was something unheard of, yes, it is comparable, to give a good example, to a testicular cancer, as I have heard about it, where the growing tumor causes your balls, both or just one, to grow to the size of a melon. Freak-show, in other words. But once the freaky and the abnormal is over, well, back to normal: one makes so and so many billions a year, the other one can't put enough on the table to kill his own hunger, let alone his kids' and his woman's. Yeah... That might, just might, be the explanation of our time's success – why do we deserve a separate cage in the world circus. Swollen balls... We may even get one, too. I strongly suspect they'll invent something like that. And if by then I'm still around and still strong enough to go out there and talk publicly, hell, you bet that's exactly what I'll do. I will go out there and tell them that our success was due to deaths of guys like Cluski or Irving... You know? We – mind you – we, me, my friends, we were the chemo, we stopped the cancer, at least for a while. Our doing. Marching. Boxing lessons. Fighting. All the training in any possible sense. And the not-giving-in-by-one-inch. All that... You know?

Eve and Kim

"Tell me briefly," Donovan says. I think he was right having chosen the Beetles for the background – most everybody in here is our generation; the sound is coming to us, very delicately, from the invisible overhead speakers. "If I were asked and had to say something quickly –something to the point, like you have to say shit for the press people. Being, Psyche, Consciousness... Can you?"

"Consciousness versus the world," Kim says. "That's all the drama I'm trying to portray. And I think some of it at least is really there. These people... People... Consciousness as a trial..." In her right hand she has a glass that remains relatively immobile, with her left hand, palm actually, she's trying to catch something that isn't there for a moment, not yet, but wait, just wait, it'll show up, materialize –she moves her fingers slowly, groping. "A shot at being it cannot be. Trying to put on a coat, all the time, a thick rubber coat - that would be the psyche of an individual with its respective Ego - and then trying to lubricate it with this side's lubricants... lard, butter, astroglide, fuck... and then try to enter... And it's most of all about some borne yet differently than that, without anything, that is, no coat, nothing given them at that birth... or maybe they just took it off themselves at some point later on, so many means finally today to take it off, right, to feel even more, who'll ever know... God... their paintings hanging in all the museums of the world, their books and music. They also try to go through the walls, thick red brick walls," she smiles, she's obviously talking about her own picture they are now admiring, without the slightest movement of her head towards that same hero-picture, where a father, blood still gashing out of the wound in his side, naked and skinny (I thought when I first saw it, after she had called me and asked me to come over and look, because it was done, finished), that I never saw anybody really naked, so friggen fragile in that nakedness of theirs, yes, fragile, lost – and strong, stubbornly refusing their fate; fate as appearance only, I thought, nothing's real, all of it's just strawberry fields for ever, let's then lean on our hands as best we can, although the head is getting heavier and heavier, a big friggen, formless stone for no purpose whatsoever, we can even manage a smile, kid's tiny, delicate, porcelain white hand in his, father's, - both of them just had gone through the wall – brick, deeply, bloody red, now behind them, half way ruined, - and here we are... right? "Are they successful?"

Donovan's nodding in the affirmative; he's happy, obviously –he's already got offers, the guys he considers important already promised to write, just in case... Yeah, I think, he is happy.

The Beetles get to us, descreetly, from those well hidden overhead speakers:

...life is easier with one's eyes closed...

Zambowski, who just joined Donovan's right side, with a high glass half full of something clear, asks Kim, obviously trying to be witty at her expense - he is known to make people cry with his tongue that's been a lot of times compared to a wasp's stinger - if some of the ones she was just talking about might not be trying, by any chance, to take that astroglided cover off, for their eyes to be able to see better, which in turn would implicitly suggest that they have eyes on their dicks, and she answers, right away, that the main thing, as it seems to her, is the fact that they have eyes at all, wherever those eyes might be positioned, on their dicks, their asses or yet elsewhere…"

She smiles.

"Did you try going the other way?" she asks him then, to Donovan's incessant and unsilencable roar.

He is not over two hundred, I can tell.

"How do you mean…?"

"At that birth, you see," nodding her head, Kim takes a slow sip of her poison, whatever it might be now, "just the coat, that thick rubber coat we were talking about, comes out, with nothing inside but astroglide, no eyes of course, what would those be for in all cases of that kind, right, and that's all that ever comes out to all the knights' greatest misbelieving… Huh? What do you think? A lot like that?"

"Don't even try!" Donovan said, now calming down. "You'll be the one to cry, pal, I'm tellin' you!"

Zambowski just turned around without a comment and slowly walked away, towards the main wall with Kim's picture on it. There was a sizable group of people there, talking, and whenever the music got silent, their murmur would unchangeably come to us.

Kathy tells John that only the dead know Brooklyn

In the last bar I had… the street I was on after that did not have an end and I turned sideways, onto one that was a lot shorter and got me to the water: out of which protruded huge, half rotten posts of very old, brown wood, like a grove of death from some fairy tale, obvious remainders of a jetty, well, some structure that was there at some point but now was there no longer, and I sat down, right there, on the edge of that concrete pier I was still on, looking at the water of a color very much like steel also too long exposed to bad weather, scum bubbling at the line where the water would touch the concrete shore, pieces of probably everything ever created by man, and, sort of outstanding, temporarily held in check by one of those also half rotten wooden posts, there was a terribly swollen body of a dog floating among all that garbage. I felt nausea. I saw, suddenly right there, before my very eyes, again – one more time - the gray, clean, cleanly neutral, painted in half glossy oil wall, and I thought this time I wasn't going to make it: my own bad headache I felt like something distant, not really concerning me, here and now, and slowly going down the concrete steps that lead to the water and then would gently disappear under that bubbling non-transparent surface, I felt a strong vertigo that was, I think, more uncertainty than anything really physical; I had to concentrate not to fall, my hands stretched out sideways, balancing. The water was cold; at least I felt it as cold. Once I got deep enough to swim, to about my chin, I had to push the swollen dog's body aside; somehow it didn't look like it before, I mean when I was watching the whole thing from that concrete pier I was standing on before, that pushing it away might be necessary at any moment, that it would be in my way; no! Well, it was. And I had to push it away and it felt soft, like also half liquid shit. I had a stomach cramp. Strong. I had to cough. Farther from the shore the water was cleaner – the current, of course; I was finally in the river, wasn't I? Even in this frame of mind I knew that I couldn't swim to far out, because if I did, I would never be able to find again the place I got into the river in the first place, and, hence, would never be able to get hold again of my cloths I had left on the pier; with my wallet, keys, and – most importantly – the Jack Daniels flask in my jacket's inner pocket. I turned around. I got back to the steps and, suddenly, I felt all the dirt I was surrounded by; I was submerged now in the essence of dirt, sheer excrement of the big city, yes, shit of all sorts, barely liquefied by the East River water, there was a swollen dog that died so long ago it was probably about to pop, and getting out of, well… I suddenly threw up one more time. I felt shudders shaking up my body and I also felt a sudden urge to urinate –so I just turned around and complemented the contents of the river. Then I sat on the edge of the pier. I reached back for my jacket because I felt that now, on top of everything else I was just plain stinking, my naked body in a bad need of a shower, that for the time being wasn't attainable at any rate, I pulled the jacket towards me and got hold of the bottle. I took a slug. One. And then yet another one. Deep. My eyes were itching and I felt tears flowing down my cheeks, just like they've been doing ever since I got out of the hospital. I had yet another slug and then simply kept on looking at the dog, what was left of him – I saw him running in the street, sniffing the corners, lifting his hind paw, jeez, maybe he found a partner at some point, too, a she, one just like him, I even remembered a little dog movie about dog love, maybe, shit, who knows, and now he was there, in front of me, about to pop…

"What you doin' there?" a voice asked suddenly above me. It was a cop, trying to do his job.

"I feel like shit," I said. "I'm sick. I got fever… Death in the family."

"Oh!" He nodded. "Sorry pal!" And then: "Really! I been there meself!" And yet a moment later: "Why you naked, though?"

"I just took a bath."

"What?" He bent over me. "Jesus, man, you stink like shit! Bill!" he turned around calling his colleague, who came over almost right away. "There's an auto-shop, right there," he pointed his finger towards the industrial buildings behind us. "Go there and ask them for a bucket of water, would you? He can't put his cloths back on like he's now! He's gotta be rinsed off first! Fuckin' thoroughly!"

"Yes, Serge!" the other one said, strangely respectfully, turning around really quickly and leaving.

He came back only minutes later with the bucket, found a half broken wooden box, a lot of those around there, climbed on top of it, and called me; that was how I took my shower. Once I had my cloths back on, they asked me where would I live and I told them – where I lived and, generally, what the scoop was."

"You drunk!" he said.

"Yeap! Badly!"

"Yeah…" He looked briefly at the other and then back at me. "Do you have any money?"

"I had some," I said. "Let me look."

I had almost hundred bucks in cash and my credit cards were also all right there, in my wallet.

"OK!" I heard him. "We'll let you go, if you agree to take a room in the hotel. There is one right there, right around the corner, we take you there, and you sleep it off. You promise?"

"Yeah…" I said to that. "Sure!"

"Sure!" he said, looking at the other. "He says 'sure!' Did you hear that?" And then, after his pal had nodded, to me: "Let's go!"

In the hotel, first thing, I took a real shower and doing it I realized that my feet were hurt very badly – blisters, so bad, that I thought I may really need a doctor, well, a health professional of some kind, to get them back in shape any time reasonably soon. That was from walking day and night and then this day, whatever the hell it was, up to now. I felt pain, suddenly, in my legs, in my – most of my life plain lousy - lower back, and I thought I should lay down for the first time in… what the fuck ever. I reached out for my jacket with the flask, but there was no flask because they'd taken it, them sonofabitches, cocksuckers… I put my cloths back on and went downstairs, where I offered fifty bucks for a bottle of whisky to the receptionist –keep the change! - and he obliged; it was really a-quickie. I had my whisky in just a few minutes time, and I thought, again lying on the bed, right there on the covers, with the bottle in my hand, about the hospital, and then I turned to my side, half way onto my belly, and I released a howl into the pillow under my mouth that stopped only when I started to chock. I took a long deep breath, then another slug of whisky, and howled again into the pillow. How long? I've no idea. And then I was in the streets again, walking under the sun that was hard to bear, really burning, and I remember having wondered why wasn't I trying to figure out where would I actually be going: was there any end to that? I remember then the shadows getting longer and longer and the contrasts all around sharper and then even more so - to the point where things would cause pain, and I thought that yet another day was up, and I was walking along a street, some street, when I suddenly saw a girl, toll, slender, with a short blond hair, thick and strong, covering her head almost like a cap custom made very precisely to her head of thick wool would, she was right there, ahead of me, walking in the same direction I was, and then a pizza van passed by on the roadway and the light of the sun reflected from its side window blinded me for a second, and I felt a soft, putrefied body of a dog, swollen to the point where it would pop, do just that: pop – inside me, in my stomach, and I had the reaction quick enough to kneel down, on the sidewalk, and next thing I remember was the ceiling of my room in Connecticut where, as Redhead later on told me I was brought from a police station in Brooklyn by herself and Jim, after the cops had called the house, telling them about me having been picked up from the street in Brooklyn, close to Coney Island, where I had lost consciousness and fell. They found the address and telephone from my documents in my wallet. Jim then took Redhead and off they went.

Redhead was telling me all that dressing my feet, at that point really badly wounded, pouring the yellow antibiotic powder into the really ugly holes the walking carved in my skin.

"You walked around three days, you know? God… Without food, just drinking!"

She wrapped some bandage around my right foot.

"One's gotta be out of it…"

Then she did the second foot. And after that one was done too, she bent over me and kissed my forehead.

"I'll pray for her, too!" she said and I, suddenly, felt that if she had taken a freshly sharpened big kitchen knife and pushed it into my belly with all her strength, the pain I felt there for a moment all anew, wouldn't, couldn't have been any sharper: I saw the gray, oil painted wall above the hospital bed right back in front of my very eyes and I felt again like leaving my own skin: like I had to just get out of it, not even seeking salvation of some kind but plainly avoiding annihilation, to fulfill which I had to go there (where?) and then go somewhere again and do something. What? I didn't know. Again. What? I asked Redhead for a drink instead and she, murmuring and mumbling something I couldn't really understand (I'm sure nobody ever could), obliged nevertheless. I lay there then, remembering, looking at the ceiling. There was a fly walking towards the window, in irregular snatches, left and right, and then forward again, throwing an abnormally long, all senselessly jerky shadow, and I thought…

Communists

Eve wants to hear the story –I think she wants to hear it again, I am almost positive about having told her the whole thing already – at least - once. But I really – strongly - suspect I did that more than once. But she also says she would never get bored by it.

"Go ahead! Please!"

For a moment we just look at each other. I am gathering my thoughts – memories. And then I am beginning to see.

Yes, Christmas time; the tree is already made, we used to use regular candles back then instead of electric lights so popular today. There are few things in my memory that used to be back then and are no more – quite a few in fact… I think it would even be save to say the world from back then does not exist anymore at all, and the one I could see, should I be willing to stand up and go to the window, is also a different one – new; glitz, shine; you have to breath very carefully, though, for that shine not to disappear under your breath's moisture, before your very eyes; don't touch, don't look too long; there will be no refunds and you will feel screwed up.

We drink tea – my mother and I. From the two old, gold reamed pieces of china and at some point she starts telling me about the Christmas father came home only to tell her he'd lost his job. There'd be no cakes this year (he used to stop off on his way back home from work at a pastry shop to get stuff that was quite fancy and she, mother, would pile up reproaches each and every time he did that for the money wasted unnecessarily… for nothing, she'd say). Nothing such in that particular year we are talking about now.

She sighs and then takes a sip of that freshly made tea before she actually starts going into the details. And then I see him, too: going down the steep steps of the basement in that impressive edifice where the police headquarters are (he spent some time before that trying to prepare for what he is now about to do – young fellows whom he wants to 'open a channel of communication' with are students, political sciences, - relegated from the university for their views after the third year - they treat cops like halfwits – the interviews so far have been on the rather ridiculous side: the interviewers have been subject of merciless jokes: a constant stream of quotations, proving incompetence of the interviewers on one hand, on the other showing off the academic knowledge of the interviewed), - opening the cell door and only a moment later entering that small, shabby room with those three young men inside, sitting directly on the floor – there are not even bunks there and there is no window, he, father, knows well that if what he is doing, his whole presence there, is to make any sense whatsoever, he has to be at his best – because it certainly won't be easy. The air is stuffy and stale. Breathing becomes difficult after only a short while. There is mildew on the walls which adds some to that breathing difficulty. He starts, or tries to start that conversation – who they are, what they do, where, and for what. It's gotta start somewhere. But they don't seem to be willing to talk this time at all, and so, just to kill that heavy, dense, almost at times unbearable silence, he starts the whole thing by telling them how serious the charges against them are, what they implicate, which is to say what's to be expected now, how is their life going to change, when one of them suddenly and unexpectedly - he, father, had already almost given up the idea of communication of any possible kind altogether – seemingly the youngest, as he then told mother, lifted up his head up until then just plainly hanging down, onto his breast, sort of, and, looking father in the eye, asked: "Are you a lawyer? And as father just said no, he asked again "Journalist?" To father's another answer in the negative his new inquiry was if father might then be a man of letters. Father denied that too and the youngster started talking, this time more exhaustively: "It is the peculiarity of privilege and of every privileged position to kill the intellect and the heart of man. The privileged man, weather he be privileged politically or economically, is a man depraved in intellect and heart…"

"Is that something you came up with," father asked, "or have you read that somewhere?"

"Bakunin…" the boy answered. For the first time he sounded frank. Father nodded.

"Do you know what Bereza means? The camp? You may or may not be able to live beyond one week's length of time there. What's that going to deprive you of, you think?"

"Others," the boy says, he doesn't look at father, he doesn't look at anything in particular, he looks and speaks straight forward, ahead, as if there, on that mildewed wall, was somebody he cared to convince of his reasons, "the careful ones who work a name for themselves, whilst the revolutionaries work in the dark or perish in camps; others – the intriguers, the demagogues, the lawyers, the men of letters who occasionally shed the soon-dried up tear over the tomb of the heroes, and pass for friends of the people – those are the ones who will occupy the vacant seats in the government and will cry "back!" to the nameless ones who brought about the revolution…

"Bakunin?" father asks.

"I'm not exactly sure," the boy says; the 'science' suddenly dropped, interrupted by father's simple question, he sounds frank again. "Could be! Sure!"

"Yeah… You got one life, kid. One shot at it. Once it's over, it's over. And if you screw up now it will be over, I can promise you that. Sooner than you think. Bakunin's teeth, all of them, no exception, fell out in Schlisselburgh. Did you know that? There is an orifice in your body right now with no teeth. Perhaps I should bring you a mirror to make you realize what you gonna look like if you live long enough to see that happen? Huh? What'd you think, kid?"

"The world…"

"The world will go its way. With you or without you. Regardless of the fact that you have or have not any teeth left. Don't tell me what the world is going to do 'cause you simply know nothing about it. Not yet anyway. Huh?"

The boy shakes his head – quickly. Then he resumes former impersonality, his eyes on the same spot on that wall behind father's back.

"Accustomed in his capacity as lawyer, journalist or public orator," he quickly distances himself from father again, one more time resuming his walk over the scientific lands, "to speak of things he knows nothing of, he votes for all the questions with only this difference; while in the newspaper he only amused with his gossip, and in the courtroom his voice only awoke the sleeping judges, in parliament he will make laws for thirty or forty million inhabitants…"

"Who's that?"

"Kropotkin," the boy says.

"Why?" father wants to now.

"It analyzes the state. I live… we, I, but you too, live in a state. We have created a monster we have no idea how to deal with. That's why. Something will have to be done, sooner or later."

"Why?" father repeated himself. But, as he talked about it later, trying to explain all of it to her as best he could, at that moment he really wanted to – as he put it: sort of 'make his own' what those young fellows would really think- what had gotten them into that cellar. The kid's voice was still the same: as if bored a little, monotonous, ironic.

"It creates an army of office holders, sitting like spiders in their webs, who have never seen the world except through the dingy panes of their office windows and only know it from their files and absurd formulae – a black band who have no other religion except money, and no other thought but of sticking to any party, black, purple or white, so long as it guarantees maximum salary for a minimum of work."

"Are you quoting again?" father wanted to know.

"Yes!" The boy simply said.

"Do you… yourself… think you know the world other than through the window –of an office of some sort… home… or whatever… Do you?"

The kid looked at him then - as he delivered it to mother - for the first time: straight at him; straight in the eye, and when he decides already to start talking again father thinks there is some progress, all of the resistance notwithstanding.

"See…" there's the same frankness in the kids face now that was there a moment ago. "He traveled. In Siberia. Manchuria. He wanted to see what it is like. People. And he did see. A lot. He saw that whatever was started for the good of the country by local men was looked at with distrust, and was immediately paralyzed by hosts of difficulties which came not so much from the bad intention of the administration, but simply from the fact that these officials belonged to a pyramidal administrative centralized monster. The very fact of their belonging to a government which radiated from a distant capital caused them to look upon everything from the point of view of functionaries of the government who think first of all what their superiors will say and how this or that will appear in the administrative machinery. The interests of the country are a secondary matter."

"That wasn't my question, was it?"

"He also talked to Proudhom then, after escaping from Siberia, about the removal of the Jews from Europe. That was Proudhom's view – as long as there is one single Jew anywhere in Europe there is no point in talking about progress, freedom and such."

Father told them to get up. Reluctantly they did, looking at him all the time. He told them then to follow him. And the 'spokesman' of the group asked him, nervously, where would they be going. Father answered his question by saying that if they pissed him off some more he would just put a bullet through each and every one of them, right then and there, and that would be how the story would end for good. He took them then to the main entrance door of the building and told them to go. They did not seem to understand and he had to repeat: they were free, they could go – wherever they might be pleased. Out! Now!

"And if you're back here… This won't repeat itself again. No!"

"What are you gonna do?" was the question he didn't count on.

"I'm gonna do what I'm gonna do! None of your business, kid. Go! Just you go and don't forget what happened here – I mean that you might be back here. Got it?"

"Thank you, sir," all three of them said, almost at once.

Mother looks at the window. She takes a sip of tea and looks at me. She slowly puts the cup down on the table.

"That was the first time. He let them go and then had to explain, of course, why he did, which he did, too. If it had been the last time, you see, there would have been no consequences – he was finally the big guy, the commissionaire, wasn't he? But, as a matter of course, it did not stop there. The problem was that there were other times - he would just let them go each and every time all the same. He told me then, afterwards - and that also time and time again, that he shared some of what they preached. He bought books. Yes, all those books. Today you just go to a bookstore and buy one or the other. Not so back then, my dear. Those books were banned. They had a true unobtainium status. He had to use all his relations. All of his influence." She glanced quickly over the bookcase. "He read them, too. He forced me to read them and then would force me into talking about them with him. He wrote parts of them down in his notebook, to learn by heart things he considered important. That's how I also am able to quote so well, those fragments, in that particular conversation, in that cell – your father made me. Time and time again, as usual, so I wouldn't be able to – ever - forget. And then there was that day that you already know about, when he came back home as a jobless. They just fired him, period."

I nod. I'm trying to imagine how she felt. Her sadness. Madness perhaps? Who'll ever know? I think: who would ever care? Our past is just that: our past. Individual. Mine. Yours. And mine isn't yours – I don't know how to care just because it isn't mine. A whole bloody ocean of desperate loneliness.

She takes slowly another sip of tea.

"There was a factory close to the town where they would make cables and wires, and –since he was always mechanical, yes, he had that, mechanisms of whatever kind would suddenly come alive in his hands – they made him a maintenance mechanic there. He would take care of the machinery. That's what we would have to live on. Can you imagine? From a police commissionaire? Like that - all the way up until the war. Yeah…"

She stood up then and started lighting up the candles on the tree – one by one, slowly, with a visible satisfaction. It did give us some light, I'd say. Yes, it did. She sat down afterwards and had some more tea. And then, after that, looking at the tree, she sang at a low voice:

"They came and found a child in a manger
with all the signs of greatness given to the stranger…"

She coughed a couple of times, clearing her throat, took a sip from the cup and putting it down on the table continued, the carol now slightly changing the rhythm:

"They worshipped him as a God
And then sang out on the spot
Out of that great joy…"

She wiped a tear from her cheek. I remember. I won't forget. Then she said, a smile on her face, just a little pensive:

"He took me straight through life. Straight –up until now, all the way.

She shook her head.

Eve shakes her head, too, she, too, looking through me at the past, her past that I hope might at some point become, just a little bit, mine too. At some point. Some time. She says, the same look on her face:

"You were bred, fed, fostered and fattened from holy childhood up in this two easter island on the piejaw of hilarious heaven and roaring the other place (plunders to night of you, blunders what's left of you, flash as flash can!) and now, forsooth, a nogger among the blankards of this dastard century, you have become a twosome twiminds forenenst gods, hidden and discovered…"

"Is that Finnegan's Wake?" I wanted to know.

"Good!" she says, approvingly, smiling. "Very good!"

"You have a memory! Good Lord!" I just felt compelled to say. "I always wanted to be able to do that and never could, you know?" I also smile at her. "Tea?"

"Would be nice… You have to train you memory, though, you know? Practice."

"Yeah…" I said simply, standing up, and then already making our tea, I did not stop thinking about him: father: I thought about him but also through him, if you will, about all those others who paid as dearly as that, or in so many cases incomparably worse than that, good Lord… And just what good did that do? At some point it began to seem to me that whatever we do, we the people, down here, under this beautiful sky, so often cloudy, too, just has to turn into downright mockery of all our doings. That there is no way around that. Once we are finished with our project, whatever that might be, or at least we think we are, somebody unzips their fly and, as my mother once put it, desecrates us from top to toe. Plunders to night of you. That's how I feel about any of whatever I was – ever - able to find out about this our life down here. The tea was almost ready. Last few seconds…

Then we drink it and I look at her.

"When I say above 'what good did that do', do I sound as just another dimwitted peasant who hardly knows how to read and write, I wish to know. I think I do. Well… It was a project – this… thing here. Is it clearer now, by any chance, as to what I mean by mockery? Being pissed at?"

"Is it?" she asks back, drinking tea.

Ernie

I was ordered to change oil and plugs in the 917 and I spent quite a few hours under the car and over it, enjoying the mighty twelve and even the little things I was doing to it. And then I took it for a ride – mechanics privilege. There's a black top track around the property, couple of miles, John made me familiar with the lay-out, with a sound barrier around it, insulating the track itself from the outer world – I smiled, those who live around us here are as rich as our boss and they don't want to be disturbed. Goodness me…

The poetry of eleven hundred horsepower in a light, perfectly balanced vehicle; unbelievable aerodynamics, that make it impossible or close to impossible to break the traction: entering a curve from

150 mph well until the end of the grade I still remained solid, no skidding. I tried again, a little faster, it provokes you, tempts you, like a beautiful woman you feel badly like following, so you do too, and nothing, same solidity – like concrete. Jeez… I wish there was someone I could share it with, be it just a little bit – Mauna doesn't give a flyin' and there's no way to make her get it. John… forget it! John knows that the car, is it a Buick or a 512 Ferrari (to him both are 'just cars') - a car, hence, needs maintenance: you gotta change oil frequently, plugs, less frequently, you gotta take a look at the undercarriage, tighten up whatever might seem loose, check tires, but that's also where it stops. Driving - that's driving from here to there, without what he calls 'speeding', because you may get a ticket, - getting the picture? Yeah… No! As far as what I'm doing here, I'm alone and it looks like things are gonna stay that way – unless I meet somebody.

And then I saw him. The Boss. Little, as I said somewhere else, grayish, kind of, standing there, on the side of the track and looking at me. I felt, for a moment, kind of awkward. I was finally driving his car, the last price I saw on E-bay was three million eight hundred thousand dollars, and I didn't know all that well at that moment what to do… I got off the track and stopped. And there he was, right there, helping me with the door (it's damn hard to get out, if there is nobody to help you with the door. Awkward. Just that. But then there he was).

"How'd you find it?" was his question.

"God…" I shook my head. "I'd never driven one before, " I managed. "You've got the wrong nigger, sir…"

"Still - how is it?"

"Poetry…

"You like poetry?"

"Matter of saying, sir! Don't really know anything about that either."

He laughed.

"Read some! Use my library, if you feel like it. Don't ask anybody! Go and get whatever you feel like getting."

"Thank you, sir!"

"Ever been to LeMans?"

"No, sir. I saw it in the movie, though. The Steve McQueen movie. Have you seen it, sir?"

"Yes," he said, "I have. Do you think you could drive like that?"

"'It would take a lot of training, a whole lot of money I don't have, never had and never will, sir…"

"Again: what do you think? Your gut feeling? You know what I mean?"

"Yes!" I said. "I know… I think I probably could. But, of course, there's no telling until one actually does it."

"Yes, you're right about that. I know I can't!"

"You tried…?"

"LeMans. Seventy. I made three first rounds before I ran into the side barrier. I was chocking, I can tell you that. Melting away. The second time I tried was over here – Indianapolis. Qualification runs. The car destroyed. Out. Over before it even started. Nothing left to fix or rebuild. Boom! Period."

"Yeah… Have you ever thought, sir, of putting out a team like –at LeMans, for instance?"

"Don't 'Sir' me all the time." He stretched his hand to me. "I'm James. I go by Jim! OK?"

"Thank you, sir, well, Jim…"

We got a chuckle out of that.

"I keep thinking about it, if you have to know. I need a driver, though. As said above: I myself can't do it, period. And, Ernie, LeMans… that's not exactly here, you know. It's friggen crowded and you gotta fit into that crowd at two hundred miles an hour, and that's what makes it so fucking difficult, you know?"

"I can only imagine."

"Yeah… Next time I'll take your time on a lap, and we'll take it from there."

God! Take what from where? It kinda shook me up – does he want me to drive at LeMans at my age? No, Goodness me, he ain't stupid! Nah! It's just for the fun! Right here! And that's where it stops! He likes to dream, to see things that never could be, and that's what that is all about. He's got a fuckin' hell of lot of money and doesn't know what to do with it – and this is most probably it. Ain't it?

Agatha

We pulled up their driveway all the way to the big oak that divides their yard a little bit senselessly into two unequal parts and I could hear the snow being crunched under the tires – they didn't shovel, did they?. It wasn't deep, no, but it also had certainly not been shoveled - as opposite to all the other times we would have come here during the winter time. Agatha was standing on the porch, waving her hand to us. She was smiling. She put on some weight, I thought.

Then the usual: we haven't seen each other for quite some time and why would that have to be the case, why don't we get to visit, we, I and Eve, them, or they us, why is life such a cruel shepherd, leading to oblivion, all the way to that point (and I am actually surprised at her sudden eloquence, although ever since I can recall her, she always talked a lot not ever having much to say, and I – most probably, was my next quick reflection - should have gotten used to that, learn over time to treat it like a headache or gas, for instance, a general nuisance, something that just has to be accepted because nothing can be don about it; but also now, this very moment, as she talks about life leading us to… - it is new, I think, new, yes, somehow new just like that snow that has not been shoveled and I wonder what it actually is) leading us to where oblivion becomes a painful remembrance of something long forgotten and yet not quite dead, like an infected scar deep inside the soft tissue that doesn't want to heal - sort of…

Does her smile have something to do with it?

I asked about Rich – what happened to him. And then listening to her, willy nilly, I thought something has… really has happened to him, must have, it is not just a matter of speech, conventional exchange of words everybody practices everywhere; and the answer (answers?) did not seem to be in her words which I wouldn't even be able to repeat, but, somehow, on her face: a shadow suddenly and quickly moving over it, forcing me again to use my favorite simile because of its adequacy here too: like a cloud's shadow moving over the ground on a windy and generally sunny day: it's there and then it isn't; and you're not sure if you really saw it or not – or was it just a figment of your imagination? What has actually happened?

She tells us about a job he found in New York, Manhattan, they are building there a lot of stuff these days, and with his skills he really makes a lot of money, finally, you know, we are now much better off and that has to off-set the fact that he's never here any more (and I see that same shadow quickly flying over again, like an omen, raven from a bad dream, a bat from a Hollywood vampire movie). "But then again I am not here either," she says (she still works at the same place, she sums it up quickly: close to 42nd terminal, money is on the lousy side but the benefits, you know, for the kids, you just gotta have the benefits, a doctor's something you can't afford out of the pocket, nobody can…), " and so we have a baby sitter, you know, that polish old lady, she's cheap and she's always here, if I need her, so it's OK, I'd say, you know…"

"Yeah, I know," Eve says.

"Yeah… C'mon in!"

"Yeah…"

Inside, in the middle of the living room, there were all the 'lice neatle klinkers' as Eve called them after Joyce a couple of times on our way up here, and reigning over them is their sitter, the old Polish lady Agatha just mentioned, who right away had to also demonstrate her capability of some - although very broken - nevertheless English: "How you stool?" to which I answered: "OK, I think", although there was no certainty at any point as to what was actually meant on both sides of the question. We sat down. Agatha brought a bottle of Cognac and a snifter for me – none was necessary for Eve because Eve would go with her to the kitchen right away. They would perform culinary miracles there, as per their telephone conversation – yes, I was expecting that. The old lady and the klinkers were non-alcoholic, of course. The huge TV was on, fortunately for me muted – American cartoons: a huge, crooked, sort of, steamroller was just turning the cat Jinks into a rug of no thickness, on that one particular spot on the road the poor cat had just fallen onto from some local Mount Everest. I leant back and closed my eyes. I just listened: to their voices: Eva's, now and then, rather rarely, and Agatha's non-stop, from the kitchen, reminding me of a conveyer band in some kind of a factory or gees going south in the Fall filling up the sky with their ethereal conversations – something that does not seem to have a beginning or an end: "The kobasa will add nicely a lot of taste to the geese that I prepared yesterday already, as you see, I had them opened and they are empty now," and then Eve's quick interruption, that is really Eve's: "They are hollowed geese, they are stuffed geese…"

They laughed: quickly, briefly.

Two human beings laughing because of the same sentence at two totally different things.

I had a sip of the Cognac.

"We'll stuff them with chestnuts, see, here, and the rice, some, not much, and the nuts here, too, they spice it all up nicely, too, we'll have to watch, add some water now and then, it burns in no time really, once you neglect, and then, once stuffed and sawed up, we'll put them in the oven at three hundred fifty and have it in there for like three hours, and in the meantime, here, I'll do the pork, it'll be nice and tender, I love pork, do you love pork? With some bacon all around, wrapped up in foil, not to burn it either, one's never careful enough, you know," she had a drink, I thought, must have had a drink because I heard the clear gulp and then she put down the glass, after which she kept on talking: "the geese, stuffed nicely, the pork, flavored already, perfect, beautiful, what we need are potatoes, some kapusta, yes, why not do it right away, Eve, let's, yawp, like that, of course, careful, and then Eva's: "What's life, Agatha? What's it for?" They both had a drink and I could hear the refill, the bottle being put back onto the counter, the clicking of glasses and then those too being put back, and Agatha's: "Life? My father just died, did you know that? In the hospital. Here, in town. He had a nightshift at Wallmart, he fell just before the daybreak, and they took him to the hospital, and he lived there for a while yet, and then just… No, not like that! No! You see, you have to be more careful with those, otherwise they'll be no good, very, extremely careful! Yes! Yes! That's perfect! What's life? You want another one?" And Eva's: "Yeah! Why the hell not?"

After the drinking break and the clicking of the glasses being put back on the counter, they were silent for a moment. All of it must have been, for the time being at least, stuffed, chopped, sawed, wrapped up and shoved where it belonged because it was quiet. I thought about John, Agatha's father, she was just talking about. I considered him my friend for quite a while. Yes, whenever we would meet during all that time back then, we would discuss literary stuff, yes, and I feel quite touched for a moment, like a quick sweet smell or taste in your mouth you did not expect, yes, that, although I noticed almost right away that he had a problem to keep it together, he would each and every single one of those times drink more alcohol than he could bear, and then it would get really ugly: throwing up, sleeping for a while, and then throwing up again, and so on, with no end in sight. Unchangeable. Each time. And then I found out that he would talk about me behind my back things that were plain ugly, which was something I just did not understand, - why? was my childish question to the news, why in the bloody hell would he do that? Say crap like that about me to people who could not possibly have their own judgment on the subject. Why? And then I thought, it came to me the day he died, that he knew, instinctively, he knew, somehow, that it was over for him long time before that one final struggle on that hospital bed; that he had been given it, all of it, and pretty generously too, and all along he couldn't stand the fact that he just farted it all away, having done absolutely nothing... Even that very day of his passing away, he was not sober, I was told. His heart finally simply gave up, like any human heart would at some point passed that one limit. There was nothing out of the ordinary about that. Nothing!

The Polish lady was smiling at me, looking a little on the sad side. She put her hands together in the 'Amen' gesture and said: "Drink." She nodded few times. "Drink. And drink." She kept her hands like that for yet a while, and then produced, with that same, kind of sad smile on her face: "Papa kaput! Dat... just – a

– fuckation…" I was slow at first, but then a got it, and I had a hell of a hard time to control my face. But I think I did well in the end. I just nodded. It must have taken for her a long work with the dictionary and I wanted her to know that she did an excellent job. "It justifies anything," I simply said. "Yes, it does."

She nodded smiling, and I think she was pleased. Very pleased.

"The most important thing is the kobasa," Agatha decided to restart the lecture over in the kitchen. "It has to open, you see that, right, not crack, get out of whack, misshapen, no, open, gently, release the juices, but by the same token, remain kobasa, retain its nature, and the nature of kobasa is just that: being a kobasa, right? Then the duck will take the savor and mix it with its own, and that is what we are after here, that is the masterpiece – the stuffing, you see, the nuts and the chestnuts, all of that also gets a taste that is incomparable with anything that I know of… Want one?" To which Eva just said, quite clearly: "No!"

On the screen the cat hit a wall (the hole he tried to chase the mice into and succeeded turned out to be way too small for himself) and he turned into something that I could not recognized for a moment – something that was out of any shape that I knew of. The klinkers were not paying any attention to that, though. They were trying to press the Lego blocks into half dried puke – or whatever it was, down there, on the floor, beside the table. With an elongated thing that looked like a spatula (finally that might have been exactly what it was: a metal cake spatula; there were some left-overs of a cake, tart, of some sort, not really recognizable at this point, on the coffee table) and with that… tool they were building some kind of a masterpiece of their own. I did not feel well. No! Not at all!

I took a deep breath and let it out; then another one and this one I held inside for a moment a bit longer.

The memory plays so often jokes on us that we, at least up to a point, don't seem to ourselves to be able to understand – a certain amount of time has to pass by in order for us to see the logic so strange in the first moments and so simple, not to say obvious, then, later, after we've had a break long enough to digest… Looking at them now I suddenly remembered a story I read many a year ago, when

I was still young, in a different and far away country, a strange story about a man entrusted by a big city's counsel with a huge project – a project of a lifetime; a dream project; and how he started, all those centuries ago, all the enthusiasm right there, no obstacles are impossible to take, no effort shall ever be spared, let's just go ahead, whoever is necessary, and do it: those were times were building was an expression, pure expression of the architects intuition – no real plans, just drawings, great at times, true works of art, yes, but also no mathematics; I've seen and even admired some of those at different points of my life: the composition would develop as they went, the process was that of realization, of translating the feeling and the understanding of the feeling and its intensity downright into stone: growing, piling up, high above the city, high above everything that had been there so far; and then he got lost – there suddenly was no continuation. Lost. He prayed. The only thing he could do was praying; and pray he also did. And then, as he was sitting there, trying to put up with his desperation, with the hopelessness, a shadow fell on his face. A shadow of someone's wide brimmed black hat, quite unexpectedly covering up the sun, cutting off the sunlight. The stranger was standing there, drawing in the sand with a stick. Something. But our builder got attracted to the sight. He stood up and approached, and looked, and saw – yes, there he saw his building, right there, in the sand: finished. His prayer was answered. He saw it. It was there. Nobody could take it from him anymore. Now it was a given. They never exchanged a word. The building was finished, built of snow white stone, that only a few years later became gray, and then black altogether, all the efforts to keep it white as originally intended notwithstanding.

The little one, after having tried to glue another Lego block to the existing structure, lifted it up, looked carefully, and then spit and worked on the spittle with the spatula for a while, after which the block was glued nicely into place: it sounds plain stupid I realize, yes, it does - but I didn't see that much difference for the moment between the Koelner Dome and what I was looking at now: expression in matter of an interior: human or... whatever, I think. Whatever. Do we ever know? Are we meant to know? And then: are we... have we been meant?

Eve and Agatha came into the room from the kitchen and they sat down with us. Eve looked kind of slowed down but still OK, but Agatha, I thought was plain drunk. She wasn't swaying. No! Whatever she would say from then on, was almost fine, almost the same way she would have said it in any other occasion, without alcohol, yes, but there was also something exaggerated to it, to every word, the diction normal people don't have in their daily life, which would make one think at any rate that something was really wrong.

"I just explained to your wife," she said now to me, smiling, her eyes watery, "that the kobasa has to be treated very carefully because it is prone to lose its nature, and the nature of kobasa is being a kobasa, and not just a cracked wide open, misshapen, piece of crap, and I think your wife understood me, so I also think from now on you'll have better food, at least a better kobasa, whenever she decides to cook for you." Her smile deepened and also a little bit of over-sweetened coquetry appeared in it now. "Are you thankful to me for that?"

"I am," I said, not really knowing what else I could say.

"Good!"

The Polish sitter obviously thought she should participate in the conversation because she said, with the same gesture she made before, hands together, the 'Amen' thing: "Papa kaput!" and Agatha sobbed. After which she repeated the former: "Just-a-fuckation..." without any additions, obviously convinced that it would do here and now, it was enough, it has been well proven, it didn't need anything – no! - and that made Eve explode. But Eve got herself together very aptly and pointing her finger at the sitter, she said then: "That's great! Really!" Then with all the seriousness she could still gather, she added: "Sad facts of life, I mean what we are forced to go through, justify a lot. Yes, maam!"

They smiled at each other.

So did I.

"Justification..." Eve said, and the Polish lady repeated after her one more time: "Just –a-fuckation..."

We got a brief chuckle out of that and I wondered if there was any way to make understand the old lady what that last chuckle was all about; try to translate the word into her own language, including the intention and the gone askew phonetics, but even that seemed too complex to be really doable. We just sat there for a while yet. And I think it was then that Rich came.

He looked the same I remembered from our last time in New York, except for the cloths – now he had on a long coat over blue jeans and a flannel shirt with some sort of a fishing jacket made of two hundred pockets sawn together. We shook hands, he with me and then with Eve, and then he bent over Agatha, like if to kiss her, I thought. But he didn't kiss her – he sneezed; there was revulsion in his face when he got up.

"You're drunk!" He looked at me. "Drunk as a skunk again… God almighty!"

Agatha chuckled.

"We've been cooking with Eve," she said. "All this time… The kobasa should be OK by now. The ducks. With great stuffing – chestnuts and the rest of it," she was actually pretty coherent now. "Because, you see, the kobasa has to be just that: kobasa – it can't be destroyed by overcooking, cracked open crap of no taste, no, siree, it has to give its juices slowly up and over, to whatever it is cooked together with, our stuffing in this case…"

"Out!" he roared. "Out! Go to the bedroom! Get some sleep!"

She stood up but did not move. She was just standing there, smiling, swaying a bit now - it was suddenly visible.

"Out! Move it!" He lifted his hand up, pointing towards the hall way. "Go! Or I will help you, by God!"

She started walking.

The Polish lady took the lice neatle klinkers also to another room, right after that.

He sat down and poured himself a drink of the Cognac she had set up there for me. Some good half of the big snifter. He downed it at one draught.

"God…"

I didn't know what to say. What can possibly be said in a situation like that? We just sat there, his look focused on the top of the table, pale, and then, not paying us any mind at all, he just picked up the remote and turned off the muted cartoons.

"You want us to stay, Rich," Eve asked him, "or to go?"

"Up to you, guys," he said. "I don't have much to offer, you know?"

"You're sad now," Eve said. "Wanna talk?"

He didn't managed to answer her question, though – Agatha walked in; all she had on was a T-shirt with no sleeves, her underbelly, I thought, looking strangely bushy, and sort of artificially black, like almost dyed for some unfathomable to me reason to that particular shade of intense, unnatural black. Swaying there, she sang, to no one in particular and very off key: "Do not believe in Beatles…"

"God!"

He stood up, grabbed her by her hair, turned her around, at the length of his right arm fully stretched out ahead of him, and administered a mighty kick in her buttocks – they started looking nicely rosy immediately after that and he just, literally, got her out of our sight, pushed her back to the bedroom, where the execution started as soon as they only got there, was my impression: clear, strong sounds of a leather belt against her buttocks accompanied by her screams that towards the end of the process became really inhuman; bloodcurdling. Eve wanted to get up, for a moment I saw her reaction, but I stopped her: in my opinion it just might do her, Agatha, some real good: a wake up call.

Rich came back. He sat down. He sighed. Then he looked at me and nodded.

"I don't know what to do…" he simply said. "We were about to loose the house, you know. I started to work in New York then, I wasn't here… We didn't have enough. Kids… All that. You know…"

I nodded but I wasn't looking at him.

Was it all of it? crossed my mind. Really? But I said nothing. What can one say? And is that any of one's business, except whose ever business it really is? What could I possibly help him (her) with? How? We all, no exception, are reluctant to admit how little we want to admit; what a tiny fraction we are ready to accept as reality – and it is not just him or her; it's anyone. Life seems to be infinitely bigger than our perception of it, let alone the intellectual realization of that perception's content: that makes you just shut up, lower your eyes and wait. For what? Well, until it's over, I think...

"I'm really, really glad to have seen you both..." He was looking at me then. "Jack, I know you know I mean that! I do!"

I bent towards him and put my hand on his shoulder.

"I know! Yes, Rich!"

Driving back home we didn't talk. I was watching the road in the lights of the car, looking for potholes, and there's a whole lot of those in that road. He wanted us to stay overnight but Eve said, very categorically 'no' to that. She said Agatha, once she would wake up in the morning, if she would remember anything, would feel really bad about what had happened in the evening. It was better that way – if we go, that is.

"Can nothing last in this rotten world?" Eve asked me about half way home. "They seemed OK, didn't they?"

"She was too possessive," I said. "She never left him any room. For nothing." Still driving I looked over at Eve. "It never lasts then. You know?"

"Yeah..." Eve sighed. "Everybody wants some nook just for themselves. It's bad if they can't get it. If the other party's fear makes it impossible, out of reach. Yeah... I can relate to that. Is it that, though, what it is in this case?"

I shrugged it off.

"Who knows... That," I said then, "and maybe few other things we have no idea of, as well. Who knows..."

"Just-a-fuckation," Eve said.

"Exactly," I said. "Now you probably got it right!"

We were now closer than half way home.

"Slow down!" Eve said. She was, again, afraid of cops – senseless, unnecessary tickets we hardly had the money to pay. "You're driving too fast!"

I was. I wondered why.

John

Trees, leafless, naked, moving chaotically in the wind, violent at times, I see through the big and also naked window, and for a moment I wonder what kind of a window it is, might be, where am I – trees are leafless so its wintertime, it is also silent, nicely silent around me now, and I certainly know how to appreciate that, although I also feel, badly, yes, quite badly, that I would love to have a drink. I can feel the taste -I think it's Glen Liveth, I am almost certain – in my mouth; my imagination takes me even further: I can feel it… the calm silent warmth spreading throughout my body. God how I miss it!

Those trees… I saw them before too; and that makes me remember: there is the park behind the Wallmart and through the window in the back I was working at the moment it started happening, I could see, just like here, leafless, naked, moving in the wind, yes, strong wind out there, violent at times, blackouts guaranteed, and then, when it already started, I understood, suddenly there was the full understanding, comprehension – emotional as well as intellectual - that those trees, that park, all of it was the part, only a part of my own heart, somehow, and that I was asked, yes I was being asked in that very manner to give up all that existence, to suddenly let go of the trees, of the wind, altogether –

Redhead came. I see her talking to a nurse, carrying a bag, I hope she's got a bottle of something good in it, I couldn't care less for just about anything else she might bring, yes - she did. Good, good girl!

I thought then, with all the beautiful warmth spreading, my eyes closed, about all those – well, we say: 'all' and in all reality the ones we think about are extremely few of those we have seen up to that present we think in – places I've been at, towns I've lived in (not the ones out there – most probably still there, unchanged and not really changeable by much, but the ones for good in that heart of mine that is about to stop and they with it): what will happen to them all? What shall happen to the sadness they are all suddenly wrapped up in – the sadness that is an investment, actually, my time I spent, doing… something at any point; my life.

Redhead told me Rich and Agatha would come later and that did not mean any great joy for me as in cases like mine could probably be expected – in fact my only thought was that I've had enough of primitive stupidity when I was still out there and I think I could skip at least some of that ocean that I now finally am here: precisely because I am here I might be spared some of that lovely family Sunday kielbasa from the grill, was my quite clear, still, thought…

I had a swig. We have to pay attention: if we got caught, Redhead and I, we might get in trouble – not me, I don't have to give a shit anymore, I guess, but her. I don't want her to have problems of whatever kind…

And she'll have all kinds of problems now.

Me trying to tell her, and she is tired, that I have understood something, maybe even all of it, and I am talking about Augustine, about being in time and out of it all at the same time, being able to see the end while the end is still long way away, and that it took me almost sixty years to understand the "shall they come into my rest," the seventh day idea Paul understood so well, and I see her face, her skin, the part under her eyes, her hair – how it thinned, how little of it left there, I can suddenly – I think now: suddenly – see her skull and she used to have great hair, God, and I am trying to tell her not to harden her heart so that she might enter too, that we are not there yet, that seven day creation from the old testament was but a sketch, a base, an outline, based on which the creating process still goes on, right now, the acceptance and rejection, all the chances, and then none, - but I see right then the dew in the corners of those so terribly tired eyes of hers, and how it then slowly flows down her cheeks towards the corners of her mouth where the two lines descending down towards her chin are also too pronounced (she isn't trying to hide any of it; she is just there – and that is the way I have always appreciated in her – the way she is, she is, period, she certainly has my acceptance –as if that meant anything…), and I think then about "shall they come into my wrath," the forty years in the desert part: I see her suddenly many years ago: we were both young, she danced in a luxury restaurant taking her cloths off, moving like a cat and them guys going crazy way before she was done with it, she was friggen great, she was, and I feel now like I have watery eyes, and my throat shrinks like a paw only too big and to friggen strong for any of us just grabbed me and squeezed and I can't suddenly breath, remembering, thinking, because I know I am not saying it: "do not harden your heart..."

All kinds of problems will she have... What?

Glen Liveth, the 'yes' part.

Our discussions with Jack – the piece I never could really understand, about glorifying God with a specific kind of death, he would quote: when you were young, you'd go where you would. Now that you're old I'll take you where you don't want to go... Huh? Yeah. We talked some about late Broch the last time, I remember, the death of Virgil. Was it the last time? I'm not really sure. One of our times together. One of those long nights that would end so fast we couldn't understand the speed: the day, the gray, the dawn, the full light and the tiredness and happiness of it all.

If I just could stay sober for a little longer, shit.

School came back for a moment – not Fordham, no, long before that, when I was yet an officer in the army: first jump off the plain, first landing, the wind schlepping me across the tarmac and I just didn't know what to do and, no, I knew, I just didn't do it, that's life, traveling on your belly across the runway 'cause you forgot the proper reaction you have been taught, running amongst artificial obstacles and shooting artificial targets, shouts...

A uniform: perfectly pressed. Absolutely clean.

Fuckin good lookin'...

A tear – clearly now, not moving – tear...

New York.

Fordham – lectures. Writing. Books. Different kind of everything. Surprise. Fascination. Love... again. Yes! The beauty of it and the pain. Sunrise and sunset.

That is, yes, oh, yes, sir, entering your rest...

Redhead looks at the door; she's worried; her wet, older and older face looks even more tired and more worried now, I think, and I wish I could do something…

I squeezed my palms into fists to the point where it is painful. I took a breath and let go.

Talks – long, exhaustive and exhausting, talks with Jack. Nights – with bottles and books. Then again: not that many. No!

I think he, Jack, called here (did he?) and we have spoken. Here. Then maybe not. Maybe it's me making it all up. How? Did they bring the telephone to my bed? Maybe they did, who knows…

Redhead looks at the door. She does.

I am not making that up.

She does. I remember the same last night: the getting dark and then these things – and then the dawn; the joy of seeing the sun, of having survived one more night to see the sun.

The boat moves now through thick, mangrove like, surroundings, gnarled roots that look alive, disappearing quickly, suddenly and unexpectedly in the black water of no movement (none whatsoever and yet I suddenly realize the boat is not responding to me – to what I am doing: I just rowed twice with my right hand (is my impression)and I should be going more to the left, but I am not, there is no change at all, none I could have noticed anyway, none; so I tried again: the same thing: nothing; makes me think if its ever been any different, ever, at any point – but then again: maybe I am going to far with this, finally I am the one who's in the boat, who stays in the boat, I am the one who notices no current, the black scary preponderant stillness all around, yes, it's me), all of which is so dcnsc, so thick, so prcpondcrantly growing into one another, up high there is no sky visible, although there is still relatively clear remembrance of a sky, beyond a shadow of a doubt, and there is a thought also about light, how does light exist in this denseness and how do perceptions, - and the 'I', lonely, stripped, almost abandoned, tries… The boat moves ahead, yes, there's certainty as to the movement, and there are those perceptions, because there is some kind of a world, through which there is also a will to move, to seek and to find, what's the simplest and most unconditional, closest to the unfindable and unnamable primary, the will, yes, is there, and then there also is, no interpretation, familiarity, it is simple, - there is no idea what it is, no seeing, no perception, but I (there is 'I' – clearly, though for the first time there is nothing else) think it is me from the beginning, the movement was, has been, towards, now with no roots soaking in the thickness of the black water and no - that almost infinite - tangle of branches being torn by the black wind in the night of the skyless upthereaboveahead – me… God!

Oh, Lord!

I wish I could see something.

Something.

The mine. Jack's father.

"You know what kind of hands he had, right?" She doesn't look at me; sipping her tea she looks at the window, through it at the park trees, and I think about the day I brought the horseshoe home – when I was yet a little boy to find a horseshoe was really easy: almost everything in terms of transportation in the town we lived in was horse and carriage; used horseshoe that fell off was a very common thing. He, father, at some point - and I really wouldn't be able to tell when (a whole lot of things I just mix up - in my imagination things that took place after a certain point, seem to be there - whenever I try to recall them - before that point and vice versa, but that particular day was a very important one in my life, I think), showed me a picture of a historical figure, a king of really great importance to the country's continuance in that particular, tremendously complicated period (and just why would that be important to a single life of a child? is a question that crosses suddenly my mind; and then: I do remember it, still, today), that king sitting on his huge, very impressive throne, leaning on the back support of it covered in bass-relief with tones of gold and pulling a horseshoe apart by means of two gold sashes (picture by also a great painter, another national monument by itself – here I should probably explain that we had to travel to the capital to view it, which in turn meant almost a whole night spent aboard a train - a torture that I shall probably never be able to forget) –one of those sashes around his neck and his back, the other one around his foot, both meeting inside the 'u' of the horseshoe...

When I found the blessed thing in the street and brought it home, I was sitting on a chair since I'd gotten there, at the kitchen table, and I was fighting with it with my bare hands - no sashes - goes without saying to absolutely no avail: it wouldn't badge, even as thinned as it was by the use it had seen, there was not even the slightest trace of a movement I was so much after. Doing it I did not realize that from some point on father was watching me do it. When I finally looked up at him, he was smiling – one of those smiles I never figured out: was there a meaning to it, or was it just a grimace caused by something absurd and rather senseless out there in front of him, grimace his face would undergo without even his knowing about it.

"C'mon!" his voice sobered me up a bit, just that, and then, that I didn't react nevertheless, motioning me to hand my finding over to him. And I did, too. He grabbed it with his both hands in front of his chest, I saw his palms squeezing it, his fingers changing color a little bit, getting clearer, towards white, and he then just bent it into an 'S' in almost no time, without (except for that whiteness of his fingers, maybe) much of a visible effort – like it was one of those soft plastic toys from my early boyhood. He then handed it over, like that, in its new and strange shape, back to me, with no comment at all. When mother just said what she did – the thing about his hands – oh, yes, sir, I knew alright what she meant by that.

"He came home," she said, "and the very way he entered the kitchen told me that something was wrong yet before he even said anything. He just hissed out, sort of: "They are taking the mine, the machinery. Come with me!" and then he grabbed me with that bear paw - I had all my arm above my elbow blue afterwards, yes, my dear, blue-black-yellow, actually, and out we went, like we were, no extra cloths of any kind, no time to put something on, no, and I kept following him because I did not want to make a circus out there in the street. What would people have said, right? It was 1945. We had to take a bus, you know, a real clunker, I tell you, Hungarians I believe made them, a piece of junk that barely moved, and it stank inside, there was a smell inside of Diesel and exhaust all at once that would unchangeably make me sick, but who would give that a thought in such a moment, and we took it from where the post office is all the way to the mine's main administration building. There was no one there. It really looked abandoned. The whole building was empty, not a living soul..." She interrupts herself. Stops, looking at the park trees moving outside the window in the wind getting stronger and stronger, her lower jaw seems suddenly more pronounced than normally, she recalls it, obviously, every single detail slowly coming alive, and I also am trying to imagine the building: its emptiness – people hiding, some of them not even in their homes, scared out of their senses, hiding in the woods, or seeking refuge in other towns, somewhere else at any rate, with their families, as far away from the mine, from the Russians - from that victorious, 'liberating' army of the 'great brother' - as far as humanly possible. I see it. I read a lot about it. About the 'liberation' process: I won't forget the scene in which a family father, having obtained the message about the 'liberators' quickly and unstoppably approaching put a bullet through his wife's head, as the only answer to the good news, then liberating thus also three of his children, to finally get out of here in the very same manner himself.

"Only on the first floor, where father's office was – yes, in his very office, there they were - five of them, uniformed, don't ask me, I know nothing about the military stuff, and in front of everyone of them there was a revolver on the table, whatever for..." She remembers: quiet, focused, there is a smile on her lips, a smile an intelligent, profound effort puts there since I can remember her. She then talks about the military as a result of man's being unable to ever grow up – and then she nods, violently, sort of, at the same time pursing her lips which does away with the smile: "The only thing is, you see, that we, the rest of us, grown up or not, have to play that hopscotch too and that is, actually, what is really bad in all this, you know? The injustice of it. The nonsense. He introduced himself to them as the general manager of the mine, and then his wife, the woman here, his woman, too - just pointing to me. Nobody moved. Nobody said anything. The same motionless silence all the time since we had entered the room. He grabbed himself a chair and another one for me too and we sat down, and that was when I realized with the full strength of understanding one has only in moments like that, that it might - just might - be the end of everything for me. For him as well. Those were murderers, my dear, to pick up one of those guns off that table and put a bullet through me or him, or anyone for that matter, was really nothing to them. They murdered whole towns, once they had crossed the border." She nods, slightly. "Nothing."

I wanted to know why did he take her with him at all - what function could she possibly have played in the fight for the mine's machinery, but she wasn't sure (my memory – right here, at this very spot – makes a lousy, I think, joke on me: I see her, out of any context, walk from the stove, carrying a huge, clay pot, necessary for some of her culinary achievements, in both of her hands, its seems full of something hence really heavy, towards the sink that is on the other side of the kitchen; she gets to about where I am sitting right now, which is about half way, she is in a hurry, and right there it is as if the whole building suddenly collapsed: thunder and lightning and then aftershocks, and I see her on the floor, stretched, in her right hand she still holds the clay handle of the former pot (the only part of it left in one piece – the rest are just irregular sharp shards all over the place), everything on the floor is water, well, liquid of some kind, and blood, her blood, she had a huge gush on her forearm that would afterwards have to be stitched in the local hospital, and quite a few other cuts with a lot of bruises all over her now really tortured body– then silence, dense, full of uncertainty, anticipating, for yet that shakingly nervous moment longer; and then a moan, prolonged, *de profundis,* a true *clamor ex crucis*: 'suuuch a pot !!!').

"Why are you laughing?" she asks; she looks a bit hurt.

"I just recalled how you tripped and fell right here, the broken pot story, remember? No idea why."

"Oh," she smiles now, too. "Suuuuuch a pot, right? That!" And then: "We are plain stupid sometimes, aren't we?"

"I guess we are, after all. All of us, no exception to the rule!"

"Yeah…"

She sighs. Nods. Our lousy memory and its jokes…

"Shall I…?"

"Of course!"

She clears her throat.

The negotiations started. At some point that silence finally died. He spoke Russian like them. As far as she knew he had no accent in Russian at all, or rather he spoke the language like a Moscovite, and that was due to the fact that he went to a Russian school - when he was a young man, you see, it was a common thing in these parts, those were Russian schools, created there from the beginning for russyfication purposes, that was just the way things were, period – yes, he spoke it just like them. And then it got to the point where the name of his Russian friend fell (he, that friend, was some kind of a big shot general at that time, as far as she knew he could have been the main General for the southern wing of the Red Army moving West towards the German border, father told her afterwards exactly, and she now thought that's what he was – "God, you know, those are those things… and being all that he also was his, your father's that is, very close friend - yet from that Russian school your father had learnt the language at – yes, from that time, from his youth").

She looks up at me, having put her crochet down altogether.

"And that was something I'll never be able to forget: they picked up those guns at that very moment, I closed my eyes at first but then opened them up again and saw how they holstered all that artillery, it just vanished right then and there – and I also don't think they said much else, although I can't be sure of anything really as far as talking matters go, because of the language barrier - and then they left. Our Russian 'brothers' left, this one time without steeling whatever they could carry away.

"Yeah…" she looks through the window again at the trees that now move a bit less intensely. "That was one of those things."

"Did they say it would rain today?" she wanted to know then. "Have you listened to the radio?"

"I have, yes…" I said. "It might. That's what they said. It might."

"It might," she repeated after me. "Nobody seems to be certain of anything anymore. It might. That's a good one, isn't it? It might. And then again it might not, right?

"Yawp."

She looked on the table where the book I was perusing lay.

"What's that?" she asked. "Are you actually reading that?"

"No," I said. "That's not something you can really read. It's sports. A lot of pictures."

"May I?" she reached out for it without waiting for my answer and started leafing through it, right away, now and then wetting her finger with her tongue. "Who is this guy?" she asked me then, showing me an opened page in the book with a picture of a young athlete sitting on a rock in the middle of an incredible beach, the great vastness of the sea behind him, as if he himself was there to only stress the infinity of the sky mirrored in the ocean or vice versa.

"His name is Hubert Lapage," I said. "He does the same thing I'm interested in."

"Yeah..." she smiled. "A good looking young fellow, isn't he?" She nodded. "But you can also see from his beautiful face, and that right away, that he wouldn't know who Proust was, now would he?"

"I've no idea," I said laughing. "He looks to me like he might have been more into Greeks – Sophocles, Euripides. Poetry, I don't think... Sapho? I guess we will never know the answer to that one. Right?"

"I guess not," she said, smiling, only then finally getting my joke: she just croaked up – suddenly quite wildly. "Right!" she said then calming down to her usual, very toned (I tend to think about it as 'gray') level.

"Wind..." she said then, looking up at me. "I thought... You know what I suddenly have thought about? It must be the wind and the trees, moving like that, they were moving like that when he was missing for those few days and I thought it was over, they got him, that was what I really thought and I started praying for his soul, forgiveness, - God would have such a lot to forgive him - going through his things looking for some indication, something, as to what to do, and there it was... the receipt – the one I already told you about, the party thing... which only turned my suspicion into certainty: I knew, all along, you see, that he'd been doing something really stupid, like only he was capable of, but then there it was... The prove. God!"

"Yes?"

"Exactly like this, my goodness... Wind like that... 43... or 42," she shook her head. "I'll never know which. I've looked it up a lot of times. Yeah. It's age, I think, you know? Horrible." She smiled, embarrassed, kind of. "43, I think..."

And she started then telling me about father founding a cell of the Labor Party in the mine he worked in. (She's found the receipt – the day was just like this, she wants to stress it for some reason one more time: wind, the trees out there moving just as they are now, kinda crazy looking, aren't they, like they got mad at something or somebody). One of those long lonely days during the war.

She keeps then telling me, in a detailed manner, things and also how she ever got to know about them, who told her about the conditions, who told her, for instance, that the Nazis, if he ever got caught, would use the services of a regular doctor and a full blown hospital apparatus in order to prevent his dying ahead of time, which is to say before they would get whatever information they might have expected from him, and that they would get their certainty that he be telling them the truth and not something he made up, for instance, because of the pain he was unable to bare any longer – they would get that conviction in some cases in a week's time or longer yet, after which only they would finally let him die... Yes, there are times, here, on this Earth of ours, in our times, when death is a luxury, a commodity we can only dream of. Yes. She nods – I see it again, as if she were sitting there, in front of me now, as if she had never passed out of this dimension of tears and pain, and memories that are oftentimes just like that Nazi chamber of interrogation with a white coated doctor in it and a full blown hospital apparatus so you may not die too soon. I saw him then: not at that moment, not during the time I just recalled, time of that particular conversation with my mother, but later after that, few years actually later, in a hospital where he had died a few days before, on a bed – and then, the next day, in the morgue of that same hospital, in the basement, where I also was asked to help tu put his cloths my mother had provided and they had them in a plastic bag right on him, on his belly: yes, I see him quite clearly: little, unusually young looking, naked at some point of the process, which strangely made me feel a lot more like his brother than his son. I was doing that, that helping, together with a huge fat drunk they had there to that purpose, and I remember, quite clearly in fact, that I felt time and time again like hitting the son of a bitch in that stupid, soulless red face with my fist, for mistreating his body… (my feet, I see, I pulled the socks off and the grass caresses my skin, I have to close my eyes for a moment and even then, after that moment, I can't open them to the full extent because of the sun blinding me with that overwhelming, immense flood of light from the deep azure sky, and I lay down feeling the grass, its green softness, on my bare chest, watching a little awkward brown insect slowly moving up the green thin, stock; there is a road to my left we came here on, a dirt road, one can feel the intense smell of the hot dust, and on its side, opposite to where I am now on the meadow, there is a long row of poplars, toll, impressive, distinctly talking to me always, whenever we, father and I, come here, always ironically inviting, giving me high brow, sort of –inviting nevertheless – greeting; their tops now dissolving in that light that makes me half way close my eyes: I can hear his voice: he is talking – to me).

"He did that in the time, " she says suddenly and I feel lost – for just a moment, but the change comes about very quickly, "he could have paid dearly for doing it, and then… 54, I think, I'm not sure again, but I guess it was 54 because you wcrc little, quite tiny yet, fragile, like a piece of porcelain… when it was time for him to become a king, like all those other," she pronounces the word 'comrades' in such a manner that I think for a moment she might really throw up right here, on the table, without even attempting to go to the bathroom, "he dropped (poor dumb imbecile) the whole thing – he left the party. I asked. You bet I did. Only to get from the inside of all that shrewdness of a five-year-old: 'What it is now is not what we back then risked our lives for…' that was all I ever got from the poor son of a gun." She looks towards the window – on the outside the trees are moving again: we smile at each other. She drinks her tea. I think the feeling I have could be described, if I had to do it with one word, as - precisely - grace.

Martinique (Kim &Eve)

Ordering Jack's papers (I think against any of my expectations I have in the end become Jack's secretary –which I think is honor enough not to be paid for what I'm doing) I've found a whole bunch of things I just couldn't place within his strange – and in my opinion extremely rich – life so I decided to call and then simply asked Eve what was their story with Martinique, for example, because going through the paperwork I had, suddenly and quite unexpectedly, found all this stuff about the Island and their stay there - and she told me – very simply - that at some point Jack was just sick and tired of what was happening to him over here, of the not being able to publish anything, well… tired, you know? Can I relate to that?

"Sure… You bet I can."

There is a note, I told her then, which seemed to me out of any context – he does not elaborate on that at all:

God created Thomas Mann and Tarsius the Monkey
Both walking this planet as two-legged ones
With the same initials and nothing else the same
A gal who put the two together they gave Nobel price
Not that long ago -

…and would she comment on that?

"He told me he would like to get out, to go some place else, see, and deal with some other people. We talked, she said, to a certain fellow he knew in DC, and it was him, that fellow precisely who came up with the island – tropical paradise; you are going to fall in love with it, you won't probably even want to come back here at all. I was more cautious, my advice was to go and see first, spend some time down there, like vacation, before any type of a more final decision might be made. He agreed. He had to get a new passport which to him meant Calvary, of course, you know how he loves formalities, offices and such, right? But he did that, too. He went, that is, to all the respective offices, whichever ones were required for him to get his documentation completed, and then we started looking for trip packages, with the traveling agencies here as well as down there. Yet before we got down there, though, Jack found out about the volcano, The Mont Pélée thing, and the explosion of 19… something and that kinda slowed him down a little. The article he read was talking about the deadliest active volcano in the world positioned right about the middle of the island. The quite recent earthquake, you know, 7 point something again, and he has been in one like that before in San Francisco so he did have an idea of what it is like, well, all that caused that we were flying down there with very mixed feelings – beautiful vacation, probably, great getaway, no doubt, a place to spend of whatever you've got left on Earth, well, you know… Not quite, probably! No, Siree! After the first euphoria was over and the relative sobriety had set in, it just was not the same thing anymore. And then the airport came along, if I may say so. OK?"

"How's that?"

"We landed. And, as is usually the case wherever you go in this beautiful world of ours, we too had to go through customs. And there it was: the worst case of stupidity one could ever have a nightmare of being exposed to: the black, Arawak or whatever they are, 'Douanier,' who started correcting Jack's French; can you imagine? Kim, Jack lectured in France at some point, Jack published some poetry as a young man back in Paris, and here we were: the black who spoke only Creole, which basically is pretty broken, primitive French of a five years old, give or take, yawp, the dummy started correcting Jack's French. I don't speak the language enough to appreciate what was really happening there, but even I could hear the very- really terribly - crippled pronunciation of that 'functionary' versus Jack's Paris TV standard and the almost non-stop 'qu'on pale pas com ça…' crap, and he was doing that only because Jack had American passport he saw there in front of him. The bloody primitive couldn't even hear the real difference between their way of talking; and so finally Jack just did not make it, so to speak: he turned him, the monkey, around and simply, simplistically, if you will, booted his black ass a couple of times to the accompaniment of some pig's squealing, being fixed right there, at the spot, with which – Kim, I want you to believe me here – I couldn't possibly agree more. You know I am a peaceful creature, right? Nobody hates physical violence more than I do. You do, right?"

"Yes," I just had to say, because it is true, as far as I know her, and, damn it! - I think I do. If anyone does! "I do!"

"He was then sentenced," she picked up, "already at the governor's mansion (it came to that – to the governor's personal intervention after my call to DC from a telephone right there, at the airport, to that fellow, Jack's friend, who had initially recommended the island and then his call in turn to the governor's place to save Jack, and then the invitation to the governor's property, too, where we listened to and talked about Wagner's Tristan all the evening, and in the meantime, whenever the conversation, a bit artificial at any moment any way, the governor's wife would show us memoirs of Gauguin's staying there, and then the guys, French or local or, finally, American, whoever wrote something about it – all that kinda OK, too - and in the very end, late at night, after all that friendliness, Jack was handed the sentence nevertheless) to a fine we had to pay, pretty friggen steep, I would say, everything considered, and he had to spend almost a week (five days or so, if I'm not mistaken) in their fucking jail there. Goes without saying he was pretty pissed off after they'd finally released him. He came back to the States and felt like, he told me that himself, like the Pope, if you remember the former Pope getting out of the plain and always kneeling down and kissing the ground like he had nothing better to do – yeah… that's how he felt the moment we got back to New York."

"You didn't go anywhere else on the Island?" I asked.

"Of course we did. Pretty much everywhere. He rented a car, a jeep, to be exact, you know how he loves Jeeping, it's one of his passions, he got the maps of the island, and off we went, as soon as his 'time' for kicking the 'douanier's' ass was up. Yes, maam! We crossed all the rivers that are there, and went through everything a jeep can go through. I won't forget one evening when we got out of the jungle, out of that rain forest patch we were in, and saw, so suddenly that it made me cry out loud, the sunset in the sea. You know? That's something. It was – well, we felt like that, both of us, - like 'Le petit Prince" – it's enough to move your chair a little westwards and you can see the sunset again and again. Here you couldn't do exactly that, but you could see the sunrise, you know, and then just drive the hundred, well, I'm not really sure, so and so many miles across the island at a proper time to the other side and see the sunset on the same day. Jack sat down then, on a bench that was there on the beach, and started telling me about the volcano, all of what he had found on the internet about the explosion in 19 something, how the entire town was destroyed, and how many people really died, you see, there's nowhere to escape… We've had explosions bigger than that, Mt. St. Helen, for instance, Krakatau before that, etc, etc, but that was all on a surface where you could move from here to there thus saving your life. Not so here. The island is small. Nowhere to go, you see? That volcano after that got the name of the deadliest on Earth. I guess I said that before, didn't I? I'm not really sure. Kim?"

"Yes?"

"I really liked it there… Jack thought it was paradise, too. Views of the ocean you get from the beaches at different times of day and night – nights on the sand, too, are then, later, hard to forget, they come back to you and haunt you, and you want to go back, you think, you want to, it just makes you think, feel… whatever else is there… that you would be happy if you went back… Paradise." She laughed up, briefly. "With death in the middle. Bold mountain – that's what it means in French: Bold Mountain, the volcano there… And yet I loved it there, you know?."

"I believe you did."

And then, that she remained silent for a longer while, I said:

"You didn't even think of staying there, now, I mean going back and then settling there, on the island, because he didn't like it. But if he did, I mean… if he had liked it, you would have, wouldn't you?"

"Probably."

"And just to think that it was you who was born over here. Not him."

"Yeah…"

"Beauty is more important?"

"Since you put it that way…"

"Yes?"

"Kim, I'm not sure, I must say. I can't tell at the moment!"

"Talk to him…"

"Yeah, right!"

"Try!"

"I just may… Who knows…"

"Do!"

"Oh!" she said then quickly remembering yet something else: "That Creole, you know, the 'Douanier', he left the island afterwards. He probably couldn't stand the ridicule… I don't really know. Jack found out about it already over here. That very same DC friend of his, I'm pretty sure. He became a border control agent at Kennedy in New York and there was never one single complaint, Jack told me, because he doesn't speak English at all. Jack thought whoever finds out about any of this from his writing will think it is, or might be, just irony, some kind of a joke on his part, stand-off comedian, almost, type of thing, - and it is not. It's a fact and you can check it any time. In those notes you've got there, there should even be the asshole's name somewhere."

"Yeah…"

"Facts, you know…"

"Yeah. Facts."

I put then the receiver down, after having thanked her for her time.

I thought about the sunset seen after sudden immerging from the rain forest; sitting on the beach and looking; the talk about Le Petit Prince; I never had that, actually; I think I wish I did - very much so. I sat down, too. I made myself a drink. Sitting in my wicker chair I slowly sipped it, thinking. Yes, I think, I would like to live with Jack. That sounded wrong, damit! Someone like him, I meant. Yeah… Hell!

I think I'll tell Eve about that later.

Not now, though! No!

Maybe I should call her again?

Later…

William HCE (Notes – Kim's work in progress)

"You're late!" she yelled from the kitchen. "What happened?"

"I went to return the movie to the gallery," William yelled back. "It slows you down, see, kind of…"

"Oh…"

He went to the kitchen and gave her a kiss, after which he went over to the kids' bedroom, where he picked up the kids food can and started reading the label. He then opened the can with the fresh pulp, it was the better one made in Jersey, he liked a lot more, and not the one from New York he didn't like the smell of at all– not at all; the Jersey product was evidently more subtle, delicate, Shauna would not spit it out right away; no; there would be a smile on her little round face with those well pronounced, not to say protruding lips, her eyes closed, well, shot into two slits of pure enjoyment. He gave her a spoonful and then watched. And one more time after that. And until the can was empty, time and again. Her sister Shema was asleep. Shauna wanted more pulp and William had to go to the kitchen to get a new can from the fridge.

"Don't give her too much," Annalivia said. "She takes after you. She has tendency. You know that!"

"She wants more," William said.

"She always wants more. We all do."

He gave Shauna few more spoons after coming back from the kitchen and watched her smile grow – her eyes, two Chinese slits of, right now, almost lust, he could swear to that. He did enjoy it.

"Anything new?" Annalivia asked.

"Jody brought today the differential from his tractor," he said slowly, as if not quite certain. "It's nineteen twenty… I'm not really sure. Yeah! In that neighborhood, anyway. He wanted me to find him parts for that."

"Did you?"

"You kidding, right?"

"No, I'm not kidding! Isn't that your job?"

"Nobody goes that far back, you know? Nobody!" He looked at her. "Are we gonna eat something?"

"You hungry?"

"Yeah, I am."

"See, mom was here and we talked, and I didn't really have time… We could order some pizza, if you want."

"I'd eat something," he repeated.

She went out of the room. He could hear her ordering and then she was talking again to somebody. Few sentences down the road he knew she was talking to her mother. Love you! crossed his mind. Love you! They kept talking and he thought that the two of them, like in the movie he just returned, could be talking across a river and then morph into a tree and a stone, now couldn't they? He smiled.

The smell was excruciating and he stood up and started changing the diaper. Loaded, of course. Expression, he thought, folding the old one that was full and putting it into a nylon bag. Ex-pression. The waist gathers up in her intestines and she then, feeling it, presses it… ex? What is that? Obviously stands for 'out.' Latin probably. Or some such. Jack must know stuff like that, he thought then. I'll ask him next time I see him. Does it have to smell like that, though, Latin or not? It's beastly. Brutal!

"I'll go get mom!" Annalivia shouted from the hallway. "I'll take your Jeep!"

"I won't be here," he yelled back.

She showed up in the door, the sun stopping on her breast in form of a clear patch of light. She coughed slightly, clearing her throat.

"And just where will you be?"

"Jack invited me to the range. He'll bring his Olympic rifle – for me, to shoot. He wants me to join the club at West-Point."

"We can't afford that!"

"Of course we can! Don't I work my ass off? Every fuckin' day having to put up with that ignorant imbecile, yes, every single day having to put up with all those tones of crap? Don't I?"

She approached him now and, putting her hand on his very short, military style cropped hair, she petted the top of his head. Then she gave him a kiss on the cheek.

"Of course you do," she said. "Of course. But, love, you also have to understand that we have expenses. Now, with Shauna here, a lot more than we had ever so far, and you don't make any more than you did before she came. Huh?"

He swallowed and then coughed clearing his throat.

"Jack will bring the gun today. He'll supply the ammo, too. Doesn't cost anything. He certainly doesn't do it because he wants me to pay for it!"

"Of course he doesn't! That is not the point, though, love. The point is that you might and most probably will catch the fever. See? And if you do, other things will also start., won't they? You'll need this and you'll need that, and that is precisely what we can't afford right now, my love!"

He was looking at her. Strangely with all the sunlight on her as well as behind her now he saw her on a boat he had seen in that very movie he'd just returned, in half dark, oncoming night, sort of, and she was sitting in that boat, immobile, a bit like a sculpture, and a very old man was rowing, standing upright on the back of the boat, and between them, right about the center of that slick, strangely long vessel, there was sitting a three headed dog, each of his heads expressing a final warning. Is that memory? Does his memory recall that before his eyes alive to this degree? She lifted up her head, turning it at the same time towards him, as if, and her voice in this omnipresent is quite clear: I shall sail rightly in my bark. I am not afraid in my limbs, I shall see light-land, I shall dwell in it. If they morph into a tree, his thought morphed now into an almost clearly pronounced in his head, finished sentence, and a stone talking to each other across the river, she would be better in the role of the stone, now wouldn't she?

"I'll take off for the range as soon as you come back with your mom," he said. "If you're not back here before five thirty, I'll call the sitter."

115

She threw her head to the right and up, like a horse would do, he thought, and snorting, too.

"You can't do that, love!"

"Yes, love, I can and I will! Be back here with your mom before five thirty. OK? Love her too!"

"I'll be very disappointed, my love, if you do that! Terribly disappointed." She touched his hair again with her hand, in a petting gesture. "But I know, I'm sure that my treasure here won't disappoint his love like that, right? My love?"

"Be back here before five thirty!"

She shook her head, smiling, sadly, kind of. He thought there was something scary about it: a sudden unknown ghost speaking out of the face he knew so well. He made a step backwards, unwillingly.

"Go up on the great west side of the sky and go on the great east side of the earth. See you, my love!"

She turned around, still smiling in the same manner, and for yet a moment longer he saw her walk towards the main door to the house, through whose glass the late afternoon sun was now really flooding the hallway, sharpening things. He heard the door slamming. Then there was silence.

He sat down. Thought about the generations before and those that will come after them and why it is the way it is – and does it really have to be this way? He thought... He will go down to the circle of fire without the flame touching him ever. Memory does turn life into a dream. Sometimes.

Pizza was brought to the door and he had to pay and take it inside; he ate. He felt he was very hungry.

Eating the fresh wonderful slice with everything on it (no anchovies) he was wondering if he knew enough to make that kind of assessments: his own mother and father – how were they? What would he, father, have done in this situation. There were kids, too; he, William, had brothers. Nah! Too many a thing missing. Way too many! Too many things neglected – they should have been delivered to him in a proper time and they have not been... Yeah. He should've been explained. Told. Things. Yes! He nodded a couple of times and then stood up, wiped his hand with a napkin, and went over to the telephone. He dialed Jack's number and then left a message because Jack wasn't there yet – a message that he would not be able to come this afternoon to the range: his wife had invited cousins to a dinner, already quite some time ago; and she's already made the dinner, too, so it would really be a pity, you see... Some other time, Jack!

Dinner. Mom. Jeep. Boat. That dog... He thought he should go to the gallery and rent the movie one more time. It was suddenly even more fascinating to him what the memory was doing with the day – what it *could* do. That was what he really felt like doing. He thought it was not only interesting and, somehow, very true - although it, sort of, lets you hanging in the end... Annalivia's brother – and she wouldn't even have to come back here with her mom (together with his own brother, too, oh, yes sir! no doubt there) - would definitely kill him if they only could – now, would they then also say that he rose from the dead before they could eat him? Something like that. Like Jack once said in the store: look before you leak, dears! Yes, he thought he definitely should go and get it one more time. He went to the small desk in the corner of the room and from the upper drawer he had to open with the key he pulled out of his trousers' pocket with a big bunch of other keys he took out a thick yellow envelope and out of it he pulled his will. He did not read it. He was just looking at it. Looking at his signature, then, in the end, in clear wide lettering, made there in a very traditional way with an ink pen in black ink: William H.C.E.

He smiled slightly.

I'm twenty five and I don't even remember myself from when I was twenty. Was I different? Do I know more now? I'll soon be thirty. I don't think I shall know so much more then – in fact, I think I know less know; know may not be the best word... Understand, I think, is better. As years pass by I understand less and less of it...

Then he nodded.

For all of it is mine...

The journey to Prag

So many times already I have given a eulogy concerning the highways and the possibility of traveling in this country that has been so far developed to the point where it is now: you can go wherever you want at any time. I was now driving east towards the New York border and the highway would give off a rhythm that spoke about comfort and safety, all that in the clear evening air slowly getting reddish, and right there ahead of me there was the sun – huge, really impressive, like a dramatic, really heavenly, almost divine warning of the oncoming night. I passed a semi-trailer, gigantic looking, and got back into the right lane. I rested my head against the head support and I thought I wished it was possible to close your eyes: aboard a plain it would be: you could – even if you were the only pilot – simply put it on automatic, but they haven't so far developed anything of that nature for a car; you, in other words, have to drive it: no closing eyes. And yet over the years one develops the ability that puts one very near just that: move, to be able to move away, somewhere else, far away, to the other side of the globe, for that matter, while you still drive, control, that part of you which is necessary to exercise whatever it takes to more or less safely drive towards the point one had set out to get to unhampered, undisturbed in any possible way, you still can go – and yet I remember the night aboard a train, the rhythm of the wheels against the tracks, my father sleeping, his head against a head support, pretty comfortable besides, the window to my right a black square, that blackness only rarely interrupted by towns flying by, blinking, inviting colonies of little flickers of light from the dept of the blackness, stops, stations, platforms I could see, and then, towards the morning the border, control, nothing really unexpected, just a longer stop, hot tea, a cake whose taste I still remember (remember – I remember words, situations, I could tell what happened and what somebody in this or that particular situation had said – and here I just have that taste in my mouth: it is, to some extent, a taste of the rubber crocodile I loved so much, its tail in my mouth – then it popped, my brother in law (that's my family, too: my brother in law was twenty four years older than I, he was a lawyer then and I was just a little boy) over-inflated my love, playing, stupidly, senselessly, I think just showing off what a big guy he was, and then it was over – rubber, shapeless, covered with whitish powder I never suspected inside of it, on the floor, pain in my heart and also hate, maybe for the first time since I was here, this side of being, with that intensity, I was ready to kill him, I am sure. Taste… Is that remembering?), and then the train would start rolling again, towards the dawn and then the day. Outside the window nothing changed: the same, kind of flat landscape, moving fast backwards in synchronicity with the train movement, a stop, one or two, three perhaps, and then the goal of our journey: Prag – taxi ride to the castle and the street that looked like one of my dreams I have so often since childhood: houses, little (not really – but that's how they look), following one another, and my father's words, he is talking, telling me what they are, where we are now: Vladislav had at some point two hundred alchemists working on his potential riches, should they have ever succeeded, which of course never happened, yes, some of it is history, some of it – as I find out later – is something he uses to make me remember better, sort of a fairy tale; I was sleepy, and that's what I remember in the first place, my eyes, eyelids heavy and falling, I had to concentrate not to fall asleep right then and there, and he was talking about Kafka having lived in one of those houses, and then later, once we were inside, after father's long conversation with the inhabitant (they spoke German so I could understand the language, but I didn't listen; up to now Kafka associates himself in my mind with a thick, plush carpet and he has a smell a little bit on the mildew side – we spent the night there: father explained to him who we were: Germans from Upper-Silesia, stuck there after 1945, and there was sudden, wonderful cordiality, surpassing by far any possible expectation, hospitality I had never experienced before, and then the room I was allowed to lay down and seek the way out of whatever was there around me into a rhythm of wheels and sparse, as if nervous lights speeding backwards on the other side of the window. I don't know if that was day or night. When did I get up. When have we – father and I – started our visit, going over the castles history. I don't. Up to now I remember that the

Habsburgs began to make changes in 1526, and in 1600 hundred, thereabouts, Rudolf started playing his tune there, turning it into a true European art center (I couldn't care less, really, it was all dross to me) and then we were in the room we came all that terribly long way to see: a huge, as I remember it, marble table, almost a whole wall, with a genealogy tree, where father showed me his own grand father in form of a golden Gothic inscription cut and gilded into the shiny stone – do not forget... not cvcr!

I saw him in my back view mirror: the disco lights, cop. SOB!

I took my time getting of the road and onto the shoulder. And then I saw him walk towards me, in his Stetson, not too big, average, I'd say; I opened the window and he asked me the sacramental "If I knew why he stopped me," and by now I knew it, of course.

"Yes, sir, you were doing 85," he said asking for my license and registration and whatever else. I handed the crap to him and then I just waited there. I thought it took him too long. I thought something was wrong, when I saw another cop car stopping ahead of me and then backing up towards my front. The one ahead stopped, opened the door, got out, and then suddenly unholstered his gun, pointing it at me, whilst the one behind approached my side and in my side mirror I saw that he had his gun also unholstered although not pointed at anything, just hanging down in his hand, and as soon as he was at my side, he asked me to step out of the car, which I did – I opened the door and got out, asking in my turn what was his problem, or what did I do wrong.

"Your license has expired, sir," he said.

"Is that why you have guns in your hands?"

"Yes, sir," he said, "we don't know who you really are."

"You can't see that I'm Pyjamma Alladin with the friggen magic Lamp?"

"We'll find out soon enough."

"How soon?"

"Soon enough, Sir!"

He was indifferent, matter-of - factly, I knew that there was no point in trying to talk to him. He told me to turn around and cuffed my hands behind my back, after which he told me to move over to his car.

"Where will my car be?" I asked him and he told me that it would be towed to their precinct, where I also would spend the night. There was no judge available now, regrettably.

"Regrettably?"

"Yes, sir. I regret that very much. Your inconvenience. The match will be run right away."

"Match?"

"Yes, sir. You will be fingerprinted as soon as we get there and the prints will be sent to a central FBI computer for matching purposes. We should have them tomorrow. The day after, perhaps."

"The day after tomorrow?" was my question which I asked right at the moment when he was shutting the door closed. He got into his seat in the front.

"You were asking?" he said.

"You said the day after tomorrow… Are you telling me that I should… might be in your slammer the day after tomorrow as well?"

"If we don't get the match from the FBI, yes, sir, that might very well be the case. Like I told you, we don't know who you really are."

"What about my neighbors, my wife, my friends. What if you don't get that 'match' for next couple of weeks? Am I supposed to sit there all that time, just because the system is kind of seriously impaired, to put it *very* mildly?"

"You should have thought about that earlier, sir. Now there isn't really much I can do. I or anyone, for that matter."

In the station I was fingerprinted right away – it seemed like there were not too many other 'criminals' – when I was standing with that background we all know from the movies, waiting for my picture being taken by the local 'artist'; I had the impression that it all was just a bad joke, something I should maybe not laugh, but certainly smile about; it did not deserved my attention, deeper going interest, research – no, it was something, a fragment of life around me, gone askew, as John would say: just fucked up. But then I had to spend the night in a room I would never choose for spending not only, well, let alone a night - not a friggen minute, willingly, in. That's what, sort of, sobers you up: it is not a joke, a little deviation off course: if someone like me – someone, hence, who never deliberately broke any of the existing law's precepts, gets arrested and all of the above, because a piece of ID has expired, something is seriously wrong – will I be water boarded, too? And if not, then why not? It's fun, isn't it? These guys around me look, all of them with no exception, like it certainly would be just that to them. Then why not?

The cell was green, oil painted, cheesy. There was a bunk, sort of, concrete, with nothing on it. I sat down. The light was on and I knew I would have to sleep – if I was to sleep at all – with that light on. I closed my eyes. I saw myself one more time, quite distinctly, standing in front of that frame, for picture taking: I knew from now on I was a criminal, I have been arrested, if I were to tell the truth anywhere, if asked – yes, I have been arrested. John was looking at me, smiling: don't be an idiot! OK? I lay down, putting my arm under my head and I looked at the ceiling, cracked all over actually - that paint has not been renewed since Jews left Egypt and then crossed the Red Sea. Yes, something is rotten in Denmark. Oh, yes, sir!

Something stinks – like a decomposing and half way decomposed body of a dead ass not even vultures come to visit anymore because even to them its sheer poison now.

There were weak voices coming through to me from the inside of the station, people talking, I've heard a laugh a little bit louder, then nothing, and then again just a regular murmur of a conversation one cannot hear because of a distance too great, or thickness of the wall one is behind too solid. I closed my eyes. I felt light. Relaxed. Not caring.

"Have you ever been in the castle?" I heard, suddenly very, perfectly clearly, missing the mark altogether, and then, right away: "No, but isn't it enough for me to be here?"

I saw father, quite clearly, and the guy across the table from him as well, with the snow white, pointed beard, nodding, smiling. "Yes! Yes, of course!" His wife was nodding too.

I was there and here simultaneously; right between that part of the world where everything is possible (or, rather, nothing is impossible anymore), and this side where from I still was able to perceive the faint voices from behind the wall of the room I was locked in reaching my ears submerged in what we tend to call reality. I think I was smiling: Cheshire Cat: there is this moment where the person being awakened resists the process: no, let me be where I am, do not destroy this, it is so fragile and so dear at the same time, and I am so curious, and just your voice can prove destructive here, you don't even have to move – so don't! There is no fear that is always present – to some extent at least – when you cross for good to the other side, simply because you know that you're still here, but the 'here' also gets the tinting from the other side that makes it more and more attractive – to the point where it would really prove difficult to make one's final decision: for now it is: don't wake me; let me be.

"They were chosen for circumcision," father says now, whatever the preceding part of the conversation might have been, (I know this part I'm listening to right now is important to him because I have heard it quite a few times before then): "which is big, really big, huge, tremendous, and which is never sufficiently understood: why in the bloody hell the omnipotent God who created the infinite universe is suddenly interested in one lousy piece of human skin? Why that particular piece of skin? Well…" he thinks, slakes his lips with his tongue and as if that reminded him of the glass of wine the host of the house invited him to, he also takes a little sip; tastes it. "I think, you see, it's simple. It's not about us; it's for us. What God says to his elect, for the moment, is this: I had to give it to you because I want you to multiply, I want you keep on and not to vanish, so there you go. But careful – that is also the most powerful part of you, that is a drive you will only rarely be able to fight with, so keep what is necessary, but cut off what is not… Right? St. Paul talks about the circumcision of the heart – you need to be competitive, you need to have the will to win, to be better than that other guy, because otherwise your activity would slacken and you would fall asleep. Nothing would ever be done. But also keep what is necessary and cut off what is not. The elect meanwhile…" he takes another sip, tastes it for a while yet longer, or so it seems, while they are waiting, obviously, for him to continue – they are interested in his thought (I think more than that: as is often the case with father when he talks to people he has also this time awakened their fascination; they're all ears; their eyes are also all focused on him, they look as if hypnotized, simply unable to move; he notices that too after a while and swallows heavily – mother would call him 'sorcerer' time and again, after having participated in similar situations, and I know that he doesn't like it; that it scares him a bit, perhaps, I'm not really sure. "It seems to me they got stuck on the surface," he says then, slowly, as if groping in the dark, "gestures, liturgy, if you will. They never lift up that surface, be it only on one side of that square they are on, to look what's under it, to really find out... how are they truly doing, I mean, if it is acceptable, if they are still acceptable, that is..." He smiles. "Now back to Kafka –where it all began. That's a nightmare, isn't it? The world of gestures. Just the surface, with hardly any question at any time about whatever might be underlying that surface. Opposite the words we all know: dirt will come to you not from the outside; dirt comes to you from your heart."

He nods. Our host, having taken a deep breath, seems to me to be digesting the thought. His wife, smiling, asks if we would like to eat something else yet... Perhaps?

Father, also smiling, says 'thank you, we are fine, full. No, tanks.'

The host asked father then – kind of a sudden, as I remember it now - about music, about father's musical preferences, and father told him, because of the place, because of this wonderful evening - our great, fascinating conversations this far - the remembrance of things, hence, past and yet still so dear to all of us, about Smetana and the Moldau, finally right now we are on the left bank of the river - and I saw the eyes of the host suddenly getting watery; he coughed; he stood up slowly and went over to a stand in the corner of the room we were in, and then we were listening to father's wish: Smetana's 'Moldau' by Prag Philharmonic Orchestra, from a surprisingly high quality stereo...

Kim about Ho

In New York's China Town he met his wife. Years later they had two kids – two boys. Ho had two jobs. All of his time here he had two jobs (sometimes three). God jobs – when he was talking about his jobs, one would think, and that thought was just forced on one almost without choice, sort of... one thought, hence, about those Cormorants he was using back in China to fish; they would be installed traps around their necks, slings of a certain diameter, so they would only be able to swallow really small fish and whatever was bigger they had to be 'freed' from by a human hand – yes, he was allowed to swallow the really small fish and whatever was there, be it just slightly bigger, he would be 'freed from' it almost right away. But he was happy. He would even say, he would actually say it, out loud, that he was lucky. Yes, his older son went to college – hell, college was an idea he'd been made to digest and then assimilate for a hell of a long time. Back in China he had no idea whatsoever about any educational system, any, and it has only been here that he got acquainted with one; college was the top of the world and that his own son would climb up there seemed to be an absolute privilege, absolute, mystical almost, top of luck people like Ho could ever dream of. Yes! He, Ho, could be lucky too. Couldn't he? His son went to college. To study. To build ships like the one he, Ho, came here on, or maybe yet something else, like those things now and then could be seen up there in the sky, those shiny birds that he, Ho, was once told about that people could fly, too, thanks to them, and that people were up there, in those... Well.... Yes, that was luck.

He bought himself a jacket – leather jacked like the one the overlord back then, yet in China had always on, yet in those times before his own boat got destroyed, coming for the money they owed: black, shiny leather, rich, manly, well, lordly. Yes, he was lucky. Oh, was he lucky, I tell you... Coming back from work one day at three thirty in the morning he got mugged, had few broken ribs from kicking, black eye, broken jaw, yes, that... They took the jacket. Yes! They took the jacket. They took it! Yes! They did! They took the jacket. That was also when he bought the gun. He was advised to get one and he did. A 1911 A1 in .45ACP, he won't forget that. It took a whole month of work but now he was protected. He was.

And here Pino elaborated on something one can't be certain that it can be understood not only one hundred percent, but that it can be understood at all. How can a word 'crack' be explained seems quite easy, right? One finds a crack in the wall and points to it. Nothing more simple than that, right? But how can, for instance, 'translucent' be explained if you can't talk? How? And so there it is: in how far is it Pino, his improvising technique, his inventiveness, ingenuity and intelligence, his story telling ability, not to say talent for which he must have always been admired, throughout his entire life, and in how far is it Ho – his true explorations, his intuitive, anti-intellectual search after the meaning of life; is there any way to separate the two? I guess not. Life: walls, translucent but solid, all around, in the middle of it Ho, whatever he could recall, whatever ever happened, all of that shaped by yet another translucency, inside those walls, in the center of the space they created – the walls as well as the translucent 'shaper' inside cannot ever be destroyed by anything; but things outside the walls can be changed as well as things inside them – those can be changed and they are being changed all the time; from good to bad and the other way around. In the walls there are cracks; invisible cracks but extant nevertheless; demons come in through those cracks. Even if the world outside, the yet 'unshapen' world is still propitious the demons can change what's inside to something else, to something that the propitious world did not mean as the content of the shaped. What can you do? Well, here it comes: you make noise! A lot! Firecrackers! Yes! Whatever of that nature. A pistol comes in handy, too. You can use it not only to chase bad people away but also to chase the demons… Yes, that's how you handle it.

Ho's lost his job. At first the first one. That was a terrible punch by itself. But then the second one went as well. His son had to quit college. No! Please! No! But he did. He had to (had to!) quit college. Ho was told right away the day his son did quit. Ho took the gun and went out to show them – to show the demons, yes, to prove to them that he, Ho, would not be helpless, that he, Ho, would not be intimidated and that he knew how to handle demons or anything for that matter. He started firing the gun at the sky and those rounds sounded in that high airshaft of the building he lived in like little Hiroshima explosions. Good! He could hear something! He could hear, too! Great! That was exactly what he was after. But then he was all surrounded by cops with guns pointed at him and he saw their mouths moving – they must have been shouting at him, must have been telling him something of utmost importance, and then it clicked: they wanted him to drop the gun, he understood as soon as he was shown, by a gesture, what that was they were after. Oh, yes, sir! He dropped it right away. He didn't want to get shot, no! And he certainly did not mean any harm to any living thing! No! He dropped it to the ground and let them cuff his hands, after which they took him to the car out there, in the street. He spent the night in the station they took him too, and the next day he saw the judge. They couldn't talk, the judge didn't seem to understand that Ho never learnt any English, that he was also def, he shouted at Ho, the latter could see that, judge's face getting red, thick veins standing out on his bull's neck, oh, yes, he could see all that, the only problem was that he still couldn't understand a word of what was being said – nothing, zippo, zilch. And that was when the judge decided to send Ho for psychiatric evaluation. And that was how Pino met him, already inside, several years before the day I'm writing this note. More about which later as said before.

John

I was dusting in that part of the household I like the most: art collection. And there are some pieces in that collection I think nobody would be ashamed of. Nobody in the whole world. For the last few minutes she was here with me – kinda hard actually to tell doing what... Just goofing around, I guess. She comes in, spins around like that, and leaves, and that's usual. Sometimes she talks to me. I was passing the vacuum slowly, very carefully, that's what I'm paid for – as also for dusting the pictures (she is allergic and they have to be dusted, Rembrandt, Rubens or whatever, no matter, as she puts it) I have a... thing made of feathers plucked from... Jeez, I've no idea what bird, goose fluff is stone and ice chunks in comparison with the duster I am using for the picture frames – frames only, it has to be stressed, I can't dust the picture itself, unless its under glass, and not all of them are. I was just approaching the one I wanted to ask her about – it's late Van Gogh, it's from Arles period, I've never seen it before, it's little, book size. I know they did not have it all that long. I know it from him.

"Oh, that one!" she says asked as soon as I got close enough, laughing – she has a laugh that is irritating to me, has been from the very beginning. "That one is too small. I told Nephtalí not to buy it but he has great influence over James, way too great... See, it's way too expensive for its size, it's a friggen nonsense. What did you call it, by the way?"

I told her again it was late Van Gogh.

"Yeah..." she said. "Whatever." And then: "I like that one!" pointing to a huge maritime panorama in gold baroque frame that was not a Turner – nice, though, I'd say. Just that: nice! She was smiling, nodding. "That's my niece: Golda Pinkelstein from Boston, Massachusetts. Gifted, isn't she? Yes," she answered herself, nodding in suddenly profound reflection, "we've never lost that touch, or did we? Never!"

She turned around and walked towards the door leading to the long corridor, but then stopped, suddenly, sort of, as if reminded of something she had forgotten in the meantime, turned around and smiling said: "Friday I shall be, as usual, in Paris, John... Would you like me to bring you something from Paris, sir?"

"A gown, "I said. I too was smiling. "Yes, bring me a gown from Givenchy collection when you do your own shopping. OK?"

She was laughing,

"You bet! We'll take it off your paycheck, right? It's for Redhead, isn't it?"

She turned around one more time and left for good.

They had their own business jet at the Hartford airport and the crew on call and she would fly to Paris or London once or twice sometimes a week, only to do the 'shopping', and even if she did not go, for whatever particular reason, they would have to fly at least once a week over there anyway, to get the supply of French bread and water, filtered in France, water that had been taken from the Loire. I started dusting again. I hoped she took my 'order' as a joke, she isn't bright but, hopefully, she isn't that stupid either: a Givenchy gown would mean several of my paychecks and Redhead would really be pissed off.

I was looking at the small, book size picture: bushes of some strange kind that no one would be able to find anywhere out there or looking up any possible botany atlas, under a sky cast of lead visible because of the light arrived here from the bottom of suffering and prayer that the *'cauchemare'* might finally end that it just achieved and is quickly passing the point of no return: understanding of imprisonment within one's destiny.

All of a sudden the door opened and she was back.

"John," she said to me, smiling, the big toe of her right foot drilling a whole in the parquet, "I don't want to do something we will all regret..." She looked up at me. "Did you mean that about the gown?"

"Of course not!" I said. "'twas just a joke."

"That's what I thought," she said. "Just makin' sure."

"Yeah... Just a joke."

"Good!"

She left then. I looked at the picture. The light outside, I thought, was reaching the inside, the here and now, the place I was standing upon, in a manner a little like I saw it there. But I couldn't see the sky: the skylights have been designed and executed in such a manner as to deliver the light but not the view of the sky. I sighed. The whole house had been designed in France and only then the design adopted locally to the Connecticut coast line – dining room was adjacent to a boulder bigger than it, that had to be drilled through to make a passage to the kitchen, both of them, the kitchen and the dining room, having outer walls of glass tinted in such a way that from the outside, from the sea out there, like from the deck of their yacht, they looked also like local rocks. The sky now, as far as I could see through that gigantic window at the end of the art room I was in, one level above the one I just described, did look leaden. But then again: I was too far away from the window to really be the judge of that.

Midhudson

"Honorable Nephtalí Assgold presiding!" the bailiff's voice sounded like there was nothing more important in the whole world. "All rise!" And then, once the honorable Nephtalí Assgold sat his honorable rear end down: "Please, be seated!" was also the bailiff's bleat and the same murmur of the courtroom in movement following. The prosecutor asked if he could approach the bench which he was granted, and as he was moving towards it I looked curiously to see if he would try to cover his eyes as not to be blinded by all that majesty he was approaching so boldly, but he didn't – I thought for a moment that he might already be blind, which would definitely explain it – and then they whispered for a while to one another – the prosecutor pointing to me and the honorable Nephtalí nodding with deep understanding of a modern Salomon (that made me wonder if I also was gonna be cut in two); and then the whispering and nodding repeated itself again. And then, not that long after that, the two cops who brought me to the courtroom from that station where I had spent the night, cuffed me again (cuffed me… Good Lord – that's a whole 'costume' they 'install' on one – mostly leather but also a lot of metal: brackets, rings, karabiners – a friggen Christmas Tree they turn you into; sort of forces you to wonder about lights, little glass bulbs, and fire crackers – where are those?), after which we left, heading downstairs and to their car.

"What now?" I wanted to know. Are we going back to the station where they brought me from, or somewhere else? What's the scoop? Huh?

The cop told me that he wasn't supposed to tell me, but that meanwhile I managed to get them convinced that I knew how to be reasonable, so he would tell me, in private - in great confidence, you understand - that the judge ordered psychiatric evaluation; that then was the place they were now taking me: forensic psychiatric centre. I felt stunned. Can I do something? Nope! Can anyone? Is there some form of protest? Appeal from the asshole's "decision"? I could tell they felt stupid about it, too. How's that possible in a free country? I wanted to know.

"Can happen to you too, you know?" I said. "You're no exception."

I saw him shiver. He laughed, but that wasn't a real laugh – it was more like I told him that his kid he really loved had mesothilioma and he heard me, yes, he heard me well, but there was no certainty as to the diagnosis yet, a lot more shall be necessary in order for him to believe that. That shudder came over him at the thought itself – not because of any conviction he might or might not as yet have.

"How? How in the bloody hell… To be picked up on the road, after having done nothing against the so called law," (the fact that your ID had expired is nowadays enough to become a suspect, (and a suspect of what? If I may know) - is that right? Could that be right – in any possible circumstances, and lately, add insult to injury, for a certain period of time – few years, right? it is going to be a few years by now, right? - a suspect can, basically, according to the above law, be shot as a terrorist if they deem that feasible…). "How?"

(…)

I sighed. For a moment it seemed quite strange to me because they sighed as wells – both of them up front.

"We should do something"

"Like what?" The one on the right front seat turned his peasant face to me, frowning: "Like what, Sir? Would you care to elaborate on that?"

I leant back.

Once we got to the hospital, a bunch of other ones took over and I was led inside. The new ones called themselves TA's. Blacks. Huge. Indifferent. They took me to a pavilion, where I just joined a group. A group – of, well, that wasn't quite clear to me for the moment. I knew I was in a maximum security prison. I knew that because I was told by the cops who brought me here, yet back there in the cop car, on the road. The moment we entered I remember my actual disappointment because of the lack of the inscription above the door about the hope that would have to be abandoned whilst entering here. But who were those people? Guys like me – whom the rotten system put here, or real criminals, whom nobody wants out there, including myself, real out-casts? Psychos unable to communicate with the honorables? The opposite to all the Assgold - their honors out there? I was soon to find out that it was a mix, and that I – which doesn't surprise me (not now and not back then) – was sort of an exception; in my case there was really no reason for my being here. Malice. Stupidity. Abuse of power. And yet in the car I realized, recalling the immediate past (some times, quite often in fact, we don't get something right away – few minutes, hours, days, well, some time, has to pass by in order for us to realize what was the meaning, if any, of a particular gesture, of a particular happening, and so it was now, too, with me): I saw it again: a book, and then another, in the hands of the prosecutor back there in the courtroom, actually passing from his hands into the honorable Assgold's whitish, waxy palms honorably presiding… My books. If that was the case… My God, if I was right and I was here because of my books… should I start putting together a new Gulag Archipelago? seemed to be the question for the moment. We were taken right about then to another room in a different pavilion to eat; we had to form lines like in the army, sort of, walk out of the building we were in, cross the yard, go up the hill, enter another building, to be seated at a long table in a cheesy painted something that remotely resembled a dining room (a lot of imagination necessary for that); we have all seen that table in that room in the movies and we have all seen all those poor chops seating at it and eating that wonderful gourmet food. Haven't we? The guy next to me I addressed briefly did not speak English. He turned out to be Cuban. His name was Pino. Jose. We spoke Spanish, eating – a breaded chicken that tasted like a barely warmed up shoe sole and some vegetables that didn't have any taste at all, and he told me a couple of first things that boiled down to this: we were fucked, first and foremost of all. Right? Got that? There's no getting out. The first hospital qualifying commission one would have at the end of a four year period. Four year period, I repeated after him, mechanically, sort of. Stupidly, could be said, I think, too. God… But I didn't do anything… He laughed. That's exactly what everybody says. Is it true? Who the hell knows? You need a lawyer. A good one, if you can afford one. Do you have somebody out there? Like a wife? Family? Such? I told him I did.

Good. Lawyer. Remember that. Only a lawyer can get you out of here. One thing above all: don't fight it! If you do, you get really fucked. You got that? I told him I did. I got it. Good!

"What did you do?" was my question.

"I shot my friend. He wasn't really my friend. He was a cocksucker who wanted to kill me all along. I knew he was after me, also from the beginning, so I got a twenty-two and I put a couple of bullets, twenty-two short, through his thick skull. That got him off my back. That's why we are talking to each other now. The cops, though, thought it was a pretty professional job, you see, - an amateur usually gets something big, a forty-five or so, something that literally blows the victim's head off – then they, the cops, know the guy was improvising, right? – he didn't have much experience. They really, right away, know he didn't know much about what he was doing while he was doing it. But I knew everything about it, you know? Beforehand. I knew I didn't need forty-five or forty-four magnum, or some such, I was hired as my older brother's bodyguard (he was a drug dealer in Miami at the time), and I did what I did. OK? They pinned then on me some other shit, things I didn't have the faintest friggen idea what the hell they might even have been talking about in front of that friggen judge in that stinkin' shit up courtroom, but I couldn't defend myself anyway. The lawyer was a shark: the fucker took the money, he knew, you see, I had a lot, so he took it, but when it came to the court I thought he was the fuckin' DA, you know? It really was easy to confuse. My brother told him, I know that for a fact, yet in that courtroom, that he was a dead man, and as far as I know, he is a dead man now. My brother did him in. Himself or hired somebody. Who the fuck knows? Huh? Good! The cocksucker. Well, here I go. OK? But I am crazy. I am… they told me… I never really could remember… some fucken' thing, you know? I take the medication, you see, I am sixty two, who gives a shit anymore, right? – I strongly advise you to do the same – take the shit they give you, I mean rally take it, ok? It makes you indifferent, it helps you a fuckin' hell of a lot in here, you know? Take it! *Tomalo.* And don't fight! *No luches. Nunca.* Remember that! No matter what happens, don't let anyone ever provoke you to fighting. If you fight, even the best lawyer won't be able to help you. Make sure you got that right!"

I didn't get to talk to a doctor for quite a few days after that but I talked to Pino a few more times and I really, I must say, enjoyed it; I really got to liking him. The days were passing by quickly.

Eve then scheduled a visit, they allowed it, yes, we have seen each other – during which I found out that the lawyer (I did not qualify for a public defender, I would have to be able to afford one out of my own pocked, and to do that I (we – Eve and I) would have to get the second mortgage on our house); that was, more or less, the result of her free consultation with a lawyer's office. Metzger&Schweinehund. I said we would wait. I haven't done a thing, I didn't have any criminal past, and, by George, somebody, anybody, even one of those friggen, non-English speaking doctors so many of whom were goofing around here, and that at any given moment for that matter, would sooner or later find that out, too. Things would, most probably, change for the better of their own, without having to lose our house.

I did not take into consideration the situation I had to deal with only a few days later, during the nighttime. I was taken downstairs and out, and then over the yard to the infirmary, it was like eleven o'clock night time, where I was told that I would be given a barium enema. I wanted to know why. What the hell for? I did not have a problem going to the bathroom – why then such a drastic (I knew a thing or two about barium and how it would work) enema? Nobody would bother to answer me, though. A black, some six feet seven, shaved head, grabbed my head (unshaved) under his arm instead and bent me over, and at the same time a nurse, chuckling, stupid spick who obviously enjoyed the whole thing, just as the big nigger did, pulled my prison pants down and started shoving the hose into me. I hit the nigger in the balls from underneath his behind with my right fist, and the very moment he'd let go of me I started up, using my two hundred twenty pounds from my left leg onto the right and then back, and I put all that momentum into my right hand – there is a way of throwing it without even thinking about what one is doing, it makes is faster, really, than one could possibly think of doing anything– I felt his forehead giving in, sort of... He went back, towards the door, staggering, and then tried to hold on to the air – that even looked funny because there was nothing there, nothing, he really tried to grab the thin air with his convulsively moving front paws, and only a very short moment later he just slouched down onto the floor where he remained absolutely motionless. I grabbed her – her eyes were wide open, her mouth too, but no sound came out – pulled her head towards my fist, and then laid her on the floor, too. I pulled him towards the center of the room; now her - that she wore pants, too - I pulled those pants of hers off, shoved the barium enema hose up hers now, laying her down on her belly in such a way that her pussy was right on top of his face. I hanged the enema bag back on the hanger so she could start taking it right away. In fact some of the barium solution started leaking out of her anus almost right there and then – and right onto that beautiful face of an overgrown baboon. Good! I think I said that loud. And then I walked out of the room. A night guy was there at the reception desk and he asked me where I would be going. The moment I told him I was going home, he got from behind the desk and tried to do his best to stop me. I told him, politely, to screw off because I did not mean to hurt him but, of course, the dummy wouldn't listen. I dragged him back behind the desk and sat him down in his chair, his head loosely hanging over his chest. He looked like he was just dosing off. I wished him good night. And then I walked the short flight of stairs up and to the main entrance door, the one leading onto the yard. They got me when I was crossing the yard. I don't know how many of them. A friggen hell of a lot. That was, give or take, how I ended up in the solitary for the first time. Did I mean to fight? Was that my intention? Hell, no! But, you see, when you're screwed up, as my new Cuban friend, Pino (Pino, José, is his name – did I say that already?) says, you're screwed up. That's all. From then on I was, of course, dangerous, and there was no way around that. That's just life down here, I'd say. Ain't that somethin'?

I, for one, think, it is.

You bet!

Ernie - LeMans

The first day the main track was not available – for the first time since I started working for Jim I saw that no money could open certain type of door – but we still had to register, if we were to use even the much shorter Etore Bugatti part. We did. Well, Jim did. Although he also had to register my name and that was a source of pride, strange and a little bit childish pride I think (I think I shall keep the paper for a long time to come), my name being register as the name of a driver at LeMans (It's a dream of anyone, whoever ever dreamed about driving something that was, be it just a little bit, out of the ordinary). John was the only guy I knew personally who didn't care. He never dreamt about this kind of driving, although he is here too; as is a friend of his he brought here with us – a guy I saw back in Connecticut a few times, on the property. He goes by Jack, middle size, stocky, wearing glasses, his hair turned gray already, a light beard, white like white wool, silent, almost doesn't talk, yes, the only time I heard him talk a little more was right here, in the church – there's a church here, in town, Gothic, gigantic, sort of not matching the size of the town, I'd say, but then again John is telling me that these towns around here are almost all like that: huge churches with little tiny houses all around them – apparently that's how they built back then. Once we were through with the hotel, with the track, and then the rest of the formalities that always have to be gone through, Jim wanted to go out, to see the town; he said he liked it very much, it contained a lot of memories for him, he met here once great guys, he said he met here his wife, too, which I had a hard time to believe because she never, ever, during my time at least, showed any interest as to what was parked in the stable - she drives cars that she changes, buys them like she buys shoes or pieces of her fancy garments, but also never going beyond that, the regular, I'd say, form of driving, from here to there, period, no, never - so we finally went out today, too. The church seemed to be the main point for all of them. And I heard Jack, the silent friend of John's talk about Gothic – because Jim asked him to, I think; he pointed to us the entrance, the tower, portals, the figures – it's a stress, an

136

accent, as he put it, you may not even remember it at all times but you also shall never be able to forget it: the entering – and then the walk eastwards along the ails; most of it shall be happening in the first half: newness, inexperience, the feeling of choking, of being overwhelmed, it's almost too much, one would like it to stop, or to decelerate at least, to change maybe; and then it is the transept; ways part: there are suddenly differences, unexpected, shocking, whatever might have been present without a real knowledge, you knew it might happen but you didn't really believe it would, all that without really going through it, all comes one's way at once – and you slowly cross to the other side, still throwing furtive glances sideways, towards the flood of light that comes at you where you did not expect it at all, and then it's different, you begin to feel experience, as if time had finally solidified inside of you, and it makes you, suddenly again, yes, it is sudden and almost perfectly unexpected, makes you, hence, accept it all a little bit easier, you even begin to talk (nonsensically, no doubt) about *understanding* – already looking at the altar, right there, fulfillment, the end, right there, right ahead of you. Jim asked Jack about the old testament story about a guy who dies trying to prevent the arc of covenant from falling into the desert sand – why does he have to die? Why is the will to help being punished so terribly? And Jack answered that he would well be out of position and means to answer that from any official theological standpoint for he himself was no theologian at all, but what he thinks, he himself, quite personally, is that God warns one about being to hasty with one's help: you think you love me, right? God says there; well, my dear, think twice; I'm not easy to love. Listen to your heart, yes, that's great, but also wait for the calling, true calling, my calling, and if you follow it, you may, just may, curse your life time and again, because you'll have to do things my way and not yours and that might turn out terribly difficult at times which will incline you to disobey – and if you do disobey, if for one moment you think you may do whatever you want to, this is how it might (it's not said it will, but it might) end for you also.

Jim sighed.

"He may give you gifts," Jack said then. "The first Bishop of this town called a dead man back to life, a man, then a child, yes, he performed miracles, he went down the pages of history as a saint, some will even say he was Simon the leper, in some versions of his curriculum he vanquished the dragon also – but then, at the end of his life he retired to live as a hermit at Sarthe," he smiled, kinda sadly, "Withdrawn. Isolated. Having left the world shut out – was that asked of him, or had it been his own decision? There's no telling." Jack smiled. "His hide out was where the Mulsanne straight is today, where you'll be establishing new speed records in a few days, whenever they decide to reopen it for the traffic at large." He looked around – his eyes turned towards where the St. Julian's head is today. "He was probably a Roman – this' incredibly old, the name of this town from those times was *civitas cenomanorum."* He looked at Jim quickly. "Am I boring you?"

"Hell, no!" Jim answered, quickly too. "It's fascinating!"

"Yeah, to me too."

Jim stood there, before that magnificent, strange, overwhelming altar. He nodded his head. Then touched his forehead with his palm, as if checking his own skin on it, temperature maybe, and then just sighed again, lowering his head at the same time, looking at the floor mosaic.

Then we would walk around town, get to the river. Jack would tell us about the castles along the river, about the French history we know nothing or close to nothing about, and then we'd just go back to the hotel, to sleep with all those kings and queens –it was slowly getting dark. Before we turned around, though, I managed to rent some movies. I asked at the rental place for Steve McQueen's LeMans but they didn't have it. Jeez... I've got my own back home, and I've seen it a hundred times, who then cares... And yet I think it would've been nice if they did; if I could watch it again, here, yes, right here, where it was made, with all the bells and whistles, for all those heavy millions of dollars, and then, after the movie was over, I could walk out and see the same town he drove into in the beginning of it. No? Well, they didn't have it. I also had a bottle of Kentucky Bourbon, but I had to watch it. Jim brought us here to see – and it might be tomorrow, if they open the circuit – speeds in the neighborhood of two hundred and fifty miles an hour; I can't be hung over. Nope!

And then the D-day came.

In the pits, next to us, a gentleman of certain age, tall, slender, gray haired, sort of caught my eye on a sudden; I thought I'd seen him before, somewhere. I asked Jim and, against all of my expectations, Jim just introduced me: the guy turned out to be Derek Bell himself. Jeeze... I never thought I would see a legend like that from up close. They had a 917 too, whoever it belonged to. We were talking about the inflation, and the fact that things are getting more and more expensive, not only in America but just about everywhere in the world, they begin to talk that the world economy is getting more and more unstable and that it might turn out impossible to maintain it at formerly acceptable levels, in which case this here would go down the drains as one of the first things in this very new world. I asked Jim what would it be like and he just told me that I really wouldn't want to know. Let's hope for the best. I was kinda... see... what the hell does something like that mean: 'Let's hope...' They are the smart asses, they should be able to predict –they were the ones to start the whole shtick, weren't they? And now, when a little one like me, is practically told that his life savings, a whole fucking life of work, is quite possibly, going down the drains, one hears: 'let's hope...' Fuck, man! I don't want to hope! I'd like to know that something is being done, like right now, but as soon as I said that to myself, it was time for me to get into the cockpit and start it up. And then I was on the Mulsanne straight – my only problem was to stay on the road; I was driving a close to four million dollar car at a speed I never had driven anything at in my whole life, and I knew perfectly well that the black top at that speed becomes more icy than ice; and once you lose the road grip – that's it: you're gone and the thing you're driving is beyond repair, that is, if you're still alive to worry about that. I got to the Maison Blanche, though, applied the brakes, gently at first, then in a more decisive manner (the chicane before that is nothing really as compared to this), and admired the stability – part of it my own work, too – of this thing I was in, at the wheel: there was not a trace of any pull, the car subserviently slowed down to the point where I had the impression that I was exaggerating (I knew that only from the theory – that that moment precisely was one of the worst parts of schooling at any stage: to asses properly the speed: after a longer while at two hundred and fifty miles per hour, or thereabouts, once you're at hundred, to know that you're at hundred, because that hundred, which is still deadly on a ninety degrees turn, now feels like twenty, and there, of course, is no speedometer – it's your job to make that judgment, no instrument to help you). Was I ready? I started to negotiate the turn. I was a bit too fast, for a fraction of a second I felt that fatal sway making one's nerves burst - you take in that instantaneously changing, prolonged, swaying protest of the Pirellis and your blood pressure skyrockets – all of it telling one clearly it's been too close to falling of the rope - but I didn't wreck it nevertheless: it's your hands and feet doing it for you, sort of. That was when I felt I had to get out, like right now, almost whilst still driving. Take that armor – believe me – that is exactly how it feels: armor; take that crap off. Fucking now! Breath! Have a glass of cold water. Then breath again. And then, after I got to our box and out of the car, Bell saw me almost that very moment – only seconds after he got there himself and managed to get out of his car (I had already taken off the helmet and the jacket), and he looked kinda surprised, I must say.

"What happened?" he asked, concerned, coming over.

"Nothing," I said. "Nothing really happened. I just got kinda shook up back there, at Maison Blanche. You know what I'm talking about, right? The breaking –from full speed of the straight down passed the second *chicane* to whatever is needed to negotiate that particular turn. I suddenly felt that I was melting afterwards. I just had to get that crap off." I pointed to the jacked now lying on the windshield; my helmet was inside the car, on the seat. "Ever had that?"

"Did you wreck it?" he asked instead of answering me, bending to the side to get a better look at Jim's car. "No…! You look fine."

"I am fine," I said. "No, I did not wreck it!"

"Good!"

"I think so too." I suddenly felt irate; a lot; was it the sweat, the tension of driving, or something yet else, I felt, this very moment, like kicking something, like smashing stuff. "I'm pleased with myself, if you wish to know, to a degree…"

He laughed.

"Sure thing." He stretched his right hand towards me in a quick gesture. "Considering it's you first time here – you did great!" He nodded; he meant it, I thought – that really didn't sound like a mockery. "I was right behind you – not close enough to see that particular turn, true, how you really negotiated it, that is, you got there way ahead and that's why I am asking now about the details I had no chance to see, but by the same token I saw enough of your driving before that to be able to tell you are quite a driver. A little more training maybe, more time on the course, well… let's just say I wouldn't mind being at your side anywhere out there, " he stretched his hand in gesture covering probably good half of the Department of Sarthe, "and that should mean something. You know?"

It meant…

Good God… It was a big deal - coming from him like that. A huge deal. I felt strange, I must say. I would have a hell of hard time to really express how I felt; I wouldn't want to forget the feeling, ever, if possible. Yes! Retain it forever!

"Thank you, sir!" I managed.

"You bet. A fact is a fact. That's all!"

"Thanks again. Really I mean…"

"OK!"

He turned around and walked away, inside. I said one more time, with him gone: "Thank you…"

I think now I must have been smiling; like a lucky man – not at all like a simpering idiot I felt like for these last few days – all of this here, you know… No!

Not at all!

In the evening John talked to Jim again about the economy; he just had gotten some new paperwork e-mailed from the States over the internet to the hotel's net – and was now explaining to

Jim, that he had read it first, how bad the situation really was, but I couldn't care less. Believe me, if they told me that evening, when I was sitting there with a glass of Bourbon, leaning back in that pretty comfy chair, recalling the runs and then also my conversation with Derek Bell, yes, if they told me at that very moment I was gonna be shot, I would probably just tell them to speed it up – to get it over with. I told that Jim. He smiled and then nodded in the affirmative, solemnly, maybe even sadly.

"That, you see," he said slowly, "is politics. Proper mix of this and of that. If it is proper, you can – like you just said it yourself – tell the guy he's gonna be shot and he will answer: 'fine', let's do it! That is politics. *Homo politicus.* Yes, Sir! That is our world. Its incredible vulnerability. That 'don't even touch it' type of thing. Yeah… You give Mr. John Doe," he kept on after only a moment, "and his pocket wife a house in which he will do new tiles in the bathroom, install new toilet bowl, new kitchen cabinets, here and there a new window maybe, - and then give'em also his Harley and his leather jacket, his helmet, and allow him to go once in five years to Sturgis in South Dakota to the annual Harley meeting so that he may have something to remember for some time to come afterwards, an unbelievably long time to come, believe me, and then, my dear fellows," he now looked around at all of us, "you can tell him, even on his beloved TV he's so terribly and hopelessly addicted to, well, anywhere, that, for instance, the Monsanto food he is eating is carcinogenic and it is not the question if, it is the question when and how, how bad, that is, his death is going to be, and the only thing you'll get from him will be the sacramental: 'whayeagonnado… huh?" He looked at us. "Sad, huh?" He looked around one more time. "Would you guys care to go out? I would like to see the cathedral again. Enter. Walk." He looked at me. "You're probably too tired, are you?"

I thought I was; but I also thought it would have been kinda stupid to tell him something like that; to tell that I am too tired to do something for a guy who just gave me the opportunity to drive a 917 on the Mulsanne straight. So I said 'no'. I said I was fine, and I, too, wanted to see the cathedral again, and maybe Jack would tell us something interesting one more time. I don't know if he cared about my answer or not – if he really gave a hoot at all. But I saw him smile. I think – I thought at the moment – he was pleased. We left and went over to the church and on the plaza there, just like it is in the movie, he stopped off and bought flowers from a street stand that seemed to be a permanent fix in that city, that he took with him inside and then left at the altar, which kinda surprised me a little –well, let's just say it surprised me enough to ask him about his Jewishness. He told me he wasn't actually religious at all. And also that he had sympathy for all the people who were capable in this world, this very poor, very sick, very dying world, to believe in anything that would go beyond senses; a guy like that would have his full respect – priest or layman, no matter.

Eve and Kim

"I got Pino his T-bone from at Mec's," Kim said putting on a sweater. "The one he really loves."

She was now combing her hair with a huge white plastic comb, looking into the small, metal mirror on the wall.

"Yes," I affirmed. I just had to smile. "I've seen him eat it the last time." I pulled up my new Sears' jeans and zipped up the fly. "I've hardly seen anything like that ever before. Yes," we smiled then at each other, "he loves that steak."

She tells me then (we both are doing make up now, both of us sitting down and using small portable mirrors) how she went about an hour ago, right after we got back here from the mall, downstairs to pick it up from the French restaurant wc havc on the same block and go to, both of us, to have our dinner now and then (it is not exactly cheap, we couldn't possibly go there every day, - well, maybe now with her new contract, she could, but I'm still not sure) – and I then hear again about the old "loup de Marseille', whom Kim seems to be attracted by, a little bit like a child is attracted by a legendary character – Tinman, Cheshire cat, Green Knight, I'd say - who came here so and so many years ago and opened it; I enjoy listening to her whenever she decides to tell me something about her preferences; I think it's her voice, her way of telling you something, her gesticulation, mimic – is that friendship? I think it is, yes. I certainly am not homosexual, there's nothing in any of the above of that sort of attraction on my part, and – as far as I know – she is not either. And yet I always seem to enjoy listening whenever she talks like that - that she is talking about herself, not only in this particular case, in almost any case like that, talking about somebody else: (he, the chef, once took his helper he just had hired, a little Polish guy, total newcomer to this country, to a doctor, lost in consequence the whole day in the waiting room, paid the absurdly high visit fee, because the helper had a middle ear infection, painful, perhaps even dangerous) she talks about herself, her preferences, her tastes – in this particular case she also wanted to know why he did that. She asked. He explained that he liked the Polish fellow; amongst the other reasons also because he (the little fellow) spoke perfect French (he, the chef, was sometimes embarrassed by not being one hundred percent sure of what he himself had just said - in terms of correctness); and then, which seemed to be also somehow significant: the kid was the son of some Polish count, Polish or Check maybe, he wasn't sure, and then came: 'I never had a son… Not with a right woman, anyway!' Only very slowly the story moves, shifts from her as main point to him – the chef, the strange, hard to understand guy we both like very much now and she, perhaps, I think sometimes, a little bit too much; he once told her about his alcoholic years – getting drunk every day, after work, he would listen then, everyday, unchangeably, to Edith Piaf records, getting more and more drunk, the words burning into his memory by means of that voice's beauty: about the clown who empties his bottle, for instance… (I see his face: unshaven, big nosed, his dark eyes half way closed, remembering) - and then - after having realized that he was simply dying - he turned it off: he would not drink anymore and did not listen to anything at all, and it seemed to him in the beginning like something was seriously wrong; like something or someone had suddenly died; it took him some time to figure it out: she, Piaf, sung, in a way, always about that other one in his own life (are you getting that?); or at least whenever he was listening to her, there was always with him right there yet somebody else he would like to listen to Piaf's songs together with – that other one: his sister, his mother and friends, but at times also his love he never really got to know; that was what he was really listening to – all of it: a complex, conglomerate; and all those most important people, whoever they might have been for the moment, did not (or just pretended for the sake of the game that they did not) speak French at all and he was translating it for them, explaining: he guided them through Paris he always wanted them to be able to see, those endless streets of melancholy of his own youth, each and every single one of them described in the smallest detail in the work of the greatest ones he still loved so much...

Kim stops painting her face, her hand is still, suspended in the midair, she then looks at me, dead serious. Yet a moment later she picks up where she had left off.

And then he knew at some point; he just knew: we – whatever can be called that – we, that's the other; I am because he (she) is; we, that almost certainly ain't me only, you get my drift, girly? He once slapped Kim's butt at about that very moment and she wasn't exactly in love with his gesture. We- the people - that's us, too – to some extent; mostly, though, it's that other fellow... Mostly! We say no! Oh, but it is! Peace, the chef thought then, getting serious and apologizing, might just be the understanding of that, as simple and as close to impossible to understand as it is. Kim laughs.

"J'm'en fous pas mal..."

Then she smiles. Gets a little more down to earth.

The chef has a way of marinating the beef: days - time's a not only contributing but decisive factor - long days submerged in a mix whose composition is known only to him; it is a huge piece, like ten, some times fifteen pounds, he puts it then in the oven – also a prescribed, known only to him, length of time, in a certain temperature. The final outcome is what gets Pino orgasmic.

Only a little later we were heading off for the hospital.

We would go there now and then. And I am trying, each and every single one of those times, not to get emotional about it. I am trying to see it as something, type: "this too shall pass..." - and I do get emotional. Then she (Kim) reaches over, touches my face, and says: "Don't!" And then we sit there, talk, nonsense mostly, little chit-chat type of thing.

I pray. Yes. I do. A lot!

Meanwhile fall came and went, and winter after that, almost unnoticed, I wrote letters to the governor's office, Kim spoke with Marsha, the hospital lawyer, and as far as I know, Marsha really did what she could. Everybody did what they could. The system, as Pino says, is broken. That's not a little benignly cancerous growth here and there on its body, no, the system has been destroyed for good. In fact - there is no system anymore: it's a dead body being torn apart by vultures, by senseless parasites, floating excrement, taking the last advantage of the fact that there is no immunology anymore and they can tear off whatever they can swallow, and oftentimes, in fact, one can see a little crap like that also choking because it bit off more than it could chew and now it too is dying on the side of that road which initially was supposed to be so luminous and turned out so terribly deadly in the end.

So we go – Kim and I (she is a great friend and in all this I, paradoxically, am forced to be thankful to the providence for having someone like that with me in this time of grief, disappointment and – at times – just blind rage); we go and visit. We sit there in that room we were given (as a big friggen favor – we can be, all three of us in one room with closed doors, and talk with each other without being interrupted by others; that favor came from the governor's office itself after intervention from a New York big shot firm, Bulshitovitz & Shtinkenscheiss, Manhattan lawyer thing of some kind Donovan found access to). And we talk. Or, rather, try to talk.

Jack is changing. He is not the same and that is precisely what scares me out of my wits. If I can't stop it, put an end to this fucking nonsense, this quite quickly moving forward process of blind destruction (almost like a bulldozer with no one at the wheel would destroy buildings filled up with priceless works of art – that's what this situation really is; and I'm trying to tell that anyone I know, and I am trying to write about it and get it published, and no one gives a shit) - there soon won't be a guy whom it would make sense to let out of here. A triumph of hardly imaginable stupidity. Negligence. One absolute fucking nonsense in these days' style. God!

The last snow outside, I think, yes, it might be the last. I am trying to point it to Jack, telling him the spring is almost over, and yet, look, there it is, quite dense, certainly screwing up the traffic, causing accidents out there maybe, and I see how bored he is –or is it boredom? Maybe something yet else, something that I would really be afraid of, some new *oeuvre* of doctor Pluplu or yet another imbecile imported here from the other side of the world to be wasted this country's taxpayer's money on. What did they do to him? I recall willy-nilly the gospel: they are unworthy to undo his shoelaces. Does he have to be beheaded too…?

John

I've noticed that Ernie takes me for a lot more in here than I ever was or am or will be, for that matter; it may very well be because I got him this job, and he sees me now and then dealing with papers, sitting at the desk with this huge, plasma screen computer Jim sometimes sits at too. When I dust or vacuum, he seems to think I do it because I am trying to save some money, which would make me just greedy. Now wouldn't it? Ernie doesn't seem to realize that none of us has any real importance in this… thing here. I'd even say Jim, our boss, the owner of this house, does not have all that great importance in our existence as certain type of - I really wonder – unit… I should say perhaps. 'Organism' doesn't seem to do it justice. It functions as long as it functions. As long as the arrangement out there functions. As long as the market is capable of carrying the… well, us.

I've tried to talk to Ernie because I like him very much. He is a straight forward, working guy, who finally gave up his business, functioning, too, carrying him on, him and his non-working wife, as well as his kids, daughter, college, son, a mechanic – the latter stayed there, in the old shop, trying to make it on his own and he oftentimes calls dad on the phone with questions – business and otherwise. That at least is not lost. I think he could go back to his

147

former shop, should this become unable to fly any longer. And for now it looks bad. Jim wants me to read the stuff that I get… we get… he gets from Wall Street, Frankfurt, Hong Kong, etc, etc, and that's how I know that it may not (in fact I should probably say at this point I know for a fact it will not) fly much longer. The world, yes, our world, is unstable and cannot be stabilized – the greed, the nonsensical belief that human brain has no limits and no borders, has finally lead to the point where it all starts crumbling and against all the babble I hear nobody – and I've listened to quite a few people so far, people who really are in the know – really knows what's going to be next. How to prop the crumbling building they built up according to pride a lot more than to reason or experience. Nobody. The sand it's built upon just doesn't carry anymore. I actually am surprised it didn't turn out a quick sand altogether. They look for salvation. They take loans – from the Arabs, amongst the other 'options'. The largest bank group in America took a loan from the Emirates. We, people living here, shall receive driver licenses with electronic tracking devises built in, billions of dollars spent on that nonsense, but by the same token we take the prop from the guys that the above is supposed to be protection against. I think listening to all that… there's never been so far on this planet Earth of ours such a pile of stinking lies – I think that is, or at least might be – the Babel tower one more time: something truly global, yes, a limitless Satanic lie spreading all over the globe, covering it like a lichen, to choke, suppress, destroy - by means of the chosen ones on top.

That mistake Ernie makes in taking me for somebody else –as if I were doing something that is outside my competency… I feel like more should be talked about that. I am beginning to think that there is more of choice in that, a deliberate, purposeful choice (yes, choice, not accident, not because it just so happens…). People do whatever they do at the level that is, as of today, the lowest possible one (their intelligence kept there, like you keep a dog or cat), and it's easy to see that their efficiency could be improved immensely – by starting earlier: good, efficient school, high quality teachers, comprehensive didactic programs - but none of that is the case – it simply is not. Why? I smile to myself, sadly. Because at that lowest possible level they do not question what they are doing, how, or for what purpose. They are unable to see that purpose – even if there is one.

I wrote a book, here, in my time, based on my access to data, in which I analyze what is happening in America in this new century and once I was through writing it, I started looking for a publisher. Talking to people 'in the business' I had the feeling that I was in some kind of a cabaret, talking to stand off comedians, helping them rehearse – yes, my fellow man, education today is a joke, and that is deliberate. Period. Mass media are not information-flow-related –media; they deliver what's convenient, public opinion (if there's still such a thing at all) shaping bits and pieces such as to bent those left overs of that opinion towards the end that is the private end of the owners of those very media, which in turn is that of the owners, period. Stupidity is a very efficient, sought after, tool – certain type of stupidity, of course. High IQ, no general education, culture (kulchur – as the poet says), no scruples, no moral. High salaries – incredibly high, in fact. When one hears about what a young snot of that kind can make, one really wonders…

And only a few months later things became noticeably different.

And then, yet a bit later, I saw Jim with the real estate agent, going around, and yet a month from that moment I heard him explain that the collection of art, except for some pieces, really dear to him, would also be for sale. They'd go up and down, all around the property – the agent wanted to know what ever was obtainable in terms of quality, age, names – the latter sometimes the most important, decisive factor; then it was banking and Jim just called me –it would be my job to dig up all the paperwork – titles, promissory notes, transaction records, ctc, etc.

What about me?

He was sorry.

"John, any kind of references you might need. I'll make you a loan, again whatever you need. Anything…"

Now, when I am trying to remember, recall as much as I can, it is a lot like a knife in my belly. Our house: nothing really special – an old house, fifty years or so, in dear need of work, but the piece of land it stood on was impressive, I think I mentioned that somewhere already, almost ninety acres, and I had negotiated a really good deal. Good God – really good. And then we started. Redhead and I, mostly, in those two days we would have to ourselves at the end of each week, a little bit also done by my son, that too, well, not really much, ever, he wasn't the one to do it. But we saw a slow progress. Yes, we did. And I loved walking over the property, as I already said that before: towards the river that was the southern border of it, and then along that slow moving dark deep water, with Redhead, because she liked it too. We would slowly go up the hill then, within the dying light, towards the house that was closer to the road, way ahead, slowly, talking – that light getting denser and denser, more and more majestic, calling into existence things we did not suspect existed. I thought my life had a sense. I just have been rewarded for all the crap I once was forced to go through, for all those lean, sometimes, oftentimes in fact, downright hungry and miserable years when it all looked just plain hopeless, yes, now I saw, I felt the reward. Goodness. Are we going to be able to keep it? We'll try. That's for sure.

Ernie would go back to his shop; his son was still there, I was right about that, and with Ernie's advice he was doing just fine – if I am not mistaken, of course. Bob, the guy they had there ever since Ernie has started the business was still there, too – no big drama at that point; those are the quite small lives, just not meant to touch the cross' thereabouts: whatever happens they just go along with more or les the same speed, feeling the same: when I told him only few months after the above what the situation was and that he would have to go back to doing whatever it was he had been doing before he came here, he just nodded; accepted it as it came (he didn't, for instance, sell the house he had back there, which I, for one, would have done; a touching gesture on his part: he was asking me, at some point of our conversation, if he could help... he felt like he had obligations here).

Few paintings were sold - Jim always wanted to be there, whenever the transactions would be finalized; the packing, preparing for the transport, that part of the whole business - that was my job.

I remember, pretty clearly, one of those days, evenings, actually.

WILL THE MERCHANTS DIVIDE HIM

We were standing there, in the art room, looking at the sunset, when I asked him, Jim, that is, for the first time since here, since I started working for him, about the picture, a simple photograph, framed and under glass, of a river, few trees on the other side, a house, very far away, all of it kind of bluish. He told me that was the place he once loved to fish at – La Seine after actually passing the main part of Paris, Billiancourt then, goes up north and the place is shortly before it makes the left turn west...

He smiles.

"Blue Picasso, you know, I see the big guy, massive, he knows what he is looking at, and the boy doesn't yet, the boy's still dancing, and it's all like that: blue, bluish, grayish, getting slowly dark, a tear, quite lonely, slipping down your cheek..."

Like the whole evening were about to start crying.

He looked towards the mighty window (it wasn't mighty from this distance), yet another picture of the maritime evening itself, with the sky getting more and more intense - and looking at it he sighed.

"John, do you honestly believe that we ate that apple? Or that it mattered?"

Was he waiting for an answer from me? Those were always my difficult moments. I would always wait up.

He smiled.

"I think we just would rather accept our own monstrosity... we accept the fact that we screwed up, rather than to accept that the author of all this beauty and sensibility all around might be a monster. Wouldn't you say? That's how the apple story came about. We are afraid of loneliness. Or more simply yet: we are afraid..."

I caught myself nodding in the affirmative. He kept on smiling.

Doctor Srakrishnaprookva

"Too yoo pyoo Ginglis?"

I smiled: I nodded with conviction, I was all the will one could gather to cooperate with any progressive force I could encounter anywhere in the world (including right here, very much so...).

"I pyook it, I foock it, I wheeze it and tweeze it – I rully anydung…"

"A ding," she came then solemnly – not a trace of smile on her Indian face, whitish, her facial reminding me a lot of a typical New York Cheesecake in a typical New York deli with a huge cockroach taking a slow walk right in the center of the upper crust, around the maraschino cherry "need inerprootah…"

I just kept smiling – my will to cooperate with the science, the progress and development, the general furthering of mankind on Earth was plain unshakable.

"And a ding," unchangeably I was decided to keep contributing to the furthering of progress in the Valley of Josaphath, "a inerprutoh wild be more utfoortsable…"

All this time, as I noticed almost right away, her broadly scientific mind was trying to figure me out – and that incessantly. From Pino I knew she was psychiatrist level II, for only 132 thousand a year. Also from Pino I knew that annual cost of one patient in here would run an average American tax payer about half a million dollars. He has been here long enough to find his ways and methods for finding out whatever he was after; he'd been diagnosed with schizophrenia (by doctors, by the way, just like the one I had in front of me right now), he almost didn't speak English himself, so he was not suspicious to anyone – people would just answer his questions, inquiries conducted always in the same manner, which is to say like a complete idiot would ask a question out of any context – in an absolute naiveté, childish gullibility and unmistakable readiness to instantly forget (not to remember whatever he was told any farther than the present and the immediate future) – so he would get his answers, too, sooner or later. Looking at the 'doctor' in front of me I just couldn't help thinking about quite a few people I got to know now and then in the cities I have lived over here in, people who spoke real English, had also real European education in their background, at a level she would need the Palomar telescope to see looming up above her thick scull, and who were forced to make their living in New York's, San Francisco's or AL's sweat shops way below the state minimum because they simply couldn't find any better employment. They had the bad luck to be White European Christians. Yes, that's the global progress, global warming and global fuck. Next Nobel for the next sly half-witted opportunist! Let's listen to wrap! Modern Art! And it's all so bloody global… How far still would the nonsense go? How much more sick will this already half ruined abode of ours still have to get? When will I – or anyone for that matter – be allowed to say out loud, publicly, what the cancer of it is? Talk about our allies? What type of chemo should be used in this particular global case?

Only a few days later it was Pino again who told me that the interpreter they hired for the conversation between me and my Indian doctor had refused to interpret because, as he- the interpreter - put it, it wasn't the patient who needed interpreting, it was the doctor – he simply couldn't understand her gibberish at the introduction time. She would speak to me then herself –no inerprootah…

Right! I was all for it; all ring and ready. And it took place only one day after my conversation with Pino, in the same pavilion I was 'stationed' in. Upstairs, though.

"Huh yoo doo eeng?" was the beginning of our fruitful cooperation.

"Uh doo eeng fuuhn!"

We were in a room with a window giving onto the yard where some kind of drill was going on, door closed and locked, although through the big piece of tempered, incredibly thick glass I could see people moving in the adjacent room too. She asked me some medical questions, absolute basics, and I understood and answered them not because they were put to me understandably (they were not!), but because they were as basic and obvious as they were. I was by now beginning to realize the hopelessness of this whole situation; most of this 'personnel' here were like that; on top of being what they were they would not give a hoot if I was still alive or dead already – they would come here every day only because they were paid amazingly well, their total incompetence taken into account, 'professional expectations' were zilch (if one of the detainees died, poisoned by a wrongly applied medicine, well, too friggen bad… Sorry, pal!), they would actually come here to chat, exercise in the gym, use the pool in the pavilion up the hill, they were the only ones who would ever use it anyway, the employees;

some also to read – I got to know a guy who actually would read books; he shocked me by telling me his favorite American author was Faulkner; when I tried to confide in him a little, though, he'd back off instantaneously – became ice cold and totally distant, well, he finally was from around here, I thought then, wasn't he? Yes, it was slowly – still quite slowly, certain things just don't fit into one's head, one has a hard time to 'internalize' them, because they are from a totally different world - it was, hence, slowly dawning on me, that if I wanted to ever get out of here, I needed a lawyer, and that we might be then forced into taking that second mortgage no matter what we decide to do.

She was looking at me now.

"Repierdol…" I heard her saying a moment later.

That was something I so far did not take into account at all: incredibly powerful medicines – used by people who, on one hand, did not give a flyin' about my health, mental or biological, on the other did not at any point have enough knowledge to apply that kind of medication to any form of life on Earth. I may just be better off dead than coming out of here as a permanent brain damage case. Ain't that right? All of a sudden I had goosebumps.

"No medicines!" I said.

"No teek no dung no good. No thuut? Shite teek some dung. Ghoot!" she made a rotating gesture with her right hand around her belly and then repeated oner more time: "Ghood!" She had then a shot at a smile. "Yooh no? Repierdol ghoot!"

"No, doc," I said. "No medicines! I refuse to take anything. I don't need it. Read why I am here. Read the cop report!"

She kept on looking at me and I wondered if there was any intelligent thought under that Indian Mona Lisa – New York roach cheesecake smile. She came then:

"Yhoo hat icideenat. Mhun closet death. You no nheet no dung? No!"

I thought it wouldn't make any difference, but I tried nevertheless. One has so few chances, so few possibilities in here, that one would quickly give up dignity, logic, one's old customs - one would only try to fit into what now was the sad, fucked up reality.

"They were trying to rape me. I was defending myself. That's all!"

"Whut rape?"

I had no idea how I could explain that to her.

"Rape… Violation," I made the gesture commonly understood in the whole world as far as I know. "Rape!"

She nodded. Whatever for because almost right away after that affirming gesture, she just said:

"Nah! Eem pusseebul!" Nuh! Potolican guhrl thuh too, huh? Shee thooh closet death, huh?" She wrote on the sheet in front of her with a French Waterman pen, saying it also out loud: "Re-pier-dol…"

I'll have to try to spit it out, I thought. Somehow.

Then I was led downstairs to the 'dining room'; it was dinner time. "Sheet man!" Pino said in English after I was trough telling him what the scoop was. "Try to get out as fast as you can. I told you that the first day you got here, remember? Otherwise you'll be worse than I am. They'll fuck up your brain. And what good, I ask you, is getting out of here, if you're a tree trunk? Huh? Whatever you got out there, what good is it? Or will ever be? Huh? " He ate the shitty, watery soup; noisily, kind of. Then he put the spoon down and looked at me again. He nodded, pointing his eyes in one particular direction. "You see the little kike with the kepi on, the one who thinks he's Lenin? He's right as to one thing. We, Christians, whatever else he might think about us, have, just like they, the Jews also do, the precept to help one another. We do! Not so the Indians. See, they think that if you're in such predicament as you are now, you're in it because Krishna or some other fuck like that intended it for you. Trying to help you, in other words, would mean interfering with the will of God, or Gods. You don't do that! Do you! Why would anyone? Yeah…" He went back to his soup for a moment, and then looked up at me again. "You gotta get outta here as quickly as you only can, make sure you got that right! Make sure your wife got that right! Otherwise try to get to the roof of this building and jump off. It's only five stories, but if you hit the ground with your head, you may, just may, get lucky, huh?"

He nodded. Then smiled.

"Do you know how to get to the roof?"

"No," I had to say.

"I show you sometime…"

Ernie's come back to life

I parked the truck in my old spot behind the shop and then walked around the building to the door but did not enter right away; I just sat down on the steps – there are few wooden steps with a banister made there to compensate the two different levels the property is on. I sat there. Bob was inside already – I could hear him move around the shop, so the coffee was already made too.

The day would probably be nice, I thought, the sky seemed clear, just a few clouds now and then, - definitely it looked like it would be a good day to work: not too hot. Then Bob came out. Seeing me he showed a little bit of a surprise, even though I had called a few days ago and spoke with him, telling him exactly what the scoop was, - that I was coming back for good, that Mauna would be there with me, and he sounded like he even liked the idea.

"Coffee?" he asked me now and I said 'yes' to that.

He went back inside and then came out again, this time with my old coffee cup in his hand. It is a blue one with a white inscription 'I love my grandma' on it. I'd have to say I never got to know my grandma: she'd died before I was born – I still like the cup. I thought it got lost in the moving process and just you look… Huh?

I know Bob –I've known him for however many years, goodness me, since I opened the shop. There was something about him now that I thought was new to me and I wanted to know what it was. The kid… He was evasive, I thought, he didn't want to talk. Or maybe he wanted to, just didn't know how.

"What about the kid?"

He sighed; puffed rather, well, made a sound that I couldn't interpret in any way; something new; something I really didn't know.

"This is… How shall I… See…"

"Bob!"

He shook his head.

"All right! This is a very specific kind of work. Right? It's hard work, very physical, you gotta be a strong guy, right? But it's also very specialized, right; it ain't exactly diggin' ditches, right? Darn it, I don't have to tell you, do I?"

"No!"

"Right. You have to like it, see, even love it, I'd say, yeah, man, love is what it takes to make it work, and nobody knows it better than you do, would be my guess. There is no other way! None!"

"And?"

He looked at me.

"Shit, man… He doesn't like it. Ernie…" His eyes lay on the tree line for a second and then he looked at me; he looked me straight in the eye, for the first time today. "He hates it, Ernie, you know? You take a look at him… That is fucking hatred. OK? He is on the cross, in pain, and all he wants is to get back down. Now you got it. OK?"

I took a sip of coffee; it felt good, fresh. Great!

"He had a couple of jobs before this," I said then. "I thought the same thing then… Hell, crucifixion… I thought this here might just be the solution. He is on his own, he doesn't have a boss, nobody to push him around, that's what I thought, you know?"

"One would think that," Bob said. "I would think that. Yeah!"

"Any suggestions?"

"Take it back! That's the suggestion. If you don't, there'll be no shop in no time and I for one would like it to stay the way it is - still is, as yet - amongst the other reasons because it is my friggen livelihood, too, ain't it? The way it's been for all those years: good, renown competent small business people'd appreciate coming to. That's all! You build that investing all you've got – time, patience, money, knowledge, all that, all of fuckin' that, right? All of it! Not to trash it overnight once built, right?"

"Trash it?"

'Trash it!"

"That bad?"

'Fuckin' worse!"

We were sitting there together on the steps, until my son came. He drove in, parked and then got out of his pick-up and came over to us, shook hands with Bob and then we kissed and hugged; I haven't seen him yet since we drove back from Connecticut last Saturday.

"New truck?" I asked, half way, sort of. "Never saw it before."

"I just got it." he said, smiling. "F-150. Nice, isn't it?"

"What do they go for now?"

"Thirty five."

"Where did you get thirty five Gs?"

"Bank," he said. "Where else?"

"Collateral…"

"The shop."

"The shop."

"Yeah…"

"The shop… Wow!"

"Gotta be good for somepen'"

"No good otherwise?"

"Dad, good for a lot of things. Sure. And don't you think I don't appreciate it. Because I do. But I needed a truck, too. That's all! And that's it!"

"The truck isn't the matter," I said.

"I thought it was!"

"No, it isn't! Business is. See? People who come here. As well as those who work here, too. Can you relate to that?"

He just nodded.

"Sure!"

We went inside then. He had to take a transmission out of a Porsche in non-driving condition so we had to push it inside. We did. Right between the posts of the second hoist that was free now. He thanked us, Bob and me, for help. I watched him, out of the corner of my eye, cleaning my old bench, I watched him kick the paws of the hoist under the car without looking where the lifting points where on the underbody, and then he just went over to the post and yanked the lever; the pump started screeching and the hoist moved; the paws grabbed and started picking up the car, slowly but surely, until something like a gunshot could be heard and it stopped. Or he stopped pressing the lever, scared by the sound – I wasn't sure which. I saw him at that moment get down to look. Now…?

"Fuckin' shit!" he yelled then, once he got up again, throwing both of his hands forward and then letting them down, just falling down along his sides. "Fuck!"

He looked at me.

"I hate little shit like that! These cars are no fuckin' good, you know? Fuckin' overrated little Kraut-crap!"

His face was red – I mean red. He was trying to catch breath and then just spit on the floor, half chocking.

A growl came out of his throat, like a dog's growl. He was moving his head from right to left and back for a longer moment now.

"I've enough of this shit! Fuckin' enough!"

He looked at me one more time.

"Enough!"

He turned around and walked towards the door that he then opened and got out. I heard the engine of the truck being turned over by the starter and then, after it'd sprung up to life, he just took off – I could hear the tires moving on the gravel in front of the shop quite clearly.

"See what I mean?" Bob was there the very same moment. "No exception, mind you. You could think it just happened, right? Just happened. No, siree! I tell yee. No!"

"What'd you do?"

"I get Chris from at William's. He's good. He'll weld a piece there to patch the fuckin' hole and then patch up the paint as well. But then it rots, you see? There is no access to the weld from above, once finished. Darn it, I don't have to tell you, do I?"

"You don't!"

"This'll never be the same car again. And what am I supposed to tell the guy? That I'm sorry! Darn it, I am, you bet... All I am is sorry! And just what fuckin' good is that? Buy'em another one just like it? Can't afford it, I'm afraid, now can I? I wish I could. Not here, not with that off-spring of yours! No, Siree!"

"Yeah..."

"Ernie, take it back! Come back and do it, you hear!"

"I hear you!"

"Good!" he said. "Fuckin' good! Somebody finally hears some-fuckin-thing!"

I felt sad.

He was biting his lower lip, playing with fingers of both his hands on an invisible keyboard.

"Yeah?"

"Yeah."

"Good!"

I took a deep breath; I'm not a shaky person, I'd say the very opposite, but my hands now felt kinda funny and I put down on the bench the air ratchet I was just cleaning, it and the clean red rag I was cleaning it with, I nodded to Bob, and I walked out of the shop, outside, just for a moment to have a bit of fresh air. I sat down on the steps. At the line of my property, right where the red land survey markers are positioned, there are trees: ashes and a bunch of oaks, too – their leaves rustle in the wind and, sometimes, I like to just sit there, right there, amongst them. I thought that I liked it here; this was my land; home... Don't wanna get sentimental, hell no, that ain't me, but suddenly I felt like that was important: extremely important. For whatever reason. Somehow. The sky was almost clear now, just tiny pieces of cotton up there the wind was quickly carrying south... I sat down on the wooden steps, shiny from all those years of use. I thought that I would stay here. Yes. I would. I would stay right here...

Annalivia PB

Mom says I should have my feet, both of them, solidly on the ground-always . Yes. Romantic involvement is good, no doubt, but it is not the base for everything, no! Such base is sobriety, intelligence, calculation, proper evaluation and then proceeding cautiously and intelligently, with consistency and perseverance, steering straight at where your business is – yours and your children's... Introduction – that is also another thing of utmost importance: presentation: how they see you so they'll receive you, as mom says. And so will you be able to arrive at what's yours. Solidly. Once you take aim, establish what it is you want, nothing – and I mean: nothing - can change your resolution. Like mom said: once you start swimming you can't stop, or you'll drown; you gotta keep on till you there. William says I haven lived my life yet so how would I know? Sometimes when I look at him, he seems to be flying in the air, I could almost swear to that: like his feet are not on the ground at all; not on the same ground mine are, anyway, like he sees things that are not there, almost, and one has to fight with him in order to just stay on the road, because he would pull us off – he just doesn't seem to understand what life is all about; that it takes a lot of consequence, yes, take the house, for instance: anyone can go to the bank and get the money and then buy a house. Anyone! How much push does it take that he stay in that job – and why not? Because he gets bored. Bored! Nothing else – easy job, he doesn't have to dig ditches, for Christ's sakes, he stands there at that counter, people like him, he knows cars, there is no problem then, none whatsoever, and yet – if it hadn't been for me, for my pushing, constantly, how long ago would he have lost even that! And I need him to have that job –well, job, of some kind, because if I take a job nothing ever gets done – I've had that experience with the bar I accepted – yes, as a bartender. No bloody good! From the beginning to the very end when I finally said enough! No good! And now that new friend of his – the Jack guy! Who the hell is that? I think that guy has a bad influence on him whoever he might be; they talk politics (men!) and Jack tells him about economy, about what's happening to this country in such a manner that William seems to lose it – like there was no tomorrow, like everything has already gone to hell and all we've got to wait for is the Apocalypse. That's no good! I think we need a little, well, maybe not downright lie, no, but a little prevarication, maybe, a little cover for the misery out there no to be visible so starkly, because then one loose the spunk, that... thing that drives you forwards no matter what. Once that is lost, I think, in this world as it is of today one's better off putting a bullet through one's head. And I want him to stay alive. Oh, yes! I need him to work so I might be able to raise the kids – we need this house for that, we need regular income. Don't we? I still have my sex to steer him with –yes, he still wants me. I can see that easily! Not that much longer ago than last Saturday I spilled broth on my gown and I had to take it off. Seemed pretty natural thing to do, goodness me! I did. I was standing then at the stove in my breaches only, and my bra, yes, those breaches are tight, and then I looked at him – for some reason I just had to stop doing whatever I was doing at the moment and look at him – so I turned around towards the table where he was sitting and eating and I saw how he was looking at me. His right hand with the spoon was moving towards his left eye: he didn't see what he was doing, he was all absorbed by the sight of my ass – and I wasn't even naked. No! That's powerful! I just gotta know how to use it, that's all! What mom says about the kitchen being a good trustworthy instrument of control too, well, that might very well be over – I mean with these prices, a saw a steak, William loves steak, and I saw at Weiss's a nice porterhouse steak William would love for 17 dollars. One steak! He'd eat that like nothing. In no time. Seventeen dollars! And who in the bloody hell can afford that? I bought nice pork tenderloin for thirty bucks instead, but that'll last a good week, breaded and fried as pork chops. With vegetables and potato, a little fresh butter on top. Yes, sir! I've been good at it so far! No doubt! Good! Well, we have this house, don't we? And William knows that I know how to keep it clean for him, and I take good care of his kids, I hammered that into his head al right! We also have our cars and all is legal about them, insurance and registration, has been so far. It's all my doing. Calculation. Persistence. Consistency. I was even able to help out mom last couple of months – he can't know, ever, about that, though! And he won't! I'm good! I am friggen good! Aren't I? As years go by I understand more and more. I guess I got it!

Pino

"El diablo se apodero del mundo ya por completo…" Pino said to me, as we sat down to eat. "The devil took over the world for good.

He started telling me then about a guy in Florida's State Prison, on death row, diagnosed with weak heart who have been, for State money operated on, imagine, thirty and something hours surgery performed by a sizable group of top guys, seven and a half million dollars, usual for the heart transplant, to be fried in the chair only a few months down the road... 'Ain't that somethin'?

He also told me he had heard Doctor Pluplu from Srilanka was about to take my case because doctor Srakrishnaprookfa refused 'taking care' of me anymore. My comment to the last part of the news being that it might just be the break I was waiting for. Pino objected and I wanted to know why not, to which his explanation was Mactoy's example (Mactoy was a cannibal – a book has been written about him). He once was... all right, he was what he was - but back then he was able to talk, OK? – he was even, Pino couldn't stress that enough - intelligent, you would say, a sentient being, in a way; he spoke Spanish; not perfect, no, not by a long shot - but you could talk to him about movies, he would also read books and would say now and then something about them, and now... "Just you friggen look!" Mactoy was now deep catatonic; immobile; mute; I don't think he knew where he was or why he was there.

Then Pino started giving me other examples – all of them from his own time in here, first hand experiences. He pointed to me the guy at the window – always sitting at the window, during the groups or any other time for that matter - that seems to be his last thread unbroken as yet with this world, the light coming in through it, or whatever else it might be to him – he always goes to the window, unchangeably. OK? That's the work of Doctor Pluplu. And before that Doctor Srakrishnaprookfa. And yet before that Doctor Pookafka also from Pakistan, who isn't with us anymore (one beautiful day he overdosed morphine and they couldn't do jack shit however hard they had tried, he just flipped...) And he, the guy at the window, had come (shit, man, was schlepped in, wasn't he?) here as a more or less regular guy, like you and I now – talking, walking, laughing, watching TV and so on. There are others. Quite a few. Also wasn't one single and only that ever died in here. You have guessed that one, haven't you? Those who died are not a problem; they just are not there any more – as simple as that. You got it? They are not there! Complaints are also covered up by the soil!

"Does one have the right to refuse a doctor?" I asked him. "Is that possible at all?"

"I don't know," Pino said, after he had thought the matter over and over as he usually would do – comparing the possible answer to my question to what he could remember or was told, at least, by others. "I don't know! You're English, you find out. And if there is, do everything you can. If you care to stay the way you are…"

He looks at the plate Kim brought for him with a great steak he loves so much– when? Now – that is important; I don't want to ask him yet, not yet, because I know he had already told me and I should know. I have time. If I can't, I'll ask. As simple as that.

He picks up the plate. Then he starts going over his pockets for utensils he'd improvised of materials that may really stunt one; it is a true example of prison ingenuity.

"Christo dice…" Pino says then, "Christ says that no one can be his servant who does not hate his own life and," I cough - this old Cuban, I think to myself, clearly, hearing words, sure has a strange manner of laughing – it grabs you, sort of, like a gentle hand, a palm around your own heart, squeezing, gently, it isn't meant to harm you in any possible way, no – just you look, think a little, maybe, "he seems to make sure we do it right. Yesterday when I was praying at night I found that and at first I thought I misunderstood something, misread, you know, my old eyes… But then it hit me! Yes, sir! That's where we are, that's what we are doing. Now… See? Then I thought, you know, it's dark, you can't sleep, so you think, is there only so little up there, you know what I mean? Do they have only such mediocre little crap to offer to those newcomers we all are in the beginning, that you have to get to hate this shit down here so badly – so badly - in order for you to appreciate what ever little might be up there? Is it like that? Only when you swim in shit for some time, would be my guess, will you appreciate drowning in clear water in the end? Is that it?" He shakes his head. "I wish I was wrong, you know? I think I am beginning to be afraid. Can you?" he looks at me – I know I'm the only friend he has left in this world – he nods, he shakes his head again. "Can you imagine finding out that God is a gigantic spider, for instance, with a lot of eyes and a split pea brain. That he stinks? Spiders stink, did you know that? Can you imagine that you finally get there, after all this shit down here you're finally there, you see it? – and there you are: you get to see God, you do, you're finally allowed, so you lift up your old head, pain in the neck notwithstanding (knowing my luck precisely that will be the moment for me to find out I'd lost my fucking glasses for good), so you strain yourself to see the best you can with your old tired eyes, and then you just have to take a puke. Huh? What then?"

"Pinito, we know nothing about that..."

"I know. Of course I know that. What'd you think? All that time I've kept on kissing ass of that Indian idiot so she wouldn't destroy my brain altogether. And she didn't, I am, more or less, OK. Now! Let me tell you! My other fear is, you know," he looks at me, with the same smile I wouldn't be able to describe, smile, that makes me remember my childhood, places, which, although I still love them with the same inexhaustible love, don't exist anymore, and all those wonderful people who died already so long ago, "the fear that we're already there - in Hell. That this is it! And no way out! And some day, in the end, we shall be given the site of our Got down here: that huge spider I imagine so often, who created all of this crap out of his split pea brain's stinking power for his own amusement without consulting it with anyone who would have had a little more upstairs before this... well, whatever... had called this absurd into existence.

I just moved my head: when? Was it... God, when?

I saw them, the TA's, three of them, to be sure, and then they were all three of them on top of me as soon as I got to bed; a little prick of the needle in my arm, and then I was let go of... Fine. I felt very sleepy and I also fell asleep. I don't remember any dreams, although I have the feeling – I've no idea in how far justifiable – that I did have dreams. Then I saw Pino's face and I remembered that I used to like that man, now, is that a recollection... Do I remember? Well, I know the guy, yeah...

I also felt an ugly headache and nausea.

"What time is it?" I asked him and he looked across the room at the wall clock on the other side.

"Five!"

"Five what?"

"Five pm," he said. "It's afternoon. You slept more than two days, you know? They were beginning to consider if you needed intravenous feeding. I sat here. I waited for you to wake up, you know?" he smiled at me. "I wanted to say something to him – something simple: a joke: like: you got used to our conversations, right?" That's, give or take, what I wanted to say to him, and I couldn't; having started the sentence, I couldn't remember what had to follow, so I tried again, I built the whole sentence in my head and tried then to only express something that already was there, done, finished, ready to be expressed, but I got lost again – I did not finish what I had set out to do, because I couldn't remember what was it I had set out to do, goodness... I liked the guy who was now looking at me and I tried, intensely, to remember why –what has he done such that I would like him... And then I slipped away: into a deep sleep: I had dreams, though: he was talking to me and I remembered: I knew, yes, there was nothing confusing about it: I was there and he was there too, and he was talking to me, he was telling me, now, what? What was it he was telling me – I could understand him perfectly well, his Spanish was strangely cultivated for someone who hardly had gotten any schooling at all, it was all clear, he made sense, yes, just... I'll get it. There's no problem with that! None, whatsoever!

And then a whole lot of things would happen – they were like a river, swollen, mighty river, whose movement gets you scared, gives you the absolute certainty of your inadequacy, insufficiency of your abilities and capabilities, suddenly confronted with all those gigantic tree trunks carried like that, like matches by the mad brown water with the accompaniment of the incessant thunder that is all ugly white– you're just there and it moves in front of you towards a goal you know nothing about at a speed that is breathtaking, and then I saw Pino sitting there, on the edge of my bed, and he was smiling. He was pleased, I thought he was very pleased, when he saw me with my eyes open, looking at him.

He nodded a couple of times.

"Good! My good God! This is good!"

"How long...?" I wanted to know.

"A long time, Jack! I don't know... Long time. You're out of it now because your great doctor is on vacation in Pakistan or that other crapo... wherever else she might be from. You OK?"

"I think so. Yeah... I guess I am.

"Try to remember things. Whatever you can remember. See for yourself. You know what I mean?"

"Yes," I said. "Yes, I think I do.

And I tried to remember, and I thought I did just fine, but then he told me that Eve has been here twice and that I did not recognize her. Yeah... Eve was here twice and I didn't recognize her. How am I doin'? Good Lord! Kim, then – the gal he, Pino, liked best, toll, good looking, and she liked him too, he could tell, he always could tell something like that, such a woman (una hembra asi...), Dios mio... she's been here a couple of times too, she wanted to talk, she had questions, but nobody could understand you, Pino said. Strangely, I seemed to recognize Kim, she was here obviously during one of my 'ups' and I wanted to tell her something but the sound that would come out of me was just plain inarticulate and, although they both, Pino as well as she herself tried their best, there was nothing they could put together into a sensible whole...

"I think your lawyer came too. A time or two. And the lawyer talked to somebody up there, would be my guess, and the lawyer promised to talk to somebody at the governors office, too, and that's why the Pakistani or Srilanka idiot was asked to take her vacation now..."

Pino asked me then where have I been in all the meantime and I told him I have been in a whole lot of places – some from my childhood, I was there with my father, we were walking in places I really loved back then ..."

He moved his head in a strange way; a little like a spirited horse would do: he threw it up and to the right, all at the same time, saying quickly: "Me too," interrupting my train of thoughts without any regard to what I might have to say. "I too went back.

You know? Through my whole life." It obviously was something very important to him and he wanted to share it with me; he had a hard time to wait, the matter was more than pressing: "Jack... goodness, my God, there's been such a lot of goodness, that, you see... things, you know, those things I can't stop being grateful for, even now, here... I think we shouldn't be afraid."

I nodded, I know that.

"My wife..." I said, half way to myself, but he heard me, I knew he did, because he now stopped right away and waited for me; there was silence that was also an invitation: my start was, most probably, exactly what he was waiting for; I kept on: "I thought about that a lot. Her. How I met her and how it was in the beginning, how we tried to put stuff together, make something out of nothing, and how it would change, me as well as her, where we would be then. Now!"

"You have kids, Jack?"

"No, no kids. Not with her anyway..."

He nodded.

"We forget." He said. "Too quickly. And then fear sets in. And then you're really fucked and stop thinking and remembering – and the memory, I think, your own memory, would be enough, should be enough, if you but knew how to use it, yes, it should be enough not to have to be afraid ever again. Ever! Again..."

He took a deep breath, through his front teeth, which made a strange, whistling noise, and then he was just busy with the remnant of his steak: the paper plate held down on his left thigh with something he improvised for a fork held now in his left hand, and with his right trying to cut of a manageable piece with something that very remotely bore a resemblance to a knife; whatever he had made it of.

I thought I've seen this before – somewhere. I wasn't sure and I didn't want to ask him yet; hang on – I will if I have to; I knew my reflection: about the prison ingenuity: stuff those utensils are made of; I'll know soon enough, if... then what is he eating?

"What are you eating, Pino? What is that?"

"Kim..." he said. "You don't remember? She brought me a steak from French restaurant she goes to, the best steak I ever ate in my whole life, you don't remember? It's because she asked me what would I like to eat, I mean like: what would I like to eat best of all possible things she could bring from the outside and I told her that a steak like that would be what I would like to eat best. We never have it in here. So she got me one. She asked you too what you wanted but nobody could understand what you wanted." He looked at the remnant on his paper plate. "Well done – just the way I wanted it. The little pink inside not destroyed and yet well done. Perfect, you see? I hate blood!" And then: "You asked me that already, Jack. A while ago. Any recollection?"

"Time's a mystery!"

"Ain't it?"

"Yeah..."

"The steak's good, though! Very good!"

He eats – his well pronounced, unshaven jaw moves slowly, a word 'majestically' slowly moves through my mind while I am watching him now (words now move like that – slowly, although their appearance is always sudden, even a little shocking, I'd say); I think I know this too; this – scene; these words – we've used them already, we've talked about that, shit, man...

Pino looks at me. He swallows. He smiles.

I smile too.

"I thought," he says, "about one thing. It's people, see, you and I, that make this life, this world what it is. Right?"

"I guess..."

"Only us, though? Nobody contributes? Adds? Subtracts maybe, a little? And then I though about my arrest. Yes, sir. That is the answer to it. I cleaned the pistol, right? Took it completely apart and washed every friggen bit in solvent – good, expensive, powerful solvent I'd ordered long before that for the gun over the mail. I used to practice a lot in those days. That was one of the things in this world, you see... Then, after a thorough wiping it with a rag I put it back together, well oiled, in a plastic bag. Right? All the time I had rubber gloves on. After that I took it to the swamp. I knew just a place there, sometimes I stashed cocaine in that place, whatever was mine. Huh? Only I knew where it was. Only me. OK? There where no fingerprints on it because I washed it the way I did. Right?"

There is a clear triumph now in his face. "How come then in the court they had the pistol, my fucking pistol, no doubt whatsoever, magazine emptied, barrel never cleaned, with my fingerprints all over the fuckin' thing? How?" He looks at me. Inquisitively, his eyes just two slits now, although I know he's not waiting for an answer from me – I already know him sufficiently well to know that. "No, siree! It's not just us. There's something else here – like two opposites, you know, fighting, like a bar fight, kinda slow, both of them, powerful but slow, not too intelligent – only we are the ones to pay the bill for damages. See? Irish fuckin' bar, on Friday night! And then you and I. And them. Fuck! All of us!" And then: "No! Not all of us. No! There are exceptions. Yeah… To some this is the fuckin' paradise, ain't it?

"And to some real hell," I said. "Take the Chinky…"

(They finally found somebody who could better understand Ho – the very opposite of Ho; an architect, retired, a guy who graduated from MIT, and that fellow after having gone to hell and back, after having officially reconstructed Ho's history, in America out there, as well as in here, he finally got Ho the court order releasing the latter from the hospital – not to go home, though. No! The order released Ho from the maximum security prison to the civil one, where the control wouldn't be as oppressive as here, where his hope of getting out and into the general population out there would not be just a dream anymore– yes, some day it may, may, really happen. His name was John, that's anyway how we got to know him, whatever his last name might have been. He would come now and then, and 'talk' to Ho, and it's fascinating, hard to believe maybe, but he hasn't really found out that much more about Ho, than Pino had done using his 'methods.' And yet there's a hell of a difference: everything John did had the weight of something official – something that would get the judicial machine to start turning, thanks to which, after five years of hell, hopeless nonsense, Ho was finally released to that civil joint. What shape is he in? Who will ever know? Does he remember what do they call him anymore? Maybe. Then again maybe not. There's no telling. And we were all wandering: we people who knew him and what had happened to him, and who had sympathy and empathy, and whatever else you may have in case like that, huh? Has he changed? Did that do anything? Any good? Is there an answer? Those are the questions… Now when they say, some people, that all the religions of the world say the same thing, that is of course just bunk. But what I think, based on this story, we are brothers, in that we exist truly only in suffering; those horrible things are the chisel that really brings us out – it's like a good sculptor looking at a block of marble can see the David in it, yes, looking at the Ho story I begin to see that, too. Will I be allowed to retain that?)is name was JoH.

"Yeah…"

But I've had the impression, and that actually all of the time we were talking, that we've already had this conversation – that this entire situation was only a repetition of something that has already happened at some point – when? Well, that's another story. I've no idea whatsoever.

Pino bent the plate and then folded it in two, after which it became the content of his pocket again. The utensils he had already stashed away before.

Agatha

They, Rich and Agatha, came to visit at some point and it was a real surprise (another one, also totally unexpected, was William H.C.E. He saw Eve in the supermarket and asked her where I was and how I was doing, and she told him the whole story, without hiding anything. He got all the 'data' from her – how to apply for visitation rights, whcrc cxactly, what kind of paperwork etc, etc, and he also really did all that afterwards, and then just came. We talked, right here, in this 'visiting room' as Pluplu calls it - for quite some time.) I would never have expected any of them in here. And today these two came just like him shocking the crap out of me - Rich and Agatha - and she brought me a huge casserole of her own making to my even bigger surprise. William brought me a bottle of Cognac which of course has been confiscated at the main gate. Rich and Agatha found out also from Eve how exactly and where

171

they, too, could apply for visiting rights in a prison like this, and here we were: sitting and talking. They sold the house, well… they tried not to. But Rich lost his job and with what she makes in that hotel it became pretty much impossible to keep up. Yeah… They moved back to New York and that's also where they are living now. They would never have thought how expensive it is, though, to live now in the city; apartments that used to cost 400-500 hundred are now way above thousand, reaching more, in a lot of cases, 1500 hundred and up, darn it…

He stays with the little ones, sitting, and she works still in that same hotel – now, though, with seniorities. They have benefits, you know, for the kids, that's major… Yeah.

Then she looked at me and pulled a few typed pages, a computer print-out from the pocket of her blouse. She handed it to me.

"You know, that John died, right?"

Yes. I knew. Eva told me.

After he'd lost his job, well, basically the same thing: they were trying to keep the property because they loved it but they were also close to sixty years old and the only thing they found was Wallmart, and you know what that means, right? What do you make at Wallmart's: It's famous, isn't it? They sold it. He had a night shift, you know? One night he just collapsed. They took him to a hospital and he recovered for yet a while. But then the same thing happened –and that second time around he did not recover anymore – he died in that hospital. She looked at the 'window' for a while, the latter giving onto a gym where a lot of people were doing their stuff, fighting with the exercising machines, and the only good thing was that we couldn't hear them in here. "After that woman died," she said then, he'd lost it, sort of, you know… He never actually recovered from that, I'd say…" She looked at me then. "You knew about it, right?"

I nodded.

"He left this," she pointed to the print-out I was now holding in my hand, "for you."

I knew the text. We discussed it after I had read it and found it very interesting which, of course, I shared with him. John wasn't naïve. I would never have said something like that about him. No!

But what he did with the text was just that: childishly naive: he mailed it to Play Boy, of all the possible papers and magazines, and I will never be able to figure out what genius of mockery whispered that crap's name into his ear. It was a very ambitious long short story about the green knight, containing certain anthropological aspects way transcending the medieval version – something that had absolutely nothing in common with Play Boys and such. To make it even stranger he started making plans after having mailed the story. Quite lucrative plans; buying houses, moving to better climates, down south - islands and such. He was crushed, terribly disappointed anyway, when, few months down the road, it became clear that they did not even bother to respond to his quest. When I told him about short story magazines, the Atlantic Monthly, for instance, he was still too crushed to mail it somewhere else. Anywhere else. And now it was in my hand.

I shook my head, sadly smiling.

Agatha was fine. So was Rich. They were both fine. Happy. She told me she now would never drink.

"I didn't realize," she said then, "that I had propensities, you know? I did not. For God's sake! So I stopped. I went to AA, and after a few sessions they made me realize that. And I stopped. There is no alcohol in the house now. Not ever."

I congratulated her, wanted nevertheless to know a little more about John – was she there, I mean, when he passed away?

"No, it was early in the morning, still dark outside probably... No!"

"How long before that?"

"A couple of days. We couldn't be there every day. They, he that is, and Redhead, Mom, you know, right? - were in Oneonta, in the hospital there. There was also the Wallmart he worked in – in Oneonta, and that was where they took him after he had collapsed. You know, it's a couple of hours from where we are, well, were... Yeah. He looked tired, I'd say. Just that. Tired. Like he hadn't slept for a long time – a week maybe, or so. His face sunk, you know, like old people have no teeth and he had teeth, pretty good ones, all his own, until the very end. End he looked like he had no teeth. His hair thinned too. He never had a shag, sure, he didn't, but that one day or two before the fact he looked like he'd lost it all, well, most, you know… He's buried there too."

"In Oneonta?"

"Yeah."

"Yeah…"

She looks at me. She doesn't look anything like him – like John – even though she is his daughter from his first marriage. Not a bit of resemblance. She smiled at me and I smiled back.

"And how is redhead doing?"

"She's got some kind of a state financed apartment and that's where she is. I think she's as OK as can be, you know. Under the circumstances."

"Yeah…"

"I used a lot of kobasa in that casserole. The best. Polish, smoked. And – I don't mean to bore you," she said quickly because Rich's elbow found her arm almost the very same instant she started talking about cooking, "I don't! But it's good stuff. I hope you like it!"

"I'm sure I will. Thanks!"

There was something about her now I couldn't quite put my finger on. Like a child you saw the last time some ten years ago that is now almost an adult –I'd say. Yeah, I guess that's what it was. As opposite to that he didn't change in any visible way. He just happens to be the guy whom you are going to recognize in thirty years from now on, in the nursing home you might wanna visit, without failing, amongst the twenty other mumbling and drooling oldies. Maybe because there isn't that much to change from the day one – what did I just say?

I was leaning back on the chair support, my eyes half closed; I saw them.

"Are you sleeping?" she asked.

"No," I said. "I was thinking. Trying to see what you were telling me…"

"You two were friends."

"Yes. Very much so."

"What were you thinking?" she looks kinda embarrassed. "If I may ask?"

"About that night. His thoughts. Empty window. Black. Silence. He knew that was the end of the tether. What were his exact thoughts? There is a description in Proust's *cahier 39* of a dancer," I looked at her. "You know who Proust was, right?"

"Yes," she said quickly. "I do."

"That dancer is probably Nijinsky, could be him at least, his incredible success, his number being added to spectacles that had nothing to do with the Russian ballet, and the narrator reflects, right there in the theater, about this crazy guy spiraling amongst all those other guys, in suits, in all the gala of the night, like a butterfly in a crowded street where it certainly doesn't belong… That was, give or take, what I was thinking. Life lives on in your memory, Agatha, it can revive or you may suppress it, your sadness, your fear, – what was his departure; did he revive it all, or did he feel simply cheated like most of us in those moments, duped and abandoned? Which was it?"

"Which do you think?"

"I've no idea. In fact I was hoping you might help me with that."

"When we got there he was already dead. They told us it had been a massive coronary. He had the heart of a drunk, of course. Well, he was one, wasn't he?"

"Yeah…"

"Tell me," I said then, "about the kobasa. He didn't let you talk before," I pointed my eyes to Rich, who sat there, smiling, as if a little embarrassed, was my impression. "Tell me!"

"It has to deliver its taste to the rest of the ingredients. That's the most difficult part of that particular type of cooking, you see. If you overcook, it tastes like cardboard, if you undercook it is kobasa and the rest of it; whereas it has to blend. See? Experience. Properly chosen times and temperatures. I think yours is now perfect, and I don't mean to brag. I really hope you enjoy it!"

"I know I will," I thanked her from the heart and then repeated it one more time: "I know I'll enjoy it, Agatha. I just know that, I do - you're a great cook. And you?" I asked him. "Still in that job in Manhattan?"

"No!" he said, "That's over. And then I have to baby-sit. I told you, didn't I?"

"Right! You did! Sorry, Rich!"
"No problem!"
"Right!"
I smiled. He did too.
"Yes, sir!"
"That's right!"
"I'm glad!"
I think I was; why the hell not?
They seemed to be.

The wake

The bar is dark and Shaun and Shun are drinking at the bar and the music is on the loud side, and pork and beer are ordered to general satisfaction, and Jut orders whisky, and then they play poles, everything seeming to be played to the music and everything having the taste and touch of beer, even the air sort of chunky as the queen says in the end bending forward and showing her cleavage, quite impressive in fact and getting hard-ons all around us, the dark but justifiable thought is: we are the people, all of us born *intra urinam and feces*, all of us having had a mother with no exception to the rule, and there's a night outside or perhaps a day, there doesn't seem to be any real knowledge as to that fact, there's gotta be something, though, something that could be justified because everything is there only to be justified, Jut says and there is an explosion of laughter. Justification is the foundation. (I am the suspended in the here and now confusion between where I come from and where I'm going, William HCE says. He's smiling politely, as is usual with him, ready to help. I am so confused in fact that confusion seems to me impossible altogether. I know about the night ahead, about the river, the meadows. But I know it only from a movie, I think, a movie I had to return…) There is nothing in time that does not have to be justified. Lorenz's and Gilia's analysis of chaos: fractals: yes, we can perfectly understand chaos of which the best proof is the simple statement: it will rain tomorrow or it will not rain tomorrow. And then: chances are. No fuckin' kiddin'! The pork arrives and the beer and eating starts to the general hilarity's accompaniment, and it is hard to justify the quantities of meat that are downed and rinsed over with the black ale to the Erin's exultation in this touchy air filled all with the tastes and smells everybody is in love with and I... I feel suddenly a little prick in my arm, it's not an insect and I... I am trying to chase it off but the arm is concretized and the thought begins, like wading through molasses, that one can become a monument, one can become monumental, yes, without knowing anything about it, and isn't all that fucking monumental, Jut asks and Shaun and Shun seem to be shunning the question spreading quickly in this sickly sweet air of beer and ale and male and female and the music that is definitely smelly on the loud side of pork's tenderness, the air is getting stuffier and stuffier.

"Kobasa has to give up its taste and aroma not completely just a certain percentage, very exact, and those have to be transferred to the rest of the ingredients, even if that's unjust. Justice is what one's thought is that it is. And not what it is. Only what the thought is that it is."

"And if the thought is not?" Jut asks and Annalevia responds: "Then you'll have to bend over," and the rest is given the taste of a roar in which dissolves the rest of the answer.

"If the percentage is not properly assessed, too much given up, the kobasa becomes cardboard..."

"Bend over!"

More beer. And whisky.

Pork. Yes to that. Kobasa.

There appears a thought of nausea. A wider perspective, suddenly. The bar is. Nothing actually is. There's that knowledge, very properly assessed. Professionally. Yes, that is the beloved word of this New Erin here. New Erin founded by. Later on *les choisis sont venus ausi* changing it into New Urin we're all drowning in now. Professionally. Is.

"They will take you out to the infirmary," Jut says, "in just a moment," and the music gets even louder and the light itself getting darker, denser, solid, could be cut with a knife, a kitchen knife, he

177

thinks, shit, the statue of David cut out of dark, congealing bar light, yes, he would certainly have to have a lot bigger dick than we've seen so far in this here New Erin or elsewhere. The thought is solid too. Yes!

The labyrinth in Chartre: western façade, impressive, awesome, calling and cajoling, promising, and then the walk itself: straight, in awe, in beauty, smelling incense in the bluish vast air supporting all those immensely long beams of light, until you stop: undecided: way to the right, way to the left; light, unforgettable stone lacework translating light towards: how many choose the one straight ahead where there is nothing cajoling or impressive, - a little darkness, a little night, a little unknown... And then Bramante's solution based on St. Augustin's thought – the book, the one that grew, only very slowly, grew nevertheless, until it, too, stopped.

Jut and Mutt fall on the body then with a club of that vast empty laughter and after it falls Annalevia peers over the yet living carcass and her solid hard melons ensuing death reflects wonderfully, more pork, whisky and wine, more beer is being brought in to everybody's even deeper enlightment. Right above her, peering over the body that seems to be finally really dying, sits Mark who already had died - a few days ago, quite realistically – but they dug him up bored by his death and brought him back here, and they are now drinking with him, too. His back leaning comfortably backwards is propped by means of a two-by-four stemmed solidly in the floor's crevice – the floor has a crack, wide and deep, right there. Yes, Sir! He seems... No, he does not seem! No!

In the end, at the end of the promise, there is an old and terribly bitter man instead of fulfillment, surrounded by emptiness and bunk, as he puts it himself. Bunk! The thought is, though, it's not he, not he at all: time has only separated that particular fragment of space and the process of separation caused whatever was in there before to simply stay with the main stream; he is now surrounded by emptiness. And bunk. Dr. Pluplu's face looms in the night above him like reflected in the slowly moving water of the dark river Lifey: *stupiditas stupidtatis,* Jut farted and the window will have to be opened –if there is a window, that is. Jut turning around his wide open eyes, sings, coughing: Seeking a key, each confirms a wee…

Each!

Yes!

I'm going to travel – I know!

Father

We took the tram from the steelworks station; the next was our street and then the burnt out mine we would so often go to, to just play amongst what was left of the constructions from the times before the tragedy, my father telling me stories about the fire and how it was fought with, how many people died – nobody actually ever really knew how many – father would tell me simply those have been real crowds. And he would also tell me the whole story in such a vivid, suggestive way that I saw the tongues of flame licking the night sky out of the depth of the elevator shaft, outlining the tower with its cable wheels that in the end got all red hot and glowing, and that was when everybody knew that there was no salvation anymore for those who'd been left down there up to that point, and every effort had been given up from that moment onwards. People just stood there all mute in their grief and awe.

Father told me he wasn't sure how far from the lake the last station of the tram was, he told me from what he knew there was still a long way to go and we would have to walk, but he also said that it was worth it, very much so, because the lake was wonderful, the beaches were fantastic, breathtaking, and now, that I already could swim, I had a chance to really enjoy something like that.

I have right now before my very eyes the dark stained wood of the window in that old rickety tramway car, its floor made of deeply oiled wood too, and I remember the smell that I know I will never be able to forget: on each and every single acceleration a smell of burnt wiring (I had no idea back then it was the smell of frying electrical insulation, but I do remember the smell in such a manner that I can identify it now, recalling it into my actual present any time I choose)

179

would spread and, that the windows were almost all of them open, the smell would then also quite quickly go away. One could pull that window yet lower down, even all the way down, and then feel the wind on your face: the summer wind; all the smells mixed together of all the little towns along the rout rushing onto you together on the background of one big smell of trees – parks, dense greenery of that region we both, I as well as my father, liked, not to say 'loved' so much, all of it suddenly even more alive, as if stressed, intensified by the movement of the car that back then seemed to me fast: we talked about the 'rush,' the 'impetus',- and only today I know that the maximum speed of that thing rated at about 40 kilometers per hour, would by today's measure be probably what, 25 mph? (later on we, the boys, would learn how to jump off the step of a car like that at, give or take, those speeds – that was the adventure; local wild west, the train was going to Yuma at 3.10, yes sir!), and on that particular day I had my head all the way outside the window, too, taking the full wind bath, catching those smells of summer like a young cat, the happiness rising inside me like a flood, as was the expectation of the wonderful.

At the end of the route they just asked us to get out. The question was: where was the lake? How close to it were we now? Father asked the uniformed guy and the latter looking at father for a moment longer did not seem to understand. Only then he came around. The lake... Jeez! There's actually nothing there that really goes to the lake. Father told him we were coming from town, from the steelworks station, and I won't forget the answer:

"You no closer to it now..."

People would walk. First method. Second was an automobile, if one had an automobile – extremely few people owned one back then – four, maybe five of those in the whole town. But... As it turned out his brother in law would go there (well, not exactly there, not to the lake itself, no, he would go to a fare held in the next town to get to which, though, he would have to pass by, 'kinda real close' to the lake, you know) driving a horse carriage with stuff for sale. He told father that if we wanted to do that we were welcome to go with him and ask. With any luck it might just be the day of the fare – fares took place two or even three times a week in some weeks throughout the year. We agreed, of course.

Well, we did get lucky and it was the day of the fare. Father was sitting beside him on something that was thwarting the two ladders the carriage was made of, the bottom were simply two very long planks beside one another, and that was my treat – I also have a hard time to forget my sore butt - and off we went. All the way in the back there were three or four sacks tied up to the planks with pieces of rope.

The road along the tram tracks was a regular road, just as we have them today, black top, maybe not in the best of all possible shapes, but I think it would be OK even by today's standards. Horse's trot resounded back then on that road in a very characteristic for that time rhythm that I still have in my ears almost unchanged, retained there by my memory, just as a mechanical recorder would do: precisely that: unchanged, maybe just a bit less clear. But then we got off that road and onto another one that wasn't black topped, that, in fact, did not have any top of any kind at all, it was just a plain dirt track with ruts, leading into the pine woods: the pine land; the pine smell on a hot summer day, under a sky that is the deepest blue woven throughout with the sunlight in such a manner that the light itself makes the background for the blue thus bringing it even more out and the breeze that touches your skin seems to proceed straight from it; the breeze bringing about the smells; hot resin, dry needles molten together into a thick brown mass the bottom of the grove was made of and also those that were still on the trees - and then all that immense, inexhaustible variety we never know what that actually is... I remember the slow movement of the carriage, my legs dangling over the sandy road that barely moved backwards under the two planks I was sitting on, all of it dipped in those smells; the main ones: sun heated resin dripping down the trunks and mushrooms growing out of the bottom of which there must have been myriads. I clearly remember telling father I would like to come to these woods some other day when we have more time to pick up mushrooms – only for that, and he nodded. He obviously liked the idea, too. The driver told us most everybody around that area would do just that: pick up mushrooms and then sell them on the fares; it was a source of a little additional income most everybody needed back then; the driver's uncle was some kind of an engineer in the steelworks in town and yet he would do that too in his free time, on weekends, together with his family – everybody just loved it; picking it up and then selling it on fares was, as said before, a source of income, but it also was the source of entertainment, relaxation, rest after the hassle and bustle of regular work, something they were all looking forward to during the week.

We got out of the woods and onto a large clearing which was at the same time a hillside so the road started going slightly down too; the speed at which we were moving did not change much but I could feel, almost clearly, the assuagement in the horses work. The clearing was covered with tall grass, reaching about waist high and at some places even higher and that was, as the driver commented, a lot of hay. They would also come here, himself included, to cut the grass working from the early morning, whenever the harvest time comes, with scythes, also all together, they would work throughout the day, and then the next, and yet next after that, until all of it was cut, and it would be left there, for an additional day or two yet, first just plainly cut on the ground and then yet few more days until completely dry, already bound in sheaves, until the transportation has been arranged for, after which it would be taken to people's respective barns.

"Barns?" I remember father's voice, on the surprised side. "They have barns around here?"

"Whatever one's got that the grass can be put into..."

He then would go on explaining that people had animals, like himself, not to look any further, and those have to eat in wintertime as well. Some have cows –"You know from those times when milk was hard to get" – which made father laugh – "He knows," father said quickly interrupting him, pointing to me, "exactly what you're talking about. His mother used him several times to get the milk, in those times yet when the milk-can was still almost too big and too heavy for him. People had mercy for a little kid like that. They would have killed her, probably, had she tried it. And he would ferret his way to the milk-wagon amongst their legs with that can that was almost as big as he was himself, and they were all just laughing, yes, all it did was make them laugh. And, of course, she knew that beforehand."

"Yes," the driver said. "The animals are from those times. Old cows. Horses you can still use. Like this one. I can make some money with it, too. It helps."

Father nodded.

"Yeah... Helps..."

With my eyes closed I breathed deeply through my nose – the wonder of the smell coming from those grasses filling my nostrils but also filling my very heart right now, through the remembrance of it, as clear, crisp, undisturbed by the time flow as it would have (I'm certain: it did) come to me back then: the wagon slowly moves, they talk, just a regular chat, up there, behind my back, and I keep watching the road slowly moving under my dangling legs, as if lazy, that laziness coming to it from the sun, I have no doubt whatsoever, from the heat that just keeps raising all those smells – as if by some magic we all know nothing about - extracting them from the world around us like a medieval alchemist we would like to meet in person at some point but we can't – and then never do; the only thing we do meet is the dense mystery surrounding his abode; do not approach - the weight of the curse of his curiosity burdens the forbidden terrain all around here; back off, let your questions sleep and enjoy what's allowed.

I just closed my eyes. (Right now; possibly back then, too).

After a while we get to the other side of the valley and toll pines again begin to give us some shade with yet one more change of the aroma. There is no grass here – the pine-needle covered bottom of the forest emanates the hot pine arôme again; the same. They talk – my father and the driver, and we are approaching noon. And we are way into the afternoon when we say 'good by' to him – the driver. He points to the path forking off the road we've been on so far, telling us that it would take us to the rail-road tracks, which we'll have to cross, and right there, on the other side of the tracks, we'll see the lake.

"Don't go back to the tram station," I still hear his voice perfectly clearly, himself slowly dissolving in the light pattern sipping through the branches above: "Whenever you decide to go back to your town, just follow the tracks," he motioned to us the direction, his voice suddenly a bit higher: "over that way! - They'll take you right back to the train station in it, right on the backside of the Steelworks. And that's where you want to go, ain't it?"

We thanked him and started walking. It took half an hour or so to get there: just as he said we'd cross the tracks and then I really saw it: the lake we've been traveling so long to see.

I just have to close my eyes: the shimmering of the tiny waves in that still blinding sunlight is too intense even now, in my present quick recollection of the moment: we are standing there, on that high shore; we've made it… Goodness me! The shore is high, grown over, per places only, by some kind of a wild grass and dwarfed brush I'd never seen so far anywhere else, and down there, all the way on the bottom, at the water level, there is a stretch, very narrow, sandy beach. I start running downhill towards it. I'm not thinking. I just run: each one of my steps must be several yards long, I'm more flying through the air than walking or even running over the ground, like in one straight jump downwards. A jump without a parachute and it evokes the feeling of… love? I'm not sure. Yes, I think – somehow… When I get to the bottom, already standing on the beach, almost at the water line, my cloths still on, I see father; he is right there, beside me. I am looking at him. I am pointing to his shoes that right now look like anything except what they are, they are covered with grim and dust, and I am saying: "Your shoes…" and he bents down and takes them off, lifts them up to the height of his face and, delicately knocking with the index of his right on the left one's nose, he just says: "Chamois, you know?"

"Yeah…"

Then we take our cloths off, only to retain those pieces of underwear absolutely necessary to cover what we don't want to show and we walk into the water. It is deep on this side and we lose the ground under our feet almost right away – we have to start swimming: there is about a mile of that swimming ahead of us. In the meantime

I've acquired crawl, the rhythms I can use on long distances, to the point, where I don't feel exhausted, I know how to relax, turn my mind off, just slowly move enough my hands and legs first to stay afloat and then to move forward at a sufficient rate. Father swims using a different style; he is on his side and I have no idea what he actually does with his hands and legs, he never showed or told me; whatever it is, though, I also know that he can swim me to death. He just won't get tired. I love this hanging between the light above and the greenly, from this perspective, mysteriously deep bottom down there, somewhere, not reachable without some kind of a scuba outfit; that is almost certain to me even without asking - this lake is deep, it's man made, and it was created because the coal mines all around us needed sand; well, this is it, father told me once– the source, the big hole that later on, once they dug up the sand so that there was not much of it left anymore, after which they moved over to yet another place, has been filled in with water. I asked father how they did that, just out of simple curiosity, where does one get that quantity of water, but I remember his answer that, although he wasn't really sure, it seemed rather simple to him: they had all the time that the production was going on to keep the water out – ground waters as well as the rain, you know, so once they stopped doing whatever they were doing, it just got filled up like we see it today, all by itself. It's so deep that the town church, yes, siree, the grand basilica we both admire so much, could be built on its bottom in the deepest spot and the towers would not stick out of the water.

"How are you doing?" father asks.

And I stop. Slightly moving my legs and arms, I float without actually progressing any more. We both play at being two corks.

"How are you?" he repeats and I answer him that I'm fine.

"And how are you?" I ask him.

He nods. He's OK and I didn't expect otherwise.

"You wanna keep on going or should we start back?"

"Up to you."

We keep on going then for yet a while that stretches over into yet another hour and the opposite shore is suddenly right there – with boat slips and yachts moored, we also see the club house with the funny pirate flag, skull and crossed bones, and a café on a large, sunny terrace. We get there in just a few more minutes. A big muscular guy helps us get out of the water and onto the pier to which a big nice yacht is moored.

"We've been watching you two for quite a while, "he says then. "It's a distance, you know?"

"Yeah…" father says smiling.

"You, sir" he says, pointing to father, "well… OK. But the kid! Goodness me!" He points to me now. "Where did you learn to swim like that, huh?"

"Here and there," I answered; that was my shot at indifference. "My father thought me most of it, though."

The big guy shakes his head in a sort of disbelief.

"Are you going back?" he asks then.

"We have to," father says. "Our cloths are on that beach."

"We've got a motorboat here all ready to go," the guy says. "That would be no problem, if you don't want to swim all the way back. No problem at all! Just tell me!"

He waits for us in an inquisitive pose, but father, after looking at me (I shook my head in the negative – I love this, I do, I won't be able to forget it any time soon, then: No!), turns him down on his offer, very politely, explaining that this is important to both of us – him as well as me, and the guy invites us for tea or orange juice, whatever we prefer. So we sit on the terrace and drink tea, which is what we had chosen, and it is peaceful: we are at one of the big glass tables under a huge, garden style parasol sawn together of different colors flowery triangles, we are already dry and the breeze feels good on our skin, feels like a caress - life at this moment doesn't exactly remind one of purgatory and waiting for true life that mother talks some times, rarely though, about; we both enjoy this. Both of us.

Then we stand up and father asks what do we owe for the tea.

The big guy, who is now with a whole group of other big guys, turns around and smiles.

"Forget about that!" he says. "On the house!"

Father thanks him, politely, they shake hands. He asks father, right then, if he, father, would like to be youth instructor, right here, for this very club, the mine has funds, it might help then, in fact he knows it would, it's a fact, yes, sir, no doubt about that, -father could also meet on personal basis the director so and so of the mine - that thing there is his yacht and it primarily would also be the director's son and his other young friends that would be taught - and father, with a strange smile on his face, writes the director's telephone on a piece of paper (quickly handed to him together with a pen that I think is nice, I wish I had something like that for school - that paper is more regular, though, more like something I already know) and it also has to be protected from the water – they look for a moment for a nylon bag that is then carefully folded and taped, and tied up to father's shorts rubber band. We get back into the water and some two hundred yards away from the pier I hear father cursing, and when he finally sees that I hear him, too, he looks at me and I think he looks kind of strange – I do breaststroke for a moment so we can look at each other. He spouts a little fountain out of his mouth and then just tells me that we should be so grateful, so-oo-oo friggen grateful, for the opportunity to meet the director so and so and his so and so son.

"Goodness. You know what that means? Who that is?"

"Who?"

He takes some more water into his mouth and spits is out, which makes a noise that I think is kind of funny.

"I made him what he is now, you know? Yeah… He owns now a yacht bigger than some people's houses and those people have to pick mushrooms to join both ends, and I'll be teaching his son how to become a great swimmer. What do you think?"

As I remember it now I wasn't sure what to think at the moment; I just thought that something was wrong with the picture he just painted and I thought him that.

"Yeah…" he said. "Yeah… A lot is wrong with that picture. A whole lot, my dear."

We swim. I'm curious and my curiosity grows. And then I just ask:

"Will you accept his invitation, though? To teach?"

He answers almost right away: "No!" And then: "Of course not!"

"Then why did you take the number?"

He swims a while yet.

"For one reason and one reason only," he says then. "I wanted to look him in the eye one more time, aboard that yacht." Then he looks at me. "Can you relate to that anyhow?"

I said: "Yes." And then: "Is that the one you threw the 'party' ID into the face of?"

He looks at me, this time a bit longer.

"How did you know about that?"

"Mom told me," I said.

He nodded.

"Women…" And then: "No, that's not him. This guy is simply to small for that. It would have been a waist. That one was truly big. He'd been in that muck from the very beginning too. Just as I was. And for a while I thought we both really believed."

He looks at me again.

"You know?"

"Yeah…" I said. "I think I do."

"Yeah…"

When we then get back to the beach we'd left our cloths on the day is already on the decline: the shadows grow longer, the light is denser, delineates things with more contrast: I think the world – just when one looks at it – can cause pain without any further ado, like misapplied knife that against your expectations suddenly cuts your own skin and you quickly smart seeing the blood that surprises you, or something like that. Our cloths are right there, in the same spot we had left them departing. We dry ourselves a little with the small towel we brought with us yet from home, we put our cloths on, look one more time around saying a silent good-by, and start climbing the cliff, and then, when we already are back at the tracks, we start following them towards the town.

"This is gonna be a long walk, you know?"

"Yes, I know," I said. "I know."

"You up to it?"

"I guess."

"Don't guess. Be!"

"Yes, sir!"

There's still light when we get to the orchard (it's on the right side of the tracks, there's no fence or anything, although the trees are obviously man planted and we both know right away is an orchard – hence we shall be steeling, somehow, if we take anything) - father says we'll have our supper, just as king David and the other king's people had the proposition bread they were not supposed to eat; simply because there was nothing else available. So we look for apples on the orchards bottom – it's wild, grown over by bushes and shrubs, and it is sometimes not easy at all to bent and look because of that. We try nevertheless. Father finds wood then – dry twigs, my job is starting the fire with nothing. I find the necessary pieces of flint; it's a long painstaking process in the dying light but we both try from some point on and it's really me who succeeds: two more or less regular pieces of flint – with a little previous experience it's easy to check what they are even if the visibility is somewhat limited: first of what they feel like to the fingers and second of just striking them against each other and then you know for certain; dried grass and some little dried up twigs are much less of a problem, after which, once the dried grass is pressed and rolled until it is just a bit of powder, I start hitting the stones against each other and I do get smoke rising slowly in a lazy spiral, pretty quick actually – well, then it's just the matter of careful blowing and adding pieces to it: twigs at first and after that bigger chunks, until we sit at a full blown camp fire, our apples on two sticks, carefully held over the flames until done. The first two we eat just like two pigs would: I mean noise-wise. But the next two are also not that much different – in fact I am so hungry I bite off a piece of the stick the apple is on without noticing it and only father's request to be more careful because we don't want any broken teeth manages to slow me down a little. But he isn't all that much better himself: his stick is considerably shorter too after only a very short while; I don't ask him what happened to it. We did all the apples we'd found before in the same manner: I still remember the taste and I will never be able to forget it – I said that before so many times already that I am beginning to think that it is exactly what our whole life is all about – things we will never be able to forget; when I go to heaven – if I go to heaven – I'll ask

God, I'm certain, about those apples back there: has he got up there anything that good?

We sit there a while yet, just to rest a little and then we start again. We don't have flashlights but we also don't need any – the moon is huge and it is moon landscape that surrounds us now: from sunny gold so and so many hours ago to this molten silver now. I begin to feel sleepy, though, with some food in my stomach, I'm dreaming abut the horse carriage we'd got to the lake on, but that, of course, is not going to happen. Of course not! So we walk.

"Wouldn't it be great," I ask father, "if people invented some means of communication that one would be able to have in the pocket?"

"You're dreaming already."

"We would call mother," I say and in the light of that huge moon I see him nod.

"Yawp!"

And then, only a short moment after that: "I can imagine what's it gonna be like when we get there! That woman (that means my mother) we'll grouch the living stuff out of me."

"Maybe she'll go to sleep?"

"You kidding, right?"

"Yeah…"

We just know she won't.

Then we see lights – how much later, I'm not really sure. An hour maybe. Something like that. The lights move, quickly up and down and very slowly also towards us. It's two guys with portable lamps – big and incredibly strong lamps, they turn out to be two policemen, and they ask father if he might by any chance be Mr. - and here I hear my own name. Father confirms, surprised. Why, he wants to know and they explain, very politely, that it was my mom who came to the station at some point to report missing people. Nobody really believed in the 'missing' part, but to be on the safe side, just to check, you know, to make sure…

"You're OK?" one of them asks me and I say yes to that. "Can you still walk?"

"Yes!"

"That's one tough kid," he says to the other, smiling, and I know father is proud.

We stood there yet a while, all three of us, before we started together towards the still distant train station and the steelworks, in that thick stillness of the night filled with the intense monotonous noise of crickets and frogs coming to us from the endless meadows on the right side of the tracks, all of it flooded with the moonlight in whose steady majesty the two incessantly moving long beams from the lamps of the cops that so unexpectedly drew near from the warm innards of the sleep of the town ahead looked to me like lances of two even more lost and even more absurd Don Quijotes arrived from the inside of the night completely forgotten by all the windmills of the world; I told father, whispering, that all we needed right now were two skinny horses and two pot bellied servants on fat donkeys, and he smiled and then just nodded. "Yeah..." Then smiled again.

Kim's papers

I opened the first folder and those were mostly bills – paid or unpaid, but most of all old; trash; I just went through it and then, without unpacking the folder, I really put it in the trash can under my desk where I cut my finger against a piece of pseudo marble that was still there among the crumpled paper – the dying Gaul I ordered from Italy: a miniaturized copy 5' by 8' for couple of hundreds that one beautiful day just fell off my desk and became several pieces I had no intention of gluing together anymore; I studied it, though, very, very carefully, before that happened; I did get to imagine his thoughts at that very moment I saw the sculpture before me, on the desk, once arrived and unpacked, - and then one more time that naked wounded man offered yet another chance: another shot at life, family, a son, a house, a country. I thought I had understood every single one of those thoughts – his thoughts growing in me. Then the sculpture fell. I took it out of the can now. I went out of the apartment and across the hallway to the garbage shoot; I opened the shoot door and dumped it in there. Then I came back.

The other folder was with press clippings; a lot more to it and it also took a lot more time to sort out; make the final decisions as to what do I want to do with those. Then there was the one with everything I was able to ever find about the dying Gaul – it seemed unbelievable to me how little I understood now out of my own notes from the very recent past, the ones I once spent so much time thinking through and giving the final form to, putting them on paper – and only then I finally started painting the pictures; I think I did what I had set out to do, I did, accomplished, the feedback surpassed any of my expectations (Donovan took it to San Francisco where it was for a while, I got a lot out of that, but then he also took it to Europe: Paris, Hague, Leipzig, and in the end to Italy; it happened because the new owner of the picture wanted to have the critiques from all those places, and he got it too; well, so did I; I also fell in love with Tuscany, got to understand Ezra Pound at yet different level, anyway; I too would like to end my life there, hopefully not only after spending so and so many years in an American DC institution, God almighty!) – all of it based on those thoughts. And now when I was trying to heat up anew those very reflections of mine, make them come alive one more time for me, they were in such a new guise that I was unable to recognize them at all. They were my thoughts back then, yes, there's no doubt about that, they seemed new, they seemed great, filled up with the spirit of discovery – now these here were just scribblings I felt forced too put aside completely disenchanted.

It's the way you get there – and not the fact that you got there, I smiled. I saw Eve then.

Don't get trivial, she would say, I'm certain. OK?

I thought I would have to be back to it at some point – maybe - reread the whole thing, the whole folder, sentence by sentence. Maybe. And then: why? What would be the reason for doing that?

She said: none…

And then it was yet another one: the same type of big yellow folder; it was I who put it in the folder of this type because the notes had been given to me quite differently as far as shape goes - in fact not even remotely in this form, here. John - Jack's (Eva's husband's) friend who died recently of heart attack in a hospital in Oneonta, had given the folder to Jack before he died, and then Jack, after his BS arrest, told Eve to give it to me, after we've had one of our conversations already inside the 'hospital.' There's a guy name Ernie, whose scribblings are clear to me, I have deciphered them without a slightest problem – they might even be accepted as 'nice,' if one enjoys that type of very basic story telling. Yes, I have deciphered those rather quickly. My assistant Sophie, who comes here to help me a couple of times a week, put them, after a little polish, nicely in typing, too. But there's something else: also memoir-like type of thing, written –actually really written by hand – by Ernie's father, Mr. Mackenzie, and that when Ernie was still just a boy. Those pages (pretty many of them, too) are about the Labor Unions – a shot at improvement of life of the little ones – yes, improving the blue color lives. He goes on for several pages only to repeat the added value part, almost the whole thing, from the Marx's Capital, without a hell of a change, and how then is that value divided now, in his days, that is - versus how it should be divided, how is the picture distorted by changes introduced into the process during our time and that to mask the essence of what it really is: more toys, worthless, real crap in attractive wrapping, there's no price on toys that are just decoy, bait, if you will, and nothing out there about how it should really be done so that those who really produce something might also have a gain, a product facilitating their own lives out of their sweat – and not only that sweat and plastic decoy-crap. Generally that's what the whole thing is: the history of that particular movement written from the inside, by a guy, in other words, who helped at some point to translate it, ideas, intentions, as best he and the others like him knew how and, hence, could, into reality.

I realized then, on probably the second and then the third day, that I'm actually reading it – bored, whenever he goes into theory, analyzing economy, industry, whatever is known to him out of both, and very much interested in the matter whenever he recalls things from the past: how they fought, how they prepared for the fighting, training, practice; the learning how to talk – not from academics, no, from the pal, the guy just like you – is it interesting or am I boring you? I'm not interested if the big CEO is attracted by my speech or not – he knows about steeling from the poor more than I do or ever will anyway – it's us have to understand, be made understand, at any rate, us who are stolen from in a massive way by a bunch of perfectly organized thieves who call themselves 'administration'; who call the rules according to which a blind man has to give up his white can that will then be sold at a garage sale for profit of the rich – they'll talk about 'the law', 'legislation,'' jurisprudence,' etc, etc.

I read. More and more. I know it all. There's not been in it one word I wouldn't have known of old. From the formal view point it's not exactly what I am used to as reading material either – but its having been jotted down on paper while still hot makes up for its lack of literary form as well as for the fact that it also is not revelatory as a theoretical work; it is precisely that: hot, real, true. It feels almost like a toothache - at some point, accidentally, I do have a headache - I really looked around to find my aspirin bottle. Another, separate, note is written by Jack – I recognize his hand writing. It is about William HCE, it's a sketch, like a beginning of something bigger perhaps, hard to tell what Jack's intention was at that particular point, followed by ALP, another sketch, no beginning and no end, sort of homage to Joyce, would be my guess, a testimony to Jack's fascination with great author's works… Probably a whole lot else but I'll have to think about it some more. I put them back in.

It's raining outside and I can hear the rain quite clearly.

I think I gotta talk to Jack. I also gotta get some more steak for Pino before I get the appointment. Pino will be eating and smiling at me his beautiful smile while chewing, and we'll talk – Jack and I. Do we want this to become a book? It's his stuff. Yes. Most of it, even if not all of it. And he's the only one who could decide such a thing, even though he does get progressively worse – and then yet worse than that. His memory. His coordination. In fact I wouldn't be surprised if at some point he did not recognize me anymore. Next week I have an appointment with Ann at the governor's office in Albany. I'll just drive there I think. We've got to do something.

I wonder what did Ezra Pound look like the moment he decided to go back to his beloved Tuscany after his release from the DC 'hospital'... Did he still recognize any of it once already there?

I'll have to listen to Pluplu cantos again, goodness me, Jack owes me big! Big! Friggen big!

Eve seems a little weaker than I thought she would be in this: but no wonder: she loves him and precisely that is her weakness: I've no idea how I would be watching someone I love being pushed into madness by a stinking bunch of foreign imbeciles, who's salaries I am paying on top of everything else, without being able to do a thing within the broken, sick system we all are forced to live in. God have mercy on us! God have mercy on us!

Jack

I felt a little assuagement now; I did not have much of a problem to recognize the guy whose face I saw – I knew his name was Pino and he was looking at me, - waiting for my reaction; that was my guess.

"How you doin'?'

"You slept again... Jeez, man, days on end. You know where you are?"

"Sure I do! What'd you think?"

"Did you go somewhere again?" he asks. "Somewhere far away, like you told me the last time? Did you?"

"Sounds like you really want me too, donit?"

"Well, did you?"

"Yes," I told him, smiling, whatever the real outcome on my face might have been. "Yes, very far away. I was again the teen I once was - in fact."

His smile widened. He nodded, once, and then one more time.

"Beautiful... I never seem to do that. Shit!"

"Think about it some more!"

"You think it'll happen if I think about it before I go to sleep?"

"Chances are."

"I wish you were right. Yeah... Why don't you tell me about it?"

195

"I will."

Then he told me that my wife Eve brought us some coffee – the kind we both, Pino as well as I, liked. The coffee we were given here was just awful, watery and tasteless piss. One was better off, we both would agree on that one, drinking faucet water. He had the thermos she brought it in, strangely they allowed him to keep it, right there. And would I want some?"

"You bet!"

He gave me a cup and it felt wonderful. It did. I asked him to tell me some about Cuba first, I told him one more time I've never been to Cuba, I once went with Eve to Martinique, though, and we both just loved the island (I must have told him that few hundreds of times) but after that he obliged again – in the beginning kind of awkward, but then the story really picked up as it would usually, and again I saw the Island (just as he, most probably could see it through his own words – the same grand emotion, epiphany, some times our entire life comes to us within): the beach, large, wide and sunny, they lived right off; the sea; I also saw him fish when he was a teenager, off a wooden boat, standing in it with a wooden spear. I saw a lot, I'd say. A whole lot. Yes…

And then he asked me, also as he would always do - and as soon as I started telling him about my dreams and where I went, I saw a small recorder in his hand and I saw him press a button, and I thought it was Kim or Eve who gave him the blessed thing to get the recording. But I also didn't mind. Nope… Not at all!

"Will you go now?" I heard him ask me.

"Let's see," I said still uncertain.

Strasbourg

Uli said to me, all in thought: "Mom just read something, you know, a brand new book, some kind of a bestseller, in which God is simply one's friend. You have to let him be your friend, though. You have to know him and you have to demand from him, mind you… Demand from him!"

"What did your mother tell you about that?"

"That it was BS. Sickly nonsense. One more piece of nothingness by means of which to destroy what's left of us. That's, give or take, what she said."

"I think so too," I told her.

We were sitting on the balustrade of the museum's terrace giving onto the river. I reached out, didn't have to reach out far, and touched her hair.

"Look!"

"Yeah…" she answered me. "I see!"

Uli was born in Frankfurt and her mother brought her over here because she wanted Uli to steepen her French, she wanted for Uli to become in the future a great translator - French to German and German to French. And Uli seemed to like the idea. We became friends almost as soon as I said in class, loud, forced to it by the teacher, that I wasn't French myself. Our first lesson in French literature started with the introduction: *"Comment appelez vous, Monsieur?"* Here I gave my name which was of no consequence; I had no accent and my name could be from anywhere in the world, well, almost, and so the teacher kept on smiling. *"Êtes-vous de Strasbourg, Monsieur?"* Was her next question; there was a whole lot of those who were not – she wanted to know.

"Non, madame," I had to answer to that, *"Je viens de Katowice."*

Her smile vanished. She looked at me with sympathy, was my impression, but also with great curiosity; I could've told her I was from Somalia or Algeria, or something like that. She was obviously trying to recall where Katowice might be. Only then she gave up: *"Et c'est où ça?"*

"Silésie, Madame."

"Eh, bien. Vous êtes Polonais alors. Comme Chopin!"

I told her then my father would have answered to that very energetically in the negative; we were Silesians; not Polish, hence, and not German. She had a defensive movement of her right hand towards me. She said we weren't here to go into that kind of historical-geographically-ethnic detail and Silesian was OK with her. We shall leave it at that.

"Et vous parlez Français, monsieur, comme ça, parce que…" She wanted to know where did I learn French like that –and I told her my mother spoke it just like her. *"Ma mère le parle justement comme vous, madame."*

"Eh, bien, je supçonnais quelque chose comme ça…" she smiled again, she seemed relieved. "I suspected something like that."

"Elle est Française, madame vôtre mère?"

"Allemande…"

She frowned and then shook her head.

"Bon bain…"

But she still smiled at me, with the same unchangeable sympathy.

Uli told her, only a moment later, she was German, from Frankfurt. I had the impression she liked Uli a lot less. If it was true, though, I must say she never really showed it: not the slightest trace of that very first moment's shadow quickly crossing her face like a cloud on a sunny day crosses the ground: she treated Uli in the class in the same manner she treated any of us – at all times. Always.

We both, Uli as well as I, liked her very much. We both thought she was great as a teacher as well as a scientist,- she published a bunch of manuals, a set of essays on French letters, the best in my opinion about the Saint-Beuve, Chateaubriand, de LaRochefoucauld, we would read forth and back all the time we were there, and a separate large study in NRF on Proust, my mother fell in love with (I mailed it to her and she mailed me back her own writing on the subject); we, Uli and I, thought a great deal about it, too; she also loved Alfons Daudet - probably as much as I did, we both, as it turned out later dreamed about buying some day, whenever our lives finally improved from the financial standpoint sufficiently to make that kind of purchase, a windmill in Provençe, also preferably with a great horned owl living in it from before our time.

I am now smiling too.

When I reached out, though, and touched Uli's head at that moment I suddenly had a recollection that I just didn't understand at first: it was a kitchen sink, I was washing dishes with a steel wool ball, and now I also saw the Rhine, the sun setting and the water reminding one in those moments of all the poetry in the world, trees, windows of the houses on the other side reflecting the light that would probably be an impressionist's dream, and I wonder what is actually the feeling under my fingers – it's Uli's hair: shortly cut, strong, thick; she's not backing off, she takes my caress, although she does not look at me, she looks at the water, the on-coming evening.

"Would you like God to be your friend?" she asks.

"He isn't your enemy," I said.

"No, I didn't figure he was… But he isn't like you either, is he?"

"He better not be," I laughed. "There's a whole world out there that's waiting. Right?"

But the impression I just had is still fresh and makes me wonder. Then I ask her:

"What do you think about love?"

"It's how you know that there's none anywhere," she said, "nowhere in the world!"

"Have you ever loved anyone?"

She looked at me and smiled. She shook her head then.

"I think so…"

"How long ago? Long time?"

"Not long ago at all. Not at all!"

I hugged her and I felt her arms around me, too. Our heads were also touching. We were standing there, at the balustrade separating us from the water, all immersed in that terribly intense on-coming evening, the city setting out for the night, the museum's building right behind us as a shadow getting darker and darker, quickly approaching the darkest shade of blue.

"We shall always be the stupid virgins," she said, not trying to change our position, though, she too obviously comfortable with it, I thought. "But I'm OK with that. You?"

"Me too. Yes, me too!"

"If you ask me we are very lucky, you and I. Would you agree with that?"

"Yes!"

Then we talked about the incomprehensible complexity of most everything around us – like the cathédrale we both love so much: infinite, inexhaustible combination of *dentelles de pierre* in which the basic immensity of architectural thought was wrapped up in its incessant prayer to the already *couronée* – like life itself: infinite meanders amongst infinite amount of possible senses, pleasant, filling you with joy but also those that make you pray for death, that too, with almost no intermediary passages.

"That Sainte-Beuve?"

She read him a lot then.

"Non, monsieur," she answered, smiling, *"c'est moi!"*

Uli quoted then Athalie; she stood still, focused, reciting without any pathos, just delivering the meaning:

"Mon Dieu, qu'une virtue naissante
Parmi tant de perils marche à pas incertain!
Qu'une âme qui le cherche et veut être innocente
Trouve d'obstacles à ses desseins!"

Looking at her and listening to the words we'd just gone through at school I got their meaning only now, suddenly: it struck me right there on the stone terrace at the river, in that beautifully cool slow evening breeze – absolute simplicity within unlimited complexity. Quoting Racine she just told me something I've had a premonition of for a long time but did not yet, not so far, not ever, really understand – and now I got touched, grazed by lightning, sort of, if you will. I told her that and she said she would like to have a feeling of that sort, too, at some point… – seeing the shore of America emerging from the mists of the ocean; she never had it; never like that. I walked her home, well, the place she lived at with her mother – whenever her mother would come to visit her from Frankfurt - after that. I never knew if she was serious with me or just joking. She sure knew how to pull one's leg. We kissed good night, and I mean really kissed, which we had never done before – this was our first time. Going back to my place I bought a post card and then, already in my room, I wrote father about it. As best I knew how.

Next day I did not go to school: I went to the old city, just as I came here for the first time from the train station directly after my arrival in Strasbourg –along the same street, walking slowly towards the Cathedral (the itinerary I found out of the map I had with me yet from Munich where mother was and where from I came here, too), a street one would take so that until the very last moment one wouldn't be able to see it; only then, after that last look on the map which tells you that you are right there, just lift up your head, - and you do: you lift it up and the shudder goes down your spine and you have to take a deep breath: it is there, in front of you... We read about it from Geothe's *Dichtung und Wahrheit,* and father told me he saw it while crossing Germany from North to South, walking, taking that detour precisely because of that text, of that enchantment – may even be the greatest of all poets of all times had experienced right there – and he wanted to see it too; and he did; and now I was there, experiencing the same shock, if that is the right word to describe it; if not, it is close enough to something that might take the therapy to get out of and then back on track, would be my opinion. My aunt waited and waited, as she told me afterwards, and I just stood there, looking, with watery eyes... way into the night. I'd never seen anything this shockingly beautiful in my whole life and I seriously doubt if anything ever again will evoke in me an impression similar to that one. I remember it still, after all those years, with almost the same intensity; it's enough to close my eyes and I'm right there again...

That was also where I went the next day: to stand there. To walk inside then – look up at the *vitraux* and ponder what they meant. And then Uli came. I saw her suddenly inside the church, yes, she was there, in the crowd of the main nave, quite quickly walking towards me. She said nothing, not even 'hallo', just touched my face lightly with her fingers; and I remember that there was a smile on her face and that she wasn't smiling to me - that it was a smile like on those faces up there from which the light was so richly showering down on us. We walked together – inside and then outside, she asked me about the clock, in her normal, quite natural voice that was actually surprising, somehow, and I told her just about everything I knew about it myself –what it was and how it worked, and why. Her questions were to the point, nothing emotional about them, questions asked by someone who wanted to know how a mechanism worked and she was interested in my answers, the whole thing wasn't just making a conversation, no, not at all. Then we slowly walked away from the cathedral and towards the river, and there, still in the historical part of the city, she took my hand and together we entered an old house I'd never been in before, and only after a while I realized we were in a hotel – and that only when she started talking to a receptionist and put our names into the hotel register, and having paid for the room took the key; then we went upstairs followed by the more or less indifferent gaze of the fat receptionist woman, found the room in the long corridor and entered. The air was stuffy and I wanted to open the window but Uli took her cloths off so quickly that I just stopped thinking about that, I took mine off too, and we went into the shower. Was I embarrassed by my nakedness? I always though I would be. But I wasn't. No, we washed each other's backs and I realized at some point that I couldn't take my eyes off her and that it felt kind of strange, and then I just turned her around towards me and kissed her, and she put her arms around my neck, as well as her legs then around my waist, and then I just knew that was it: we were making love, I leaning against the shower wall, and I was actually surprised that I didn't feel her weight: Uli was strong, as toll as I was and greatly built, and I felt nothing, except for what we were doing. Then we were just sitting there, in the shower, with the curtain still drawn, water falling on our heads and I was trying, I remember, to catch breath because there suddenly seemed to be no air, and looking at her after only a moment I saw her do the same, and just like that, half chocked out of our senses, we started kissing again…

In the room she took a cassette from her bag and stuck it into the hotel radio that had a cassette player. The voice of Edith Piaf started telling us the story about the two who requested *la chambre d'hotel dans le petit jour*, and we smiled at each other, lying on the bed, with the window still closed, and then she got up and opened it, and I thought she was beautiful, just that: blindingly beautiful, my God; Piaf sang that she was only *"l'hiver au fond du café"* and, through the chocking tears, that she had *"trôp de peur pour pouvoir réver…"*

And the two of us…?

And Uli came back to bed then. We were listening, we did not talk. We stayed overnight.

Next morning we went straight to school from the hotel.

I thought. Goodness… Not about Racine the class was talking about, although the *meritum* of my thoughts was probably very close to Bérenice or Andromaque, nevertheless. I felt, well, I'm not sure how I should put it: suddenly confronted with something that was a lot bigger than I, I'd say, and that couldn't be changed for the moment –although, I also think, I would have given a lot to get back our innocence from before. I was ready to go out there to kill a dragon: a big sucker that could cook the whole town with his breath; Oh, yes, I was ready – and the only problem, big problem with that, was that there was no dragon anywhere in sight to be killed; I was there, in the classroom, in a few hours we both, Uli and I, would get out and… I thought the only thing I could do then was to wait – let's see. OK?

Let's wait. Just wait up.

After school we went to the same hotel again and the same afternoon repeated itself with the same ecstasy. I called my aunt from the hotel telling her we were in the museum, after which I would go a little around; she had no objections, knowing I loved the town, and that I really studied the history of the cathedral and its immediate vicinity. From the hotel we would go to the river, we would really take a long walk, during which I had a strange impression of being exposed to the world: like there was a danger, paws and claws – something would move quickly towards us and it wasn't benign, and we were naked, unprotected; I didn't understand any of that but then we were sitting at the river shore where I saw a small plant, absolutely and totally misplaced, a tomato that just grew there, planted probably by the wind in a crack of the concrete plate and never cared for by anyone, right there at the water, and I saw Uli peering over it, taking it into her cupped hands, like she was trying to protect it from the city's noise; and suddenly I knew she felt the same way I did; I asked her if she understood the feeling, whatever compelled her to do that. She turned her head towards me and looked me in the eye.

"I think I do," she said.

"What is it?"

She asked me first if I remembered the old testament story about the old father, absolutely lonely in the world that was half empty back then anyway, to whom finally love comes with all its promises, and then, once that love is there, he is suddenly asked to kill it and burn it on the altar as an offering...

"Do you really remember that?"

"Yes," I said. "Of course I do. Isn't that the most important of all stories in the old testament? Isn't your old and lonely father the father of faith altogether?"

She looks at me. She bites her lower lip with her upper teeth. Her eyes get watery.

"I'd like to go back to the hotel," she says then. "That's how I feel about life right now."

We'd go there, to that hotel, most every day. The receptionists got to really know us in the end, they knew our first names; they never asked anything else, tough, and we were grateful for that. The fat one from the first time gave us once a huge block of Swiss chocolate that we then ate, piece by piece, in bed – because you need a lot of strength for that... I did not like the fat woman from the very beginning: she was just like that: insolent, piggy. But we both liked the chocolate. We did not talk about the future. Uli never asked me what I thought about it; if I thought about it at all; she never did.

The day I have received the letter from my mother calling me back Uli looked a bit like St. Peter on the Cathedral glass window: she knew about it before it has happened and the confirmation of that knowledge would make her sick; the sickly sadness was what I saw in her face; you wait for something, you think you're well prepared, because there's no way around it, it just has to happen, has to, there's no way around that no matter what you might do, what you or the other might come up with, and then when the moment arrives every fiber in your body bristles against it and you'd rather do anything than to agree with the inevitable...

We went for a long walk after we had spent our usual time in the hotel room, hours and hours on end, without talking at all, just going places, our legs seeking the road as if by themselves, making the choices, places we once were at as 'we', together, inseparable –

now silent, as if scared, not daring to talk, was my impression, yes, scared into silence.

We stopped for a longer moment in the church, under the glass with the virgin, because Uli knelt down and prayed and that prayer of hers seemed to have no end – she was afraid to stand up, I thought; and I too didn't feel like getting outside because the light pouring onto us from the glass windows seemed to carry assuagement; the non-remembrance, the non-thinking that felt like a blessing.

I called mother on the phone with a simple – it seemed very simple, basic - to me: why? I liked it here very much, she, mother, insisted on my French being as good as it could possibly get, then why? And mother told me about the aunt, here, in Strasbourg: my stay was getting too expensive for her, she was alone, she did not have a husband (according to my mother she said explicitly that 'something like that would take a guy she did not have'…).

"What is her fucking expense?" Uli wanted to know. "You eat like a bird. That old house she lives in is what it is if you're there or not, nothing will change after you're gone. So what is her problem?"

I didn't know. I had no explanation. I asked Uli if she told her mother about us and, after a moment of hesitation, she frankly said she did not.

"Did you?"

I had to say 'no' to her indagation either. Well…

When something like that, something bad, painful happens, we try, and I think, always try to define the 'why' of it, the cause –it happened like that because… and here it comes, the main cause; and only then, once that definition is already present, made up, almost a notion – no, it's not a notion at all, it's more like a feeling, I think, it's not in your mind, it's a lot more in your heart - that negation appears, unclear, as if shy, kind of, that our main cause is something, well, other than *main* cause, that it could easily be circumvented, it is not even all that important at all, - it is altogether something else. Now what? I thought Uli knew and all I had to do was ask. But than I thought that I also knew and I didn't need to ask. I saw mother's face and now she, too, looked like St. Peter from

Münster's *vitrail*, and I thought her face was kind of painful to me too, just liker the rest of it.

The day a bought my train ticket we didn't see each other. I took a long walk, I went over the most cherished places, from early morning way into the afternoon; I thought I loved Strasbourg, I thought I would love to live here for ever without this painful necessity of thinking about going back – that there is something else, yet another place in the world where one is from and will have to go back to, whatever for; I wish; just stay right where you are, look at the river that in the meantime has become a part of you, old trees at the edge of the slowly moving water, the building of the museum where we had, actually both of us, I as well as Uli, so many great moments, great discussions, great illuminations… That it might be yours, no need to go anywhere.

Anywhere…

But then you get to know: going somewhere is part of it: most of what you do is going somewhere and then arriving at that place, and trying to grow roots of some kind so you may have a base, so the autumn's wind won't carry you like gossamer all around the world, and then, after yet a while you start waiting for the moment when it shall become perfectly clear that you have to move and then to keep going again, so you just bent over and down and pull them out of the ground with your own hands, wipe the blood off and start walking…

The train's departure was in the late afternoon, almost evening, so I had first something to eat – I had left in the morning without even saying good by to the aunt, I just didn't want to pretend, didn't feel like it at all - how thankful I was to her, because I just wasn't, no, never really was, not for one day, from the very beginning I felt that there was something terribly false, something twofaced, about her; she never bothered me in any way –we were more like the owner of the cave, whoever it might be and a spider or something small, something that doesn't mean much of a bother – just be careful not to step on it: that, I'd say, was our relationship from the very beginning. So I did not say good by to her. I ate the very little I ordered, and then just went straight to the station, where I was told that the train was already on the platform. Walking there I was passing along a long row of glass windowed boutique-type stores selling flowers, books, woodcraft and such, and in one of them I suddenly saw a face that got me really scared: eyes that must have been huge in the past, now swollen beyond recognition into two slits, looking very sick in that white, half way transparent rest of it, a mouth, twisted into the sheer expression of pain; the creature was looking at me and wouldn't take those wild, dying eyes off me for one single second. I wondered. I just walked by, towards the train, and only there, already after boarding, I realized that it was Uli. That bloody slow! Friggen halfwit! I ran out of the car like crazy to back there, to that boutique I saw her in but she wasn't there anymore. I stood there, looking around, suddenly hoping I would see her one more time, until they said over the loud speakers that my train was about to depart. I ran back to the car. Inside already, after I had sat down and opened the window – there was nobody else in the compartment - I wondered: if she had been there, if she had waited that short while longer, what would I have told her. That my body felt too small for me; like shoes you would like to be one number larger because they cause you blisters…? I think she knew that, though. We had talked about that and that also was how she felt about herself. Yeah… I know I would have kissed her – hugged her against my chest so strongly she would pant. We both would have. And I would certainly have told her that I loved her.

Man's Wake

The noise is getting more and more pronounced at the bar, unbelievable lots of food are being consumed without any mitigation, as well as alcohol, Jute says something that is not liked and he gets hit with a beer jar over the head and heavily falls off the bar stool, looking dead, he does, which seems to be agreeable at this point (seems to have become his profession in the meantime), he was not generally liked, so to hell with him, but on the other hand Mutt shall from now on be alone which does not represent a great progress or so it seems. Cluski says then, laughing his head off, that when he went last time to make a covenant with the toilet he also walked out for a moment, not for long because the fresh air outside caused him to have a vertigo, but there was a bus, he is telling now Irving who stands right there beside him, a big, modern, very beautiful bus with a group of dwarfs aboard going to Gran Canyon and Hoover Dam, and did anyone know that dwarfs now had unions, that they really got together, them poor sonofabitches, about fucking four feet tall, about, no more, with any degree of certainty, and they are really represented, and that the motor was running he, Cluski laying down on the ground put his head to the exhaust and his vertigo went away just like that, he snaps his fingers, away for good, just like that. Mutt puts now his head on the bar and he seems to have fallen asleep or maybe he too is dead, the thought appears suddenly; possibly. Shit! Of course! One of Annalivia's breasts is definitely out in the open, she doesn't seem to know about it, though, and the poor thing is sweeping the bar whenever she moves to serve Whisky or wine, or beer for that matter, and they are talking, Cluski and Irving being the loudest, about the whoreible state of disfucktion our state is in now and pork is served again with kapusta and kobasa, and more beer, whoreible. Irving then talks about new branches of social thought he just got himself acquainted with, based on psychological and religious research, by a Welsh or, yeah, Welsh, Needle, yes, shit, Needle it seems, about achieving mastery in high fartness, and he demonstrates how he stood the book he had paid his own good many for, not that much, though, no, but his own and not stolen from the taxpayer which is lately hard and harder to believe, right on the floor and then kicked it with his right foot like he would execute the eleven meters penalty in sacker and how the masterpiece flew through the airs, a great parable, you know, a great book, really, hit the wall and bounced off straight into the metal can for precisely that purpose. Right there! Even if he tried the thing over and over only to repeat it again he would probably die first because there wasn't enough time for him left in this world or any fucking world for that matter. It was perfect. Fucking perfect! Pronouncing the two words one after another he stretches his lips at first into a pussy athwart and then he purses them like for a kiss to an asshole: need-le pur-fect! one more time.

Annalivia in a nurse's outfit now drinks a jar of beer half empty, almost at one draught and puts the jar down on the bar but it flips and makes a pool of beer on the glossy bar surface and she picks up her breast, pulls it up as high as it would go, and then lets it fall making a loud splash which causes a salvo of laughter from all sides –everybody is laughing which seems to make her really happy. Really! Happiness! Joy! Fuck!

And then the dwarfs are at the bar too; about four feet each, looking like the midwifes had been fucking drunk dropping them from the height of about a yard or so onto a concrete surface that would offer no pardon for mistakes; perhaps even a bit higher than a yard; going to look at the Gran Canyon and the Hoover Dam, no shit! One of them, a she, has a wide smile, teeth that are a bit those of a horse and she says she'll win the campaign, anyone can bet on that, - talking all the time about her campaign, that there were no dwarfs yet, not yet, mind you, but that there's always the first time. Sure! She also declares readiness to offer the vice- position to the next (only fair is fair!) who is four feet and half an inch tall (taller than her by one sixteenth) which confuses him whoreibly as it seems, as it also seems to confuse anyone else at the bar. She introduces then her great medical program everybody shall be able to profit from. It's not the first time a dwarf has profited from talking about a medical program in a country where there is none.

Annalivia brought out of the gigantic, old, still functioning perfectly fridge in the back an also gigantic New York cheesecake in which her huge, all the time naked breast is suddenly resting, right in the middle, a good half of its resting height above the cheese level, though, while she listens to the campaigning with all the kon-sen-tration she can still gather; her eyelids are clearly falling, though, and it is clear that it won't take long now. No!

It is well known now: yes, it is common knowledge. A prolonged and juicy fart resounded and the vague thought is that it might, just might, be the influence of the pork with kapusta on the customer's digestive system (s)!

(sic!)

McKenzie looks down at his son Ernie standing at the side of his father's bar stool (he looks at the boy down under his lifted up left arm and it looks a bit like he is trying to figure out what his armpit's content might be – the boy is just something else; his meaning there is not, or rather not quite, clear for the time being) and his explanation to the boy that pissing onto the leg of a barstool is a partial at least inappropria-friggen-teness (it has become a very well known truth critical papers keep repeating) because an artist giving up an hour of work to converse for that time with a friend knows that he is sacrificing reality to an illusion, as a great writer once said: (friends being friends only in the sense of sweet madness which overcomes us in life and to which we yield, though at the back of our minds we know it to be the error of a lunatic who imagines the furniture to be alive and talks to it).

"Use the bathroom," he says in the end, loud and clear. "Always!"

"Yessir!" the boy says, also quite clear.

"Always! Time's a flyin'!"

"Time is," the boy says. "Yessir!"

'Good!"

The only one without any movement right now seems to be Mark whom friendly love had dug up from his grave, already a day or two ago, there's no certainty, so he gets finally a couple of friendly jabs, too, which puts him at a slight angle to the ground, as far only, of course, as the two-by- four his back is propped against would let go – the piece is quite solidly stemmed in the crevice the floor had developed right there or so it seems – there would seem to be the clarifying thought.

"Yes, Siree!"

"Sure thing!"

"Right!"

"Crapo!"

Cluski has a black eye (his superciliary arc does not look quite like an arc, the bone is broken and badly misshapen but he eats quickly emptying his plate without paying it any mind); it has been done with a nightstick to which he obviously got used in the meantime;

only then he slows down a little: he just drinks beer and only now and then puts in his mouth also a small ration of pork with kapusta – those must besides already be ice cold. Irving has a dwarf on his shoulders and the thought is that the latter is there by invitation, somehow, and the dwarf moves back and fort like he was riding a horse against which Irving does not seem to have anything at all: he sits there, participates in none of the activities around the bar, like he had chosen for the time being not to be there – on purpose. There is no clear understanding, the general thought seems to be. None. No, siree! All of it just is – like the rest of being: ordering function of perception does not seem to exist anymore, dissolved in the loud intense – intensely loud - talk about new forms of medicare performed by the she-dwarf with the horse teeth. The one who rides Irving's shoulders says, also loud, in a screeching froggy voice, that we shall fight for the higher quality of entertainment. He is then in foreground, his hands stemmed into his sides, laughing, drawing attention to himself. "She says, he shouts then over all the voices in the bar, it's like a bird voice – piercing, your ears ache, She says her father was taller than mine. He bursts out with a terribly noisy laughter. Was he? And she affirms: of course he was, you little fuck! OK! He is there unchangeably – he is one sixteenth of an inch taller than her highness is, notwithstumbling. OK! And when he, he looks at her inquisitively, your father, would look up, see? Up high, to the sky, would he see two gigantic spheres up there amongst the clouds? Would he? And she purses her lips, suddenly offended a little, but not sure what the correct answer to that might be. He did? He's back. Huh? Of course he did, she says, now looking even more offended. That is as clear as the day, you little fart. OK! Your highness, he responds to that. OK! Those two were the balls of my father, your fartness! See? Annalivia picks some of the cake with her finger and puts it in her mouth which spreads immeasurable satisfaction on her face. The thought that somebody should open the door and to let it open for a longer while becomes overwhelming after only a short while, but nobody really does anything.

"A hand from the cloud emerges, holding a chart expanded."

"The eversower of the seeds of light to the cowld owld sowls that are in the domnatory of Defmut after the night of the carrying of the word of Nuahs and the night of making Mehs to cuddle up in a cuddlepot, Pu Nuseth, lord of rising in the yonderworld of Ntamplin, tohp triumphant, speaketh."

"Because, graced be Gad and all greedy gadgets, in whose words were the beginnings, there are two signs to turn to, the yeast and the ist, the wright side and the wrongcd side, feeling aslip and wauking up, so on, so farth."

"Open the friggen widow!"

"No, Siree!"

Les Cloches de Bâl

Going back to Munich I also wanted to pass through Basel, because of one of father's favorite books (it really was, for a long time, for years his favorite, and then it was not only not his favorite at all – but he stopped reaching out for it for good): Les Cloches de Bâle, was the title. The Bells of Basel. So I'll arrive there around two in the morning and there'll be nothing available to take me to Zürich until the day time, way into the next day already, according to the schedule I've got in my pocket, but I'm actually glad about it, because it gives me time to goof around night time Basel and there's a fair chance that with the dawn I might, just might, be able to actually listen to the Cloches de Bâle (once again: that's the title of Aragon's book father used to like so much at one point in his life – The Bells Of Basel). When I got off the train from Strasbourg it was already two thirty, we've had a little countertime on our way down here. I would then leave the train station and go out to town about which I didn't really know that much. Right outside there was a stand, magazines and papers, and that also was where I got my guide through the city of Basel. I also got myself a cup of coffee and a little sausage I liked very much. I was quite far away from the stand actually when I decided to go back and get a couple of post cards; I wrote one to father, I knew he'd enjoy this, I knew, as already said above, there were times in his life when Aragon was very important to him and he read an awful lot, novels as well as poetry, he could quote from memory which, for that matter, was never my forte… The second one I wrote back to Strasbourg – to Uli. I still didn't realize, I think, what actually had happened; no, I didn't. I knew that and I was in all reality only trying to keep it all that way for as long as I could, was my thought later. I was sort of praying that memories be kept in check, that something sudden, like a walk, talk, sudden stop and discussion, ice cream eating, a visit to the museum we cherished so much, wouldn't pop up suddenly and maddeningly. But I stopped at a closed shop window and I wrote. Both cards. To her and to father. I then post marked them and as soon as there was another open stand I would ask again where to put them. The sleepy but very polite lady explained where the boxes were and she offered throwing them in for me, if I only wanted her to, and I said yes to that. I knew she'd do it. Why the hell not, then? Not that far away from there a church offered wide steps on which I could sit and think; and I did just that, slowly sipping my coffee, I thought. I saw father's face before me, smiling, he was telling me about the French communists – made quite a detour to Louis Carroll, because he then would talk about the Dada movement and Aragon's questionable friendship with Breton – Comité National des Écrivains, the switch from Snarksism to Marxism, and then, his face suddenly saddened, he would talk about Aragon's struggle against what communism has become in the meantime. You see, in 1956 he supported the Budapest insurrection. We thought, we pondered, you see, nobody is really that blind or that stupid, and finally you'd like to know why in the bloody hell did you put your own life at such risks, and that is when you begin to know, to realize to the full extent, that your will, your wishes, your… stuff, OK? All of it is actually meaningless. You fight, struggle, you do things. The outcome is not even close to what you intended. Not even close. He, Aragon, supported the Budapest insurrection which was the absolute, perfect negation of what he had fought for. All of his life. You know? In 1968, after Prag, after millions were murdered again and nobody, and I mean nobody, had at that moment any illusions left anymore, he wrote a preface to Milan Kundera's book, known to us only because it was published and made quite acclaimed in France, precisely by him, as "La Plaisanterie."

I see him. Clearly.

He sits there, his head supported by his hand, listening to the radio, the reception plain lousy but understandable, enjoying the news from Vietnam: so and so many tons of bombs... Good! Accursed soviet cockroaches are finally paying – right now! Mother was then simply bored by that (whenever she would come to visit him from Germany which, as stated somewhere else, wasn't rare at all), and she would say to him time and time again, against my better judgment, to 'change the long play', because the monotony of it was getting on her nerves. We've had enough of that! Enough! Of any of that!

Going back only a little: she did have enough of it all; as she would, quite often in fact, explain to me, there is that moment in one's life where you think you would rather die than preserve the *status quo*; you'd do anything... Anything!

She then left the country as soon as it became possible – I know for a fact that he had helped her, he used any and all of his influential relations to get her out so she might not die there. She left with me. Munich (where she was originally from) was now my place (after Frankfurt, at first), and so I would now go and visit father - now and then. Go back. My life seemed to me at times, like a fairy tale about a bad sorcerer's curse, to be just that: an unchangeable story about going back –to somewhere or to something; and the having to leave again.

He didn't like that either, of course.

He lived alone. In the same apartment. He read, thought. Took long walks around the town we used to walk so much around together. I begin to realize what it was to him when I would come back, be it just for a few weeks, some of those times.

I'm now old too.

God!

America was really his hope then. His hope for the world, and I know, I realize that he would have freely given whatever was still left of his life for this world to make sense, whatever might ever have happened notwithstanding. A world where a pig would become pork chops and not a politician. You know? Yes, my dear, I want you to realize that. I want you to retain that, because that is and always will be your life and there's no life outside that understanding – or rather –without it, without that understanding – all there is, is slow degradation... You'll be allowed to vegetate. The world, this world of ours still has a chance to be a better place. Not all's lost! And that was also – America - where I wanted to go in the future. To study. To live.

To remember and to contemplate.

He showed me the Statue of Liberty, only a newspaper picture, explaining that it had been the gift of the French, - but, you see, whatever it was or is, or ever will be, for that matter, in terms of what's it made of or by whom – one thing is certain: it *certainly* is not a lie. You know? You can be sure of that. That is not a lie! And never will be!

He would shake his head with unshakable certainty.

I remember him then already very old.

His hospital. Sickness.

The moment comes to me, suddenly strangely alive, down in the morgue, where I was helping the hospital guy to put the elegant black suit on his body we just had washed all over with alcohol, and that dumb schmuck, red faced, stupid ass, grabbed him under his chin and pulled him up towards the heads of that bed he was on.

When I shook my head to make the present come forward, Uli came to me from the opposite side of the street, and I really had to strongly cough to clear my throat.

Slowly the dawn was breaking. The street I was on would step by step show details I couldn't see so far. My coffee cup was empty. And then, suddenly, the church bell started to toll right there, in the bell tower right behind me. In only a minute another one answered from somewhere farther away in the city. And then yet another one. And yet another one after that, almost simultaneous, and then others, al of them, melting into one mighty clangor above the city's awakening on this early Sunday morning. And I realized that I was just hearing Les Cloches de Bâl.

Kim

I called Eve, wanted to talk about the papers I'm going through, but she wasn't there. Nobody picked up, anyway. Last time at the hospital we were talking about all the notes Eve had now in her possession, notes by Jack, I mean written by him personally, as well as all those he just gathered from others, written by themselves or yet somebody else, notes that only ended up in their hands for a while and then, once having been found worth his while by whomever, passed on to him – finally all of it ended up in Eve's hands because of what has happened to Jack. The fact also that I have more and more difficulty in communicating with him, whenever I go there, forces me –as little as I appreciate it – to make some decisions of my own. I'd like Eve to help me with that, although I can understand her reluctance… Yeah… Here is one I'd love to hear what she wants to do with. She was working on Homer, translating but also writing an essay, I thought fascinating – can't find it anywhere. The translation –well, it's not a translation, really… It's work in progress, I'd say, yes, very much her style… I promised myself to keep my own comments to a minimum, should I decide to comment at all –should the book also ever get published –which, besides, I doubt – Oh, yeah, these things will have to speak for themselves. And they do, too! That's exactly what I think. I do! And yet, I also think, that a little touch here and there, by a hand of someone like Eve or Jack, people, hence, who really know what they are doing, might make that speaking a lot more pronounced… Eve oftentimes tends to just let it go… That's why I think Jack would be a lot better. Well, we'll see… Well, folks, here it is:

Hekuba?

Under indifferent sun that pains my escaping eyes an awkward wagon trundles under the empty sky, pulled by the mules too old for the sands of this shore - of unconcern; and the squeaky wheels moan out the question that bleeds from the wounded heart about the mocking lie I've heard so long ago - like a feathered arrow in the breast now chocking on the wooden air: he was to be a king, a-ruling, he was to be the one who would break the ring of this unconcern, this cold indifference of dying when what still stands is long dead already and change it into glory, he was to - I was told by whom I believed in all he said of old - then why like this in pain that cannot even be looked at amongst a bunch of thieves…

Old wagon only trundles under this empty sky of squeaky indifference those flat wooden wheels are slowly moving forward on that empty beach.

The main one's boredom among you finally dispatched that yet another devil powerful enough to stop the true evil from taking his life - so he lives as yet to make brine enough to melt all the ice ever made by you.

I tried to stop him. Yes, I did try to stop him.

"Where are your senses gone? - that made you famous once…

If he gets you in his clutches, sets his eye on you – he'll show no mercy, no respect for your rights, should you ever have any - and the waiting, see?"

Once the end draws near hope also sets in that he might be gone to one better place; but waiting – you see? When hope is dust already and the outcome still only a future that is vague and distant. Abandonment of waiting that cannot be stood. Prayer for safe return of all the enemies, ours and not ours, seems to be the line we shall have to take. Then you go for the body. Make sincere petition to all sincerity. And going you pray for a bird of omen, so you can see that sign with your own eyes and trust your life to it as you venture down.

He rinsed his hands then, took the cup from me and taking a stand amidst the forecourt, prayed, pouring the wine to earth and scanning the high skies. But there was no eagle, just heat pouring down. And soldiers standing there among a group of people not yet afraid enough, keeping watch and waiting for the God sent night to finally come and cool things down to what we can bear.

The question then arises that still can be asked resounding quite sensibly in all indifference: Have you abandoned him for good, oh, father, your favorite man of war during all this time, that in all the panic that ensued thereafter seemingly lost? All the noise of battle can stretch on a field that takes on the colors of crimson and purple, or it can stretch from one whisper to yet another one, passing from what's death right back to life, from loss to fulfillment, from want to …?

Again and again.

For how long yet to come?

The noise of the battle, the chariots falling on us, the whirlwinds arising, against the fainting hands too weak to withstand this story they're part of; into the clash of steel; through clangor of jaws, mighty teeth of iron do we come into it only to be told then: that whisper coming to us lightly right through slippery middle of unbearable noise: that love is your armor, only one you need, and that at the moment of your final knowledge that: what protrudes there shining from your painful breast is a spear of steel that just pierced your heart, to bring you assuagement from that burning sun you never could stand. Sleep embraces lightly your exhausted soul joined to the joy that the battle's over – that the full completion of pre-ordered deaths was finally able to give you the bliss - of sun anew arising: quickly seeing your children getting out of sleep and also one more time opening the wall of this leather tent of so many years: fresh and snow-white linen, spices, olives, wine, shall accompany you in that ceaseless dream now that the noise is over. Only spear-like question unswayingly sticking from the painful breast: growing, learning, journeys, answers and inquiries, the sun that instead of burning would gently warm your skin – and mothers and then lovers, first pain and first teeth … and Oreck vacuum cleaners – what size paper bags will you have to purchase in the supermarket on this day of hiss…

I won't comment on that either!

What do I feel?

I think I've got to talk to her – I just have got to! I also hope that Jack today may show a little bit more interest in his own work and what's ahead of it. Finally I am only trying to prevent it from disappearing into oblivion – if they don't do it, nobody will. Nobody!

I did talk…

God!

I never expected this. No! And yes! I think she did, somehow, she knew that this was gonna be the outcome, maybe even right from the beginning. She did. Hell… Today we… I have found out, right at the moment of our arrival at the hospital, right then and there, yes, I have found out that Jack had passed away last night. I mean I found out, and as son as I did, I was standing there just plain dumbfounded; and she didn't even seem surprised to me. Then we came back here, together. We didn't talk. 'Much' as the quantificator here would be a sheer nonsense. We did not talk at all. We just sat there. I poured her a drink because I thought it would do her a lot of good - but she refused. No! We just sat there. In the evening, still with her sitting like that, no stir, no reactions, nothing, I started going through the notes again, thinking that she was there at some point (and not just one time – no, she would go to the hospital now and then without even telling me about it), without my knowledge, without that basic, well, basest of all the information that she had gone to the hospital without me (am I mad at her? – now, that's ridiculous in this situation, isn't it, and yet…) that she would go there without even telling me about going there, - or would she? - and I suddenly found what seems to be her last note, this:

Hand

He wanted his right hand freed; why? Who knows… Doctor Gloogla Pluplu did his best to dissuade me from doing it, but I insisted. His argument was based and then went time and time again back towards the situation in which, after they had freed his right hand (this was not the first time he requested that – but it was the one time they did follow his request), with that very hand he hit TA Poopumba, a black guy six foot seven, three hundred pounds in the middle of the latter's forehead knocking him out for quite some time – took a lot of doing to get Poopumba back on track.

I had to sign a release. I did. And then I approached him, in his contraption, right there in the middle of the room. He looked at me. His eyes saw me – I knew that. He saw me. He was looking at me. Yes. I knew his look. I would also swear he was trying to say something to me but his mouth would not follow his will. He gave it up. I could hear him breath, though; heavily. And then I felt his right hand: yes, he touched my forehead – that's what he wanted it freed for: he made on my forehead, very slowly, like it cost him a lot of effort, but also very distinctly, there was no way to be confused about that, the sign of the cross...

When I looked up at him then I knew that he wasn't there anymore; it was just a body.

Lake Estates, 08

ABOUT THE AUTHOR

My background: Master's Degree from the University of Breslau (Wroclaw), then continued in Vienna at the doctoral level. Publishing essays and press articles in Austria as well as in Germany. Writing fiction most of my life, some of which has seen daily light, too. In the mid seventies I also studied anthropology at the University of Paris, among the others under Mircea Eliade. In that time also I traveled to Ireland to write about the situation in Belfast for Canard Enchaîné in Paris. Arrived in America in 1981 I took (and would keep taking too) odd jobs, not in any way related to any kind of literary occupation. I wrote, though. I have seven books written, finished – ready for the publishing process. Some of them – like the one I'm sending – has also been critiqued, with a very positive outcome. I've done that in one of the internet places where the author has to pay to be critiqued.

What is the book about: America of today – through the eyes of a whole row of characters – contemporary as well as going back to the times when labor unions were being created and the wealth, known and admired internationally, quickly came into being. What is art and what is its function in our lives? Two women help us see that – painter and writer, and it is the husband of one of them who also is the main guy – the one who gets arrested and ends up in the Forensic Center as a patient directed there (senselessly) by the judge for the psychological evaluation (more frequently the case than anyone could think – I worked in one of them and happen to know that part of "reality" on first hand bases). Worked into the main intrigue are several other lines of narration with lesser people – all of them representing, though, something that we all know from our daily lives; something that represents our time and the changes we witness, willy-nilly, equipped with super keen senses or not at all, geniuses or complete dull-wits; from that incredible, internationally acclaimed wealth of the blue color that seemed to be unique in the whole world, towards where it all seems to be headed as of right now... Whatever that might be.

I think if someone reads at all (which is not that common today at any rate) and enjoys, let's say, John Grisham or Dan Brown (let alone complete trash of which there is an immeasurable flood out there), they certainly won't enjoy my work. But if someone's pass-time is, as opposite to the above, Faulkner, Hemingway, Fitzgerald, Dos Passos (Proust, hopefully, and Joyce, Sartre, and Camus), they'll also enjoy my writing – I can assure you of that. I think (in fact I know) that there is a niche in America – people who seek and cannot find (not in sufficient amount anyway) this kind of literature and it is to them that I address my book. This one as well as the others I've written. Well, here it is...

Sincerely,

Jack Haberek

CPSIA information can be obtained
at www.ICGtesting.com
Printed in the USA
BVHW070743260121
598726BV00001B/85